R

A **TOM WAGNER** ADVENTURE

Thriller

Copyright © 2022 by Roberts & Maclay (Roberts & Maclay Publishing). All rights reserved. No part of this book may be reproduced in any form or by any electronic or mechanical means, including information storage and retrieval systems, without written permission from the authors, except for the use of brief quotations in a book review.

Translator: Edwin Miles / Copyeditor: Philip Yaeger

Imprint: Independently published / Paperback ISBN 9798848157895, Hardcover ISBN 9798848157956

Cover Art by reinhardfenzl.com

Cover Art was created with photos from: depositphotos.com: pstocks, Antartis, irabel8, digitalstorm, dechevm, zacariasdamata, Krivosheevv, Croisy, iLexx

This is a work of fiction. Names, characters, businesses, places, events and incidents are either the products of the author's imagination or used in a fictitious manner. Any resemblance to actual persons, living or dead, or actual events is purely coincidental.

www.robertsmaclay.com

office@robertsmaclay.com

GET THE PREQUEL TO
THE **TOM WAGNER** SERIES
FREE E-BOOK

robertsmaclay.com/start-free

CONTENTS

Chapter 1	11
Chapter 2	14
Chapter 3	18
Chapter 4	21
Chapter 5	25
Chapter 6	29
Chapter 7	33
Chapter 8	39
Chapter 9	44
Chapter 10	47
Chapter 11	51
Chapter 12	54
Chapter 13	57
Chapter 14	60
Chapter 15	66
Chapter 16	68
Chapter 17	74
Chapter 18	77
Chapter 19	83
Chapter 20	86
Chapter 21	89
Chapter 22	91
Chapter 23	93
Chapter 24	95
Chapter 25	99
Chapter 26	101
Chapter 27	103
Chapter 28	106
Chapter 29	108
Chapter 30	111
Chapter 31	116
Chapter 32	120
Chapter 33	122

Chapter 34	126
Chapter 35	130
Chapter 36	133
Chapter 37	135
Chapter 38	139
Chapter 39	143
Chapter 40	150
Chapter 41	153
Chapter 42	158
Chapter 43	161
Chapter 44	164
Chapter 45	169
Chapter 46	174
Chapter 47	178
Chapter 48	184
Chapter 49	188
Chapter 50	194
Chapter 51	200
Chapter 52	204
Chapter 53	208
Chapter 54	215
Chapter 55	219
Chapter 56	223
Chapter 57	228
Chapter 58	232
Chapter 59	236
Chapter 60	241
Chapter 61	244
Chapter 62	249
Chapter 63	251
Chapter 64	257
Chapter 65	261
Chapter 66	265
Chapter 67	271
Chapter 68	276
Chapter 69	281
Chapter 70	286
Chapter 71	290
Chapter 72	295

Chapter 73	300
Chapter 74	305
Chapter 75	309
Chapter 76	313
Chapter 77	319
Chapter 78	322
Chapter 79	328
Chapter 80	332
Chapter 81	338
Chapter 82	343
Chapter 83	348
Chapter 84	354
Chapter 85	359
About the Authors	377

"Happiness resides not in possessions, and not in gold. Happiness dwells in the soul."

Democritus

1

AN ISLAND IN THE CARIBBEAN

Opening her eyes seemed to take an eternity. Her eyelids were heavy in a way she'd never known before. She felt as if she had to consciously plead with every single muscle involved in the process until finally, as if in slow motion, her eyelids rose. But it didn't change much. A dense fog blurred her gaze. At first, all she could see were outlines.

Without warning, a new perception joined the little she could see, a pounding headache, as if someone were bashing her temples with a sledgehammer and at the same time drilling into the top of her skull.

She couldn't tell how long it took until her senses began to send even marginally useful information to her brain.

Her headache continued to pound rhythmically—no, it was more like drumming. But as hard as she tried, she couldn't tell if the hammering was just in her head or whether she was actually hearing drums.

Her vision began to clear. The blurs of light and dark took on more and more contrast, and she realized that the sounds really were coming from outside. She was surrounded by banging, scraping, drumming, rattling. Even if she had screamed, she would not have been able to hear herself over the cacophony rolling over her.

She now saw that the bright spots around her were flaming torches, set on stakes in a wide circle. But that was all she could take in—partially because her mind was still as fogged as her eyesight.

Then another perception joined those already overwhelming her senses. A pressure on her arms and legs. She could barely move. Not just her head, but her hands and feet, too, felt as though they were caught in a vise. She tugged, tore, pushed, pressed, but every movement caused searing pain in her arms and legs.

The roaring in her head grew louder, the lights around her brighter.

She screamed. She screamed and screamed again, but it was just as she'd feared: she heard nothing. And more and more, a cruel suspicion became a certainty. Even if her screams could have been heard, no one would have responded.

Before her eyes, a torch danced up and down. Her vision was clearing, but she didn't want to see any of it. More and more, she realized how hopeless her situation was.

Singing had joined the drumming, now. Monotonous chanting in a language that only the old people knew. Scraps of words she knew from her grandmother, although she had no idea what they meant. But she knew who used these words.

The area around her grew brighter and brighter. She saw a crowd now, perhaps a hundred men and women dancing, singing, and drumming, half naked, savagely ecstatic. Her panic grew.

She had heard of this, but she hadn't known that it still existed. The crowd in front of her parted and a man in a top hat, his face painted white, approached, flanked by two men carrying torches.

She vaguely recalled her grandmother telling her of an ancient myth about an undead being who wore a top hat and whose face was a death's head. The Lord of the Dead.

The man held a long machete in one hand and in the other a skull with its crown smashed out. Panicked, she tore at her bonds until the blood ran from her wrists and ankles. She didn't care about the pain. She screamed. She jerked her head from side to side, threw all her weight against the ropes that held her, but they did not budge at all.

The crowd was going berserk. The singing grew louder, the drumming wilder. The ecstatic dancing seemed completely beyond control. The man came toward her with his machete raised. She saw him set it against her throat and with a practiced movement he sliced through her carotid artery. For a few seconds, she watched a fountain of blood spray from her own body, as the man caught it in the open skull.

Then her world went dark forever.

2

AN OLD FISHING BOAT, CARIBBEAN WATERS

"Go! Get us out of here!" François Cloutard bellowed at the old seaman over the roar of the waves and hammering of the motor. With all his strength, the man guided the aging fishing boat through the waist-high surf. Few dared to enter these waters, and with good reason. Soot-black, razor-sharp rocks fringed the island on all sides, bursting from the turbulent sea. The coastline was dotted with the skeletons of wrecked boats that had lost their battle with nature. They appeared briefly as the waves receded before surging back to pound them again with merciless force. Modern technology was no help here. Only a highly experienced sailor could take on these forces and steer a course safely through the rocky labyrinth. It was one of the few situations where humanity still had the edge over technology, where experience paired with intuition was more than a match for modern equipment.

"Quickly, far away," Cloutard murmured to himself, gripping the rusty railing as tightly as he could. Nausea rose inside him, but it wasn't just the heavy seas driving it. It was the images in his head, the things he had just seen. At the start, he thought he must be dreaming, but it was sadly all too real. The young woman's screams still resounded in his head. He had almost screamed himself, but he had pulled himself together and fled to avoid sharing the woman's fate. He'd have had no chance of saving her, anyway, and would only have ended up a victim of those maniacs himself. But he'd survived, he was safe, they had not spotted him. Trembling, one hand clamped to the railing, he took out his hip flask and gulped down a mouthful of Louis XIII to calm his nerves and his gut. He had spent a lot of time on the ocean, and in his youth had had countless adventures while traveling the world in search of antique treasure. But this journey was an ordeal, and the terrible images in his head had made it worse. Another wave whipped over the deck and straight into Cloutard's face, tearing him from his thoughts. He took another swig from the flask, then put it away and clawed his way forward along the railing until he reached the ladder to the bridge.

"I thought you said the island was uninhabited," Cloutard shouted up at the old seaman.

"I did, man. But who really knows? No normal person goes near the place—and if they do, they don't come back alive to talk about it," the old man yelled back. He was clearly enjoying his battle with the forces of nature.

What a lovely prospect, Cloutard thought, although he didn't give much credence to the seaman's yarn. Everywhere you went in the world, he knew, you could find locals with outlandish stories. Myths and legends about enchanted mountains, cursed forests, remote islands from which no one came back alive. Usually, there was little behind them— usually, but not always. In this case, Cloutard doubted that the rocks around the island were the only source of the myth.

When they had left the island and its natural bulwark behind them, Ignacio Torrente throttled back the motors and climbed down from the bridge. The grey-bearded seaman reminded Cloutard distantly of a Jamaican version of an old Hemingway. He would not have been Cloutard's first choice, or his second. Just a few days earlier, when he'd sighted the remote wooden hut and the two decrepit-looking fishing boats on the shore of Hunts Bay, he had almost turned back on the spot. But despite his misgivings, he had knocked at Ignacio Torrente's door. And it was good that he had. Torrente had turned out to be a competent partner and seaman, and the tip he'd given Cloutard a week earlier had already paid off. Sure, the old man occasionally looked a little too deeply into a bottle of rum, but Cloutard was in no position to judge. After all, it was the old man who'd given him the clue that had led him here to the island.

"Did you find anything?" Torrente asked. Cloutard, soaked through, proudly took out what he'd recovered. Torrente smiled broadly.

"We have to hurry. A huge storm is brewing, man. If you think this sea is rough, you really don't want to tangle with that," Torrente said. He nodded to the west, where ugly, dark clouds were towering on the horizon. The sea was already rougher than it had been when they had sailed out just a few hours before, and waves were bursting over the gunwales of the rocking boat.

"Show me," Torrente said impatiently when they had taken shelter below deck in the tiny galley.

"It was just as you said. Right there in Blossom Bay," said Cloutard, and he set the object, wrapped in an ancient length of brown fabric, on the table.

"You actually found it," said Torrente. He reached for a bottle of rum rolling around on a shelf behind him with the pitching of the boat. Cloutard likewise took out his flask and the two men drank a satisfied toast.

"Then let's take a look at what you've found," Torrente said, sliding the bundle across. Carefully, he loosened the string and folded the fabric away to reveal an ivory rod twenty inches long and more than an inch thick. "It looks like a military baton," said Cloutard. He put his hip flask on the table beside him and picked up the rod.

Without warning, there was a muffled blast and the boat lurched to one side, flinging the two men roughly from their seats and onto the floor. Loose objects flew through the galley like shrapnel.

"What was that?" Cloutard cried, getting back to his feet.

"Sounded a lot like an explosion," Torrente replied.

3

GEORGETOWN, GRAND CAYMAN

"We have to get it!" Tom shouted, pulling Hellen along by the arm.

Hellen glanced at her watch. "Damn it, we might be too late," she said, looking around nervously.

"This place is a labyrinth. Every time we come here, it looks different! Which way do we go?" Tom asked. Like Hellen, he looked around uncertainly. They did not have the luxury of making the wrong decision now. It was literally a matter of seconds.

Tom knew that the large crowd could be a problem. Too many variables. They could not proceed as they usually would. Innocents could get hurt.

Hellen raised her arm and pointed. "I think we have to go down there. Yes, I think that's the right way."

"We have to risk it," Tom said, but Hellen was already pushing her way through the people crowding the square. He sighed and went after her.

Tom had gotten rusty in the last few months. The run from the car had already put him out of breath.

He pressed his hand against the stitch in his side and followed Hellen, who had disappeared into a throng of wildly shouting people. Tom lumbered in after her. Shaking his head, he pushed past men and women blocking his path. He was angry at how out of shape he'd gotten. Not even a year ago, during their escape from the Wewelsburg, a chase like this had hardly made him break a sweat. Now he was breathless, his heart was pounding, and his arms and shoulders ached. The air all around was heavy with the odors of meat, sweat, gasoline, and countless other things he couldn't place.

One thing was clear to him: simply lying around in the sun, eating and drinking and occasionally swimming a few laps in the van Rensburgs' pool, was doing him no good at all. He gritted his teeth and ran on. They were on a mission, after all.

He had spotted Hellen in the crowd again. She looked as exhausted as he was. Like him, she was nowhere near as fit as she had been just six months earlier. She was leaning on one of the many tables, obviously happy to have reached her destination. Tom summoned up all his strength and pushed through the last of the crowd.

"Did you get it?" he asked breathlessly, looking at her eagerly.

"At the very last moment," she said, nodding enthusiastically and holding up her prize triumphantly for Tom to see.

Tom didn't want to think about what would have happened if they'd arrived too late. They would have had to change their plans completely.

"Seven dollars, missy," said the toothless man with the greasy captain's cap on his head, holding out his hand to Hellen.

Tom nodded a little tiredly as Hellen paid, then he packed everything into a bag, and they made their way back through the market to the car.

"Not exactly cheap, but you've saved lunch," said Tom, and he pressed a kiss to Hellen's cheek.

A few minutes later, worn out, they slumped into the seats of the Range Rover Evoque convertible. Tom started the motor and they drove back to the villa.

Finding good swordfish was a nightmare.

4

THE OLD FISHING BOAT

What had begun as a harmless outing had quickly turned into a battle for survival. As if from nowhere, a boat had appeared behind them. The explosion that had almost sunk their old tub had made it clear that their pursuers were not friendly. Bullets buzzed around their ears the moment they set foot on deck—a man aboard the rapidly gaining boat had opened fire with an automatic weapon—and they were forced to take cover behind the bridge. But that wasn't their only problem. The storm brewing in the west was gaining strength and getting closer. Monumental thunderheads were already darkening the sky. Lightning flashed and rain whipped their faces.

"Who are those guys, man?" Torrente cried.

"I have no idea," Cloutard lied, although he could very well imagine why "those guys" were after them. Apparently, he'd been seen on the island after all, or they at least had spotted the departing boat. But he decided to keep that information to himself for now. He didn't want to unsettle the old man even more. And what was he supposed to say, anyway? That they were the voodoo priests who had just sacrificed a young woman on the island? He would sound like a madman.

"What are you going to do?" Cloutard shouted, as Torrente scrambled up into the bridge. He immediately opened the throttle as wide as it would go and swung the bow directly into the storm. "We cannot—"

"It's our only chance, man. I don't want one of those guys to kill me. I did not sign up for that. I'd rather take my chances with the storm," the old man said. "They'd have to be crazy to follow us in there."

Cloutard gripped the railing and glanced back. Torrente's plan did not appear to be working. Their pursuer, undeterred, was gaining. Again and again, bullets whistled over Cloutard's head or slammed into the wooden panels of the cabin. Suddenly, the shooting stopped, at least for the moment. Cloutard risked another look and shuddered.

"Where the devil is Wagner when you need him?" Cloutard muttered, rolling himself up like a hedgehog beneath the railing. "*Que dieu m'aide.*"

If it had been up to him, he would have brought Tom and Hellen on this escapade with him. He really could have used Tom's skills right now. But the two had made it abundantly clear that, at least for a while, they wanted nothing more to do with this life. At their wedding, van Rensburg had shown them the 300-hundred-year-old letter that Anne Bonny had written to one of her compatriots. Initially, Hellen had been thrilled, but after her father's sudden death and the horrible truths that had subsequently come to light, she had withdrawn. She would have to come to terms with all of that first, reconcile herself to her father's death and rethink her priorities. Tom wouldn't leave Hellen's side, wanting only to support his new bride through the crisis. All understandable, certainly. But Van Rensburg hadn't given up. Cloutard, no longer the youngest himself, let the billionaire talk him into it, and had gone off in search of the "pirate queen's" treasure alone.

When the grenade exploded, it tore Cloutard out of his wistful thoughts. A fountain of water shot up, and the boat once again lurched precipitously to the side. Cloutard could not hold on and slid across the deck and into the bow of the rickety vessel as it dipped into a trough between waves. The grenade had exploded beside the fishing boat, damaging the hull. At the last moment, Cloutard managed to grab hold of the boom the fishermen used to haul in their nets. But between the huge waves and the howling winds, the boom was swinging dangerously back and forth. When the bow surged up the next mountainous wave and the spray flew high over the canopy, Cloutard let go and slid back across the deck to the bridge. He managed to grab one of the vertical railing supports and pulled himself upright. With his other hand, he braced against the side of the bridge and, like a toddler on ice, tottered to the ladder that led up to the helm. He looked back quickly: their pursuer had fallen behind a little.

"Can't this thing go any faster?" Cloutard bellowed up to Torrente, but his shout was swallowed by a massive wave that almost knocked him off his feet. He looked back again and, for a fraction of a second, hope flashed inside him. He couldn't see the boat chasing them. But then, like a whale breaching the surface, their pursuers shot out of a trough, practically leaping over the wave. Cloutard grabbed the ladder and was already climbing up to join Torrente when he saw a man on the other boat loading another grenade into the launcher mounted on his assault rifle.

"Look out!" Cloutard cried, but he hesitated a moment too long. The grenade slammed into the deck two yards from him. He had no chance. The explosion and the pressure wave it caused ripped his hands from the ladder and flung him bodily into the sea. Everything went black.

5

COUNTRY ESTATE, CLOSE TO SIENA, TUSCANY, ITALY

THE OLD WOMAN STABBED IN ANNOYANCE AT THE RED BUTTON on her old mobile phone and followed up with a few Italian curses for good measure.

"Still nothing?" asked Fabio, looking with concern at Giuseppina, François Cloutard's foster mother.

"*Niente*. When I get my hands on him, I'll kill him," she said, and—vigorously, for her age—stomped away into the garden.

Fabio and his wife, Adalgisa, had arrived in Tuscany just the day before. They knew that Cloutard was away on a treasure hunt because he'd asked them to join him, but their Mona Lisa job had once again demanded their attention. The project, now entering its final phase after years of work, was why they had come to Italy and were visiting Giuseppina. Her husband, the old don of one of Italy's biggest crime families, had been dead for years and she had passed on the business operations to one of her capos, but she was still one of the most influential mafiosi in Italy. The other dons had immense respect for her, particularly because she was a woman. Her contacts were vast, her network tightly woven, and her mind as clear and analytical as ever. The wisdom of age and experience had made her the first person that Fabio and Adalgisa turned to when they had problems in their "business."

A young man, presumably a distant relative, entered the garden. He bowed to Giuseppina and whispered something in her ear. She nodded and sent him away again with a dismissive wave.

Adalgisa looked at her in distress. "Don't you trust us, Mamma?"

Giuseppina, of course, was not their mother, but everyone called the old woman simply "La Mamma." Anybody who had anything to do with the Mafia knew immediately who that epithet applied to—and most of them shuddered to hear it.

"Because he whispered something in my ear?" the old woman asked. "Oh, no, of course I trust you. The boy just saw that in some mafia film. You come in quietly, whisper in the don's ear, the don nods, and you leave again. The young people think it's cool, so I play along." She smiled mildly.

"So still nothing?" Fabio asked, although he knew the question was pointless.

"No. It is even worse," said the old woman. "Don Ernesto has not forgotten the Klimt."

"You mean he's still angry at Cloutard for not delivering 'The Kiss'?"

"More than that. He also found out that Francesco was going to give him a forgery."

"But I thought Van Rensburg had settled the matter and compensated Don Ernesto?" Adalgisa pressed.

"Yes, as far as the money goes, that is true. But Don Ernesto's honor has been wounded. My Francesco was planning to deceive him. That is not something a don can quickly forget."

"I would not worry, Mamma," said Adalgisa, and she laid her hand on the old woman's shoulder. "François has nine lives. I'm sure he'll be fine. Just think of everything he's been through working with Tom and Hellen. The Ark of the Covenant, the trick with the old church bell and the Holy Grail, smuggling Hellen and himself into the Alcazar, and all the rest."

"Of course, of course, but he always had Tom or Hellen with him," said the old woman. "I do not have a good feeling at all. And to be honest, I am worried about my Francesco."

Fabio and Adalgisa were astounded. Had La Mamma actually shown emotion? Real concern?

"I'm going to call that van Rensburg," she said, and she took out her old Nokia again and tapped at it nervously.

A few minutes later, she hung up. "His last contact was from Miami. He told van Rensburg he had some business to take care of in Jamaica." She shook her head moodily. "I'm not going to sit around here and do nothing. Something isn't right. I can feel it. Francesco is a dependable boy. He caused me nothing but trouble since he came to live with us, but he never did it on purpose. I have never been unable to reach him, ever."

The old woman suddenly seemed years older, and she was clearly upset. Adalgisa stood and took the old woman in her arms.

"And especially with Don Ernesto after him, we have to do something," Giuseppina whispered. A moment later, she pushed Adalgisa away. She was back to her old self. "Raffaele!" she called, and a split-second later the young reappeared.

"*Si, Mamma*?" he asked, and he lowered his head, as usual, to receive his orders.

"Call Gonzaga. We need him. *Rapido!*"

6

UNKNOWN LOCATION

A REEK OF GASOLINE, SWEAT AND DEATH HUNG IN THE tropical air, but the pungent mix had largely been blocked by the swelling and blood in his nose. *At least there is one positive side*, Cloutard thought. Not even the storm had helped to mitigate the nauseating stench. He coughed and stared up at the ceiling, his eyes sticky with sweat and blood. Then two strong hands grabbed hold of his thighs and tipped him upright again in the chair to which he was tied. Blood and water dripped onto his sodden suit.

The tropical deluge pounded unceasingly on the roof of the wretched barracks, a flimsy construction of wood, straw, and corrugated iron. The light from the bare bulb that dangled on a cable from the ceiling, most likely powered by a generator, flickered a little. In one corner, just beneath the roof, Cloutard could see the red LED of a surveillance camera.

Then the next blow came. This time in his stomach. All the air was momentarily forced from his lungs. He could not remember the last time he had found himself in a situation like this. As a younger man, he'd been on the other side of this kind of conversation more than once. Then, of course, he'd been the one asking the questions. He had never taken any satisfaction in the role but it was true what they said: money can't buy everything. Though Cloutard fundamentally abhorred violence, he had occasionally been forced to resort to a more physical means of persuasion.

But those days were long gone. He wished for a moment that he could swap roles, but the next blow brought him painfully back to reality. Here and now, his situation looked hopeless.

"What are you doing here? Who sent you?"—the same questions his interrogator had fired at him all along between punches. He hadn't recognized the man in cargo shorts and linen shirt immediately, but it was the same who'd shot at him and Torrente from the boat.

Once the pain in his gut had eased a little and he could, with difficulty, catch his breath, he raised his head.

"Hold on, wait," Cloutard said, as he saw the next punch coming. His body reflexively tried to dodge the swing, but his bonds prevented it, and his instinctive efforts resulted in no more than helpless twitching and his eyes clenched shut. Cautiously, he opened them again when the anticipated pain didn't come. And that was enough to renew his strength.

"I am a little put out to find that you do not know who I am," said Cloutard, and he spat blood at his interrogator's feet. "I do not talk with lackeys. Get your boss in here."

"My boss has better things to do than talk with the likes of you. That's what he has me for."

Cloutard looked at the man through his swollen eyes. He sensed that he took pleasure in torturing others. The man went to the small table that stood in the center of the barracks. On it lay a small case, a laptop, a mobile phone, and the items they had found on Cloutard after they hauled him unconscious from the sea: his passport and a medallion the size of a compact disc.

"Besides, I know exactly who you are. Monsieur François Cloutard." The man held up the passport, waved it around for a moment, then tossed it back on the table.

Cloutard rolled his eyes.

"Okay. So you belong to the 87 percent of the human population who can read. Congratulations. But that does not tell you anything at all about *who* I am. And with whom, when it comes down to it, am I speaking? So that I can address you by your name, which is customary among civilized people. You know mine, after all. Although you and I presumably have a different understanding of the meaning of 'civilized'."

He had gone too far. A stabbing pain shot through his head as his tormentor's fist once again slammed into his cheekbone. He fell backward on the chair again, banging his head hard on the filthy floor. *Oh, yes. He loves this*, Cloutard thought. His head droned and his face hurt.

"My name's Darius Cabrera, smartass. I'm asking you again, Monsieur Cloutard, what the fuck were you doing on our island?"

Cabrera was leaning over him again, his hands gripping Cloutard's legs. This time he simply stared down at him from above. Sweat dripped from his forehead directly onto Cloutard's face. Disgusted, Cloutard turned away. Cabrera grinned diabolically and set Cloutard's chair back on its feet. Then he turned his back to him and took two steps to the table.

Cabrera picked up the medallion and turned it in his hands, inspecting it from all sides. The disc had a hole in the center and two recesses cut into the edge. The surface was covered with countless engravings, but they formed neither a recognizable pattern nor any kind of image. It looked more like a badly scratched, donut-shaped piece of a larger puzzle.

With his other hand, he took a second disc from the small case. It looked remarkably similar to the first. Cloutard's eyes widened—his suspicions had been correct.

"What I'm wondering, Monsieur Cloutard, is where you got this from?"

7

SECRETO CARIBE, ESTATE OF BILLIONAIRE
EON VAN RENSBURG, GRAND CAYMAN

Tom's eyes were fixed on Hellen, and he could not have been happier than he was in that moment. All the madness they'd been through together since their reunion in the *fiaker* carriage in Vienna was forgotten. Even the affair with Hellen's father was now, finally, behind them.

Hellen had come to terms with it now. The worst was behind her; she had worked through her father's death and everything that had come with it. It hadn't been easy, but with Tom's unfailing support, she had made it. He had been there for her every step of the way.

Hellen came out of the kitchen with two plates in her hands and smiled. The view over the Caribbean still impressed her, though they had been living there for months. Tom stood up from his sunbed and also looked out over the sea. Like everything van Rensburg owned, this house was perfect. It was situated on a small peninsula, sealed off completely from the usual tourist hustle and bustle of the Caymans. The terrace jutted out a little way over the edge of the peninsula. At its end was a saltwater infinity pool that the two of them used often, though the sea itself was only a few steps away below the terrace. The entire house was built in a half-open design, with outside space a part of almost every room—apart from the annual hurricanes, Cayman weather was very stable.

Tom and Hellen had been on the island for several months, after having enjoyed an extended honeymoon. A trip to the United States had been part of their itinerary, and Tom had shown her a few places that reminded him of his Uncle Scott, now deceased. Like Hellen, Tom had lost a beloved relative through the machinations of the organization that called itself "Absolute Freedom." The global terror network had dominated Tom's, Hellen's and Cloutard's lives for almost two years. Only after many battles, much spilled blood, and countless tears had they finally destroyed it. But that had been almost a year ago, and slowly but surely the dust had settled.

Tom and Hellen had decided to turn their back on Europe for a while. Too many places reminded her of her father and the things he'd done.

But thankfully, all of that was behind them now. It seemed like another life to Tom—a long-forgotten life. And as strange as it sounded, he was enjoying this new routine, where the toughest challenge he faced was getting his hands on the best swordfish in George Town.

Hellen set the plates down, put her arms around Tom, and gave him a kiss.

"We've got it good here, don't we?" she said, and she glanced out over the turquoise sea before setting to work cutting up the fish they had tracked down together that morning.

"Good? That's an understatement," said Tom, pushing the first forkful of swordfish into his mouth. It practically dissolved on his tongue. "Mrs. Wagner, I've got to say: I never would have guessed that you're such an amazing cook," he added, and he moved his eyebrows up and down lightheartedly a few times. "Even Cloutard would be impressed."

"Tom, I don't want to seem petty—or, God forbid, a cranky women's libber—but we did agree that I'd keep my last name, if only because of my scientific work. If I ever want to work again as a respectable researcher, I can't be known as the wife of the guy who blew up half of Europe."

"Me?" he placed one hand on his chest and looked wide-eyed at Hellen. "I couldn't do a thing about it. The bad guys were the ones doing all the blowing up." He raised his hands apologetically, but with a sparkle in his eye. Then he impaled another piece of fish with his fork and let it melt in his mouth.

"My apologies, Doctor de Mey," said Tom, grinning broadly now, and he chased the fish with a mouthful of white wine. Van Rensburg's wine cellar had turned out to be a true treasure chamber, and Tom had learned enough on the subject in recent months to be able to hold his own, even with Cloutard.

"We haven't heard from François for ages," Hellen said, as if she could read his mind.

"Last I heard was he was doing something for van Rensburg," said Tom.

Hellen pulled a face. "Still off hunting for treasure."

Tom realized instantly that he'd hit a sore spot. At first, Hellen had been as excited as anyone when van Rensburg had offered them the treasure hunt as their first assignment, a kind of wedding present. But the murder of Hellen's father had derailed the whole enterprise. It had been the proverbial straw that broke the camel's back, and it had changed her. Too many people had been hurt, or even killed, and she had finally closed the door on that part of her life. Now, a year later, Tom had found to his surprise that he didn't miss the action and adventure half as much as he had feared he would, either.

Fishing, diving, playing golf, and cooking had become the focus of their lives. They had quickly grown accustomed to the quiet life. Still, they knew it couldn't go on forever. They couldn't live out their days jetting around the world and enjoying the good life at van Rensburg's expense. He was a businessman, and Tom and Hellen's team was supposed to be an investment. But for now, the two simply didn't want to admit it.

When they finished dinner, Tom stood up and began to clear the table. The doorbell rang as he was on his way to the kitchen.

"Are we expecting anyone?" he asked.

"No. Mama isn't coming this week after all," Hellen replied. She crossed the large, open living room, went down the stairs to the entrance hall, and opened the door, while Tom, always the good husband, began loading the dishwasher.

Hellen paled when she saw who it was at the door. The moment had come. The moment they had avoided talking about, that they had successfully repressed for so long. In front of her stood Wikus de Waal. De Waal was the right-hand man of the van Rensburgs, the billionaire couple in whose house they had been living these last months. It was actually one of several homes the van Rensburgs owned.

Presumably de Waal was there to tell them that the billionaire's patronage had come to an end and that they would have to look for new digs.

Tom stood at the top of the stairs and looked down as Hellen greeted de Waal and invited him in. He also suspected that the time had come for them to pack their bags.

"Wikus," said Tom, with pointed friendliness. "To what do we owe the honor?"

De Waal, his face marred by an ugly scar, was as dour and excessively formal as always. If one didn't know him, it was easy to imagine him to be a merciless killer. He greeted them with no more than a nod. Tom wanted to invite him out to the terrace, but he didn't get that far.

"I'll come straight to the point. Mr. van Rensburg needs your help. Monsieur Cloutard has disappeared."

"Disappeared? What do you mean?" said Tom, feeling the cracks that this little message was opening up in their perfect world.

De Waal made his way up the steps. He knew the house well, of course. Ignoring the view, he continued implacably, his eyes fixed on Tom and Hellen. "Monsieur Cloutard was on assignment for Mr. van Rensburg in Jamaica. He has not been in touch with us for several days. Master van Rensburg can't reach him. No one knows where he is."

Tom looked at Hellen. He knew what was coming.

"When you go looking for ancient treasures, bad things happen," she murmured almost inaudibly. Then she turned away and busied herself in the kitchen.

"What do you mean by 'disappeared'?" Tom asked again. "This is Cloutard we're talking about. The man has more lives than an army of cats. Nothing happens to him," said Tom.

De Waal was about to reply, but Hellen cut in with surprising vehemence.

"It's probably a setup, another one of the stunts François loves to cook up. Cloutard and van Rensburg have run into a dead end and now they want our help. But we're not interested."

De Waal raised an eyebrow and inhaled slowly. Tom was not exactly an expert on expressions or body language, but he could tell that the situation was probably a little more serious than Hellen had just painted it. De Waal opened his briefcase and took out an iPad.

"Master van Rensburg would like to discuss it with you directly," he said. Tom and Hellen exchanged a meaningful glance. They knew they had been taking advantage of van Rensburg's hospitality for a very long time. With a heavy heart, Hellen came back and joined Tom and de Waal. De Waal placed the iPad on the table. Seconds later, van Rensburg appeared on the screen. The expression on his face spoke volumes.

8

AN ISLAND IN THE CARIBBEAN

"If there's one thing I hate, it's repeating myself," said Darius Cabrera when Cloutard failed to respond to his question. "Where did you get this?"

Cloutard's eyes flicked from one disc to the other. The second had similar engravings and also had two recesses cut into it, but they were a different shape.

"Oh, that old thing? I found it while I was strolling on the beach," Cloutard answered cockily, hoping that the feigned indifference in his voice would convince Cabrera. But Cabrera only grunted, and the leathery skin of his face twisted into a menacing scowl. He turned around and carefully laid the two medallions inside the foam-lined case. He took a deep breath but didn't say a word. Calmly, with a nerve-racking theatricality, he slowly closed the lid and clicked the latches shut.

"I can see it won't be easy to get anything out of you with the soft approach," Cabrera said, his back still turned to Cloutard.

"The soft approach?" Cloutard repeated, and he again spat the blood that had gathered in his mouth onto the floor.

Cabrera didn't react. Leaning on the table, he pondered for a few seconds. Then he crossed to the door, opened it, stepped out around the corner, and returned carrying a rusty pry bar. Cloutard gulped. Things were taking a very unpleasant turn. Like a baseball player, Cabrera slapped the pry bar against the palm of his other hand over and over as he slowly approached Cloutard. The threat of pain was often more effective than the pain itself, as Cloutard well knew, and he had to admit that it really worked. However, he wasn't sure whether his captor knew that. For Cabrera, it seemed more like a primitive kind of macho posturing. Cloutard tugged and twisted at the ropes holding him as Cabrera drew closer and closer. The thought of what he had in mind with the pry bar propelled Cloutard's adrenaline level, already high, to a new peak.

Cabrera stopped in front of Cloutard and tapped the iron bar against his shins in turn. "Eeny, meeny, miny, moe," he murmured, staring Cloutard straight in the eye with an expression that could only be described as aroused. Cloutard's panic grew. Broken bones were the last thing he needed right now.

"Well, Monsieur Cloutard, which leg is it going to be?"

Without waiting for an answer, Cabrera took a small step backward and swung the pry bar back.

Cloutard squeezed his eyes shut and prepared himself for the worst pain of his life. He'd once experienced being shot, it was true, but somehow he feared that the impact of a rusty iron bar on his shin would be worse. But the pain didn't come. Instead, a cellphone rang.

"Shit," Cabrera said, lowering the pry bar. He placed it on the table and picked up the phone. "Hello?" he snapped angrily.

His posture instantly straightened, and he turned and looked up at the camera mounted in the corner. He listened for a while, not taking his eyes off the camera.

"Is that your boss?" Cloutard was now staring into the camera himself. "If he wants something from me, he should talk to me himself."

"Yes, sir. As you like. I'll try it." With that, he ended the conversation and threw the phone back on the table. Cabrera sniffed, clearly upset that he hadn't reached his grand finale. It seemed he had really been looking forward to breaking Cloutard's legs. He went to Cloutard, cut him loose, and dragged him to the door.

"*Connard irrespectueux!*" the Frenchman snapped as Cabrera pushed him out into the open and he stumbled down the three veranda steps, ending up face down in the mud in front of the barracks. He raised his head and spat out some of the filth.

The wind had lost much of its strength, but the rain continued to fall relentlessly from the sky. Cloutard struggled back to his feet and looked around—more low buildings, and several men armed with AK-47s were strolling back and forth beneath the porch roofs.

What the devil is going on here? Cloutard wondered. The whole place reminded him of a guerrilla drug-runners' encampment in Colombia. The low barracks were covered with camouflage netting. The men themselves wore camouflage pants and green T-shirts or stained undershirts, and each had a gun belt with a holstered pistol and a large knife.

How was he ever supposed to get out of there? *I should have waited for Fabio and Adalgisa to finish their job. Why did they have to start that whole Mona Lisa thing again now?* Cloutard thought. He should have been trying to come up with something else, but his current situation wasn't exactly going according to plan. Still, there was one ray of hope: he hadn't been in touch with anyone for several days, so there was a chance that van Rensburg had been able to persuade Tom to come looking for him in the meantime. But right now, he wasn't at all sure that he would live that long. He could no longer rely on his backup plan.

Cabrera shouted a few instructions in Jamaican patois—a dialect derived from English, that had developed among Jamaican slaves in the 17th century—across the open area in front of the barracks. Immediately, two armed men vanished into one of the buildings. Moments later, they reappeared with four women. Cloutard was horrified to see that they were shackled together at the ankles. They bore clear signs of exhaustion and maltreatment. Prodding and beating them with the butts of their rifles, the men drove the women into the center of the open area. More blows forced them to their knees. Zombielike, they obeyed, their will to live obviously having been beaten out of them. Cabrera stepped out into the rain, took a pistol from one of the sentries, and positioned himself behind the women.

"Oh, *mon dieu*," Cloutard murmured. "What is this? What are you doing?" he said, turning to Cabrera with rising desperation.

"Monsieur Cloutard, I know these women mean nothing to you, but if what my boss just told me about you is true, then I know you won't let an innocent woman die for your sake. So I'm going to ask you one last time . . ." Cabrera demonstratively cocked the pistol and pressed it against the back of the head of one of the women.

"I'll count to three. One..."

"Okay, stop, *trou du cul fou*, I will tell you what I know!" Cloutard cried in desperation.

"That's much better." Cabrera lowered the gun. "Take them back," he ordered his men. "And warm up the chopper." He approached Cloutard. "Now at least my boss doesn't have to do without the bounty the mafia has put on your head. I believe the requirements were alive and uninjured."

Cloutard flinched at the mention of the mafia, thinking he must have misheard. Why would the family be looking for him? Van Rensburg had taken care of the affair with the fake Klimt, but probably that had not been enough for Don Ernesto. Money was of no interest to the don. His honor had been slighted, and he would be after revenge. Cloutard knew only too well how the heads of the families ticked. He'd grown up among them himself.

Cabrera planted himself in front of Cloutard, glared hatefully into his mud-smeared face, and bound his hands with a zip tie. "You and me are going to go on a little outing. It looks as if you got your wish. The boss wants to talk to you."

9

SECRETO CARIBE, GRAND CAYMAN

All the color had drained from Tom's and Hellen's faces. They listened to van Rensburg for several minutes, and he was not happy at all.

"I've been trying to reach you for days, but do you pick up the phone? Do you call me back? No," he said accusingly. "It's like you're going out of your way to avoid me. May I remind you that you've been living off my generosity for almost eight months? And you haven't been living particularly modestly, either."

Neither said a word. Van Rensburg was right. Simply sticking their heads in the sand and acting as if they could go on like that forever hadn't been a very clever approach.

Tom and Hellen looked at each other, realizing that Cloutard's situation wasn't a joke. It wasn't one of his beloved stunts. There was no manipulation, no trick aimed at persuading them to get involved in a treasure hunt. It was a simple, awful fact.

"Monsieur Cloutard has been working for me for some time now, searching for the treasure of Anne Bonny. In the last few months, he's followed clues and traces halfway around the world. A week ago, he said he had had a breakthrough, and that was the last I heard from him."

Van Rensburg's tone was a mixture of reproach and concern. It was true that Cloutard disappeared from the radar regularly, especially when he was involved in one of his own "private" projects. They didn't know exactly what shady deals he got involved in on his own time, nor did they want to. Cloutard was a crook, but they had always been able to rely on him. Not contacting anyone and leaving his employer hanging like this was not his style at all.

"Where was Cloutard the last time you spoke?" Tom asked. Hellen looked at him and narrowed her eyes a little. Tom ignored her and kept his eyes fixed on van Rensburg's face on the screen.

"His search had taken him to Jamaica. He was trying to track down an old treasure hunter there that someone had recommended to him."

"And who was Anne Bonny?" Tom asked, turning expectantly to Hellen.

She gave him a small shrug. "One of the few female pirates. She was very young when she first hired onto a ship. She sailed with her husband, a sailor, from South Carolina to the Pacific. When she got there, she fell in love with a pirate named Calico Jack, and left her husband to become his bride. She had to disguise herself as a man, because at the time women weren't tolerated aboard ships. Not much is really known about her, but there are plenty of wild stories. Only one thing is certain: she brought a lot of changes to piracy. Not only did she prompt the acceptance of women, but she also helped to free slaves. But that's all I know about her. I'm no expert on pirates."

Her three listeners could all hear the bitterness that filled her voice. The whole matter was bringing unwanted memories to the surface, things she would rather have left behind. Her displeasure was clear.

10

TELEVISION JAMAICA STUDIOS, KINGSTON, JAMAICA

"That's all from us today. I'd like to thank our guests once again, Mayor Grayson Graves and his challenger, Leticia Ortiz. Who will be the next prime minister of Jamaica? The election remains on a knife edge..."

Leticia Ortiz had already stopped listening to the presenter. She knew the rest of the blah-blah-blah that came at the end of a TV debate well enough. She simply sat and gave the camera her friendliest smile until the red light went out. She also wanted to avoid looking at the man she was challenging in the election. He hadn't earned the right to sit there. She, and presumably anyone who knew anything at all about Jamaican politics, knew what kind of man he was. He didn't have a respectable bone in his body. He was no more than a—

The red light went out. Leticia was on her feet instantly. She didn't want to spend a second longer than absolutely necessary in the same room as Grayson Graves. The presenter thanked the two rivals again and Leticia absently shook his hand as she looked around the studio. A moment later, she spotted who she was looking for: Eleasha Weir, her assistant.

She stood and hurried over to the young woman, linked her arm in Eleasha's, and practically dragged her out of the studio into the corridor.

"I can't begin to tell you how furious that man makes me. He belongs behind bars, not on Montrose Road," Leticia said when they were out of earshot.

"You were fantastic. I'm telling you, when the new polls come in, you'll see you have a chance," Eleasha said. She looked into Leticia's eyes sympathetically and gently squeezed her hand. "Your mother would be proud of you."

"Thank you," Leticia said, her voice breaking a little as she swallowed back the pain. "Would you do me a favor and get me something to drink? Coffee?" she added, smiling tiredly.

"Of course. Anything at all for our next prime minister," Eleasha said, and she trotted away and left her boss alone in the corridor.

However, Leticia's moment of peace was brief. Two station employees hastened down the corridor a few seconds later. She overheard a few scraps of their conversation as they passed: ". . . only one boat went down in the storm, and the captain, uh . . . sorry, I've lost his name. Doesn't matter. In any case, he was rescued by another fishing boat just after . . ."

Leticia turned her back to the two men and stepped away. When she turned around again, she collided with Grayson Graves, who had just exited the studio himself.

"Well, well, well, Miss Ortiz, no need to be so forward. If you want to get close to me, you just have to ask nicely," Graves said with smug grin on his face. Leticia recoiled in disgust, then a cold shudder ran down her spine as his public mask gave way to his true face.

He was certainly a good-looking man, even considering his years. In his early sixties, he was almost agelessly attractive. He was well groomed, stylish, immaculately dressed, and eloquent. Women were lining up for him. But Leticia knew better.

Rumor had it that, as Kingston's mayor, he now reigned not only over the capital, but over the entire country. Corruption, kickbacks, blackmail, and intimidation were just the way he did business. Everybody knew it, but no one had the guts to do anything about it. Everyone was afraid for their lives and livelihoods. With the snap of his fingers you could lose everything—or end up as fish food in the bay. Graves had the police and the judiciary in his pocket, but he also had a small army of murky characters ready to do his dirty work. Leticia didn't want to even imagine the methods or businesses he'd used to drag himself from the gutters of Kingston to become the richest man in the country. He had ruled over the capital for more than twenty years, while the rich got richer and the poor poorer. And yet, in all those years, hardly anyone had dared stand up to his tyranny. Only Leticia's mother, an aspiring politician herself at the time, had stood against him in an election, a classic David-and-Goliath matchup. Leticia had been a little girl at the time. And her mother, it was said, had had a real chance at winning. But fate had other plans. On a trip to Charleston, South Carolina, she had died in a car accident. Without an opponent, Graves had coasted to re-election.

"Save your slippery tongue for the streetwalkers. Nobody buys the family-man image you hold up to the press anymore," she snapped at him.

"You'd better watch out, young lady," he said, his voice icy. "Kingston is a dangerous city. It would be a pity if something happened to you, wouldn't it?" He lifted his hand as if to clear a lock of hair from Leticia's face, but she took a step back and reflexively slapped him across the face.

"Keep your filthy hands to yourself."

Graves smiled and laid his hand almost tenderly on his lightly flushed cheek. Then he noticed a man at the far end of the corridor.

"It's your lucky day, young lady. Business calls." He lowered his hand, pushed past her, and strode off toward the waiting man.

"I'm so sorry. The program director waylaid me and peppered me with questions about you," Eleasha said when she returned, two cups of coffee in her hands. She nodded toward the end of the corridor, where Graves was talking to the man. "What did he want?"

Leticia did not respond immediately. For a moment, she stood and watched Graves as he talked to the unknown newcomer. The man looked around, raised a small case he was carrying, and opened it. Graves inspected the contents, smiled broadly, and clapped the man appreciatively on the shoulder.

"I'm sorry, what? Oh, nothing. His usual slime," Leticia said absently in reply to Eleasha's question, her eyes still glued on Graves. Her assistant pressed one of the coffee cups into her hand and drew her away.

"Come on. The poll results should be in any moment. We should get back to the office."

11

SECRETO CARIBE, GRAND CAYMAN

"I know you don't want to go chasing after treasures or ancient artifacts right now, Mrs. de Mey," van Rensburg continued. "But this is about the life of your friend. I'm not asking you to find Anne Bonny's treasure. You've turned down that request often enough."

Hellen nodded, then she turned away and wandered off toward the kitchen, lost in thought.

"Who'd like coffee?" she asked. She didn't wait for Tom or de Waal to answer but took three espresso cups and switched on the machine.

"Cloutard would probably be the first to raise his hand right now," said Tom. He was right, and Hellen knew it. She, too, had thought immediately of the Frenchman and his nonstop carping about the terrible coffee machine in the corridor at Blue Shield's, headquarters at the UNO City in Vienna. Both of them smiled fleetingly, hearing his protests in their ears.

"All I'm asking is that you fly to Jamaica and find Monsieur Cloutard," van Rensburg said cautiously.

"Isn't that a matter for the local police?" Hellen shot back.

"With all due respect, Mrs. de Mey, you know the conditions in the Caribbean. The police won't lift a finger," van Rensburg said. Tom nodded. He knew what van Rensburg meant, and even Hellen had to admit that the local authorities were not to be relied upon.

Hellen sighed, went back to the two men, and handed them the cups of espresso. She sipped at her own, then stood in front of the iPad and looked directly at van Rensburg.

"I want to make one thing perfectly clear. I have no interest in treasure hunts or adventures of any kind. Too many people have been hurt and died. I'm tired of constantly putting my life on the line. I'm an archeologist, a historian—not Lara Croft. I know perfectly well that we can't stay here forever at your expense, but I also know that I don't want to play Tomb Raider anymore."

She paused. She was obviously having difficulty continuing. Tom put his hand on her shoulder but said nothing. He'd learned when to keep his mouth shut.

Hellen made several attempts to say something but gave them up. Finally, though, she found the words she wanted. "This is about François. He really seems to be in danger, and he knows we're right around the corner. If he was safe and well, he would have been in touch. I have no desire to even set foot in Jamaica, but we can't just lie here in the sun when our friend is in trouble."

Tom was amazed. He'd seen how much her father's death and the events surrounding it had taken out of her. But he was proud of his wife—she had come to grips with all her problems and was putting Cloutard's well-being ahead of her own.

Almost inaudibly, she said, "We'll fly to Kingston and try to find out what's happened to François. That's it. After that we'll find a place of our own and be out of your life forever."

She leaned her head on Tom's shoulder and he put his arm around her. He could hardly believe it. They were back in action.

12

THE STREETS OF JAMAICA

Bradley Shaw sat in the back of the limousine. Through the tinted window, he watched Cabrera enter the low building. Then his eyes drifted around the interior of the luxurious car and he smiled. His hand caressed the pale leather and fine wood paneling surrounding him. *You've made it*, he thought. *After so many years and all the setbacks, you've really made it.*

He opened the minibar between the two reclining seats and poured whisky into a crystal tumbler. Pleased with himself, he raised the glass to his nose, sniffed at the expensive liquid, then drained the glass in a single swallow and put it back.

So far, everything had gone according to plan. He'd thought of everything. Well, everything except the minor incident with the Frenchman. But he would take care of that, too. The door Cabrera had vanished through now opened from the inside and two women came out. Shaw recognized them immediately and could not restrain a smile. It was Leticia Ortiz and her assistant. The two women took no notice of the limousine, but went straight across to a parked car and climbed in. He turned around and watched as the car exited the grounds onto Beachwood Avenue.

He jumped, startled, when the door of the limousine suddenly opened. Grayson Graves got in and took a seat opposite him, followed closely by Cabrera. As soon as the door closed, the car pulled away. Shaw looked at the two men. It had been less than a month since he'd approached Graves. Graves, of course, had been skeptical at first, but Shaw had quickly managed to gain the mayor's trust. Without a word, Graves signaled Cabrera to hand him the small case.

"Good work, Mr. Shaw! I must say, you delivered on your promise," Grayson Graves said, and he drummed his fingers on the lid of the case.

"Thank you, but the credit isn't all mine. We were fortunate to cross paths with the Frenchman."

Graves nodded. "Even so," the mayor said. Then he paused, leaned forward, and poured himself a drink from the minibar. He took a mouthful and went on. "How are things looking with the other clues?"

"All moving ahead. I'm confident I'll have the information within 48 hours. But keep in mind, we have a long road ahead of us. Finding the artifacts is one thing, but understanding and deciphering them is something else entirely."

"I'm aware of that. But you should understand that we're on a tight schedule," Graves said.

"Of course."

"I've assigned Mr. Cabrera here to find the owner of the boat the Frenchman used to escape from the island," Graves added.

Shaw's eyes widened.

"My men and I will take care of it tomorrow," Cabrera grunted.

"How's your girlfriend, by the way?" Graves said, turning back to Shaw.

Shaw swallowed. For someone not in the know, the question might seem innocent, harmless. But Shaw knew the mayor and his motives. Graves didn't make small talk.

"She's well. Thanks for asking. I'm meeting her a little later," Shaw said hesitantly.

"I have to say, when you came to me a month ago and told me who you worked for, I knew right away: this man is going places. And I can tell you this: you've chosen the right side."

"I know it," said Shaw, smiling and narrowing his eyes. Yes, he was on the right side. His own. He was no stranger to unscrupulousness, not when it meant getting ahead in his life and career. He didn't mind leaving a few bodies in his wake if the situation called for it. He just had to make sure he didn't end up as one of those bodies himself if things didn't go according to plan. "You can let me out here," he said.

Graves nodded. He rolled down the partition and instructed the driver to pull over.

"I'll keep you informed," Shaw said as he stepped out of the limousine. For a moment, he watched the car as it rolled away. Then he raised his hand and flagged a passing taxi.

13

A HOUSE IN PORTMORE, A COASTAL TOWN
SOUTH OF KINGSTON, JAMAICA

Leticia Ortiz replaced the telephone receiver on its cradle and looked out over her small garden. She was tired, although "tired" hardly did it justice. Recent weeks had been exhausting. She would never have believed that this project could be so draining, and she was only in her mid-thirties. How could anyone do it as they got older?

Leticia shook her head. She was running to be the next prime minister of Jamaica. What would one have to go through to become the head of a European country . . . or president of the United States? It seemed unimaginable to her.

She stood up from her desk and walked slowly through her sparsely furnished office. Originally, the room had been planned as a child's bedroom, but in recent years she'd been forced to face the painful reality that relationships weren't really her strong point. Repurposing the room had been straightforward enough: a small desk, a couple of filing cabinets, a couch and coffee table for discussions with her staff, and an air conditioner that produced more noise than cool air—that was the extent of her makeshift campaign headquarters.

Seeing her like that in her small dominion, one almost had to feel sorry for her. Almost everyone in her circle of friends had shaken their heads and looked at her pityingly when she told them what she was planning.

"Against Grayson Graves?" they'd said, looking at her in horror. "Good luck with that."

Nobody—nobody at all—had given her even the ghost of a chance. Not against Graves, Kingston's long-established mayor . . .and, as it happened, a criminal of the very worst kind.

Leticia had set herself the goal of exposing Graves' illegal wheeling and dealing. He was a self-made man, someone who'd dragged himself out of Jamaica's gutters to become the wealthiest man in the country. His machinations ranged from blackmail to kidnapping to drug deals and human trafficking. He was the biggest criminal kingpin on the island, practically untouchable. His political influence served one end: to make sure his illicit schemes went on unhindered. But there was more to it. He had built his influence and wealth on the strongest foundation that existed in the islands of the Caribbean: the fear and superstition surrounding the voodoo religion; there were rumors that he took part in rituals with his closest adherents. Many knew about it. And all who did feared for their lives and kept their mouths shut.

And that was exactly what Leticia didn't want. Somebody had to do something, and that somebody was her. She didn't want to keep her mouth shut. She was set on completing her mother's life work.

She stood at the terrace door and leaned her head against the glass, breathing slowly in and out. Every time her thoughts began running in circles, this was how it ended. Slowly, she lifted her head, only to let it fall against the glass door a few seconds later. Gently at first, but the more she felt the pain, the harder she pounded. The last time, she was actually afraid she would smash the glass, and she stopped. She stared at her weary reflection.

A single, heavy tear trickled down over the twin birthmarks beneath her eye. Every time she looked in the mirror, the birthmarks reminded her of her mother, who had had identical marks in the same spot. Then she crossed to her small safe, the first thing she'd had installed when she moved into the house.

14

NORMAN MANLEY INTERNATIONAL AIRPORT, KINGSTON

As soon as they landed in Jamaica, Tom and Hellen rented a car. "Cloutard's hotel or the charter boat agency?" Hellen asked, while Tom fired up the GPS in the car.

"Let's go to the last place Cloutard called from, 'Adventure Boat Tours.' They were probably the last ones to see him. The hotel isn't going to run away," said Tom.

"All right," Hellen said. She gave him the address and they were on their way.

Half an hour later, they arrived.

"This area's pretty run-down. It wouldn't be the first place I'd think of to start looking for our Gallic snob," said Tom as he guided the Mini convertible onto Atlantic Boulevard. Most of the single-story, colonial-inspired places that characterized at least partially the landscape of Kingston, even of the entire country, were looking shabby. Old, dented cars lined the roadsides. Here and there, local people in bright-colored clothes were picking up the rubbish and fallen branches the storm had sent whirling through the streets, but to the relief of the locals, the damage had been minimal. They had seen far worse.

Atlantic Boulevard lay far out on the eastern edge of Kingston, running alongside a branch of Hunts Bay, not far from the container terminal.

"Are you sure we're in the right place?" Hellen asked when she realized they were driving down a dead-end street. "I don't see anything called 'Adventure Boat Tours' anywhere."

"It's the address from de Waal's briefing, right?" Tom said, tapping the GPS. "This is where Cloutard was headed the last time he contacted van Rensburg."

He parked the car at the end of the street. Despite the stifling midday heat, a few children were playing soccer in the dusty turnaround at the end of the cul-de-sac. Tom and Hellen climbed out of the car and looked around. This was definitely not the better part of town.

"This should be it." Tom looked at his phone and turned in a circle. Nothing. Beyond the dead end was no more than a fringe of trees, and beyond that was Hunts Bay.

"Hey, come here for a minute!" Hellen called to the kids playing soccer, and they stopped their game. "Do you want to earn a few dollars?" The children looked at each other and nodded. They approached Tom and Hellen slowly, on their guard.

"We're looking for 'Adventure Boat Tours.' Do you know where that is?" The children laughed. One of them, apparently the oldest, held out his hand toward Hellen.

"Ten dollar," he said confidently.

"Pay the man, Tom," Hellen said with a smile. Tom took out his billfold, removed two five-dollar bills, and held them out invitingly to the youngster. When the boy tried to take them, however, Tom pulled them away playfully.

"So where do we find 'Adventure Boat Tours'?"

The children laughed again, then all of them raised their hands and pointed to a narrow driveway that led through the trees toward the bay. When Tom and Hellen turned in that direction, the oldest boy snatched the money and the children ran away, laughing.

On the shore stood an old wooden house, trees and bushes encroaching from all sides. The dilapidated shack jutted out over the bay, built partly on stilts about six feet above the water. A veranda surrounded the entire structure, and a few steps down from it, an ancient fishing boat, as run-down as the house, was moored to a jetty. Tom and Hellen crossed the veranda to a window. Tom peered through the grimy glass, then knocked on the door, where a sign hung. It read, "Adventure Boat Tours."

"What in the world was Cloutard doing here?" Hellen wondered.

"We'll ask as soon we find someone." Tom looked around. No one responded to his knock, so he grasped the doorknob and turned it. "It's open," he said, pushing the door wide.

"We can't just—" Hellen whispered, but Tom was already inside. She had almost forgotten that Tom wasn't the kind of guy to hesitate in a situation like this.

"I think we're in the right place. Look at this. Someone beat us to it," he said, looking at the chaos inside. Several empty rum bottles lay among papers strewn wildly across a large table. Clothes were scattered all over the floor. Drawers and cupboards stood open.

"Hello!?" Tom called. "Anybody home?" He moved through the large room slowly. "We're tourists on honeymoon and we're in the market for a romantic tour," he joked, moving deeper into the house.

Hellen laughed lightly and shook her head. Moments like this made her happy, because she knew she had married the right man—although she was far from happy about the situation they were in.

"Nobody here," said Tom when he'd checked all the rooms. "There's a small pantry by the back door, full of tin cans, rum, and propane bottles. The kitchen is a bigger mess than here and upstairs there's only a bedroom."

"Hey, look at this," said Hellen. She was kneeling beside a folded-back rug behind the sofa. Underneath the rug was a trapdoor.

Tom leaned down, hooked his finger into the iron ring and lifted the hatch, but below it was just the cloudy water of the bay. "Probably for loading and unloading, or maybe it's an improvised toilet," he said.

Hellen smiled. Tom let the trapdoor drop and Hellen spread the rug over it again.

"Let's go check the boat."

They went outside and looked at the dismal-looking fishing boat. Amazingly, it was still afloat—it looked as if it had more holes in it than Swiss cheese.

"Ahoy, Captain Crunch!" Tom shouted.

No answer. Tom crossed to the deck, then reached back to help Hellen cross the narrow wooden gangplank as well.

"Permission to come aboard?" Tom called. Hellen looked around, expecting the boat to start sinking any second.

"Shouldn't we have asked that before?" she said. She shouted "Hello?" but there was still no answer.

There was no sound at all apart from creaking timbers and the regular sound of wavelets lapping against the side of the boat.

The ancient craft looked as if someone had set a small, crooked shack on top of a hull. A ladder led up to the bridge, though "bridge" was an exaggeration. It was little more than a ship's wheel with a roof over it. Beside the ladder was a door that led below deck.

"There's blood here," said Tom, and he pointed to the door handle. On the doorframe, too, was a blood-smeared handprint. They hadn't been in a life-threatening situation for almost a year—not counting their daily battles at the fish market—and they had enjoyed their quiet life thoroughly, but now Tom's alarm bells were screaming "danger." Years of training had created ingrained habits, and his hand instinctively went for his gun. But there was no holster on his Bermuda shorts.

Hellen handed Tom a tissue, which he used to open the door. A sharp, nauseating smell rose to meet them. Slowly, Tom squeezed through the narrow doorway and made his way down, with Hellen close behind.

"If we want to find Cloutard, I think we're going to have to work a little harder," Tom said, pointing to the corner of the cabin.

Hellen drew a sharp breath when she saw what he was pointing at. A man lay face down at a small dining table. On his head was an ugly head wound, a few flies buzzing around it.

15

SOMEWHERE IN KINGSTON

The man's eyes were glued to his phone screen. The transmission from the mini-camera he'd set up in Leticia Ortiz's office a few days earlier was crystal clear. He watched as she knelt to open the combination lock on her safe.

A grin spread across his face. Zooming in a little, he could easily make out the combination she tapped into the keypad.

He watched as she opened the safe, took out a leather folder, and placed it on the table. He could see the relief on her face when she looked at the folder. It had to be the papers they were searching for. Their hunch had been right, and their suspicions had just been confirmed.

The man narrowed his eyes as Leticia took out a page and read it closely. The page was different from the others in the folder. It looked much newer to him. It was a handwritten document, perhaps a letter or a will. He could even see the tears that flowed down Leticia's cheeks.

The man had what he wanted. He saved the video footage, although he'd already memorized the code. It wasn't the first time he'd opened a safe. His thoughts turned to the best time to break into her house, because his employer—who had planned everything and brought him on board—could not wait much longer. Now it was up to him. He'd try to take care of it today. Leticia Ortiz was a busy woman, with many public appearances scheduled weeks in advance. It would be a walk in the park.

16

ADVENTURE BOAT TOURS, KINGSTON

"Is he dead?" Hellen murmured through a tissue she held over her mouth and nose.

"If he is, he can't have been dead long." Tom, too, screwed up his nose a little and cleared his throat as he carefully approached the body.

"What about the stink?"

"Look around," said Tom, pointing at the chaos in the cabin. Spoiled food, empty diesel cans, countless beer and liquor bottles, and a clearly overflowing latrine seemed to be responsible for the stench. "Trust me, death doesn't smell like this."

Slowly, he reached out his hand and placed two fingers on the man's throat.

"Well? Is he alive?"

"I'm not sure. I can't find a—"

Hellen jumped back, accidentally sweeping half-full glasses, uncleared plates, and filthy pots and pans from the galley counter with an ear-splitting crash. Without warning, the man had let out a grunt and turned his head, completely ignoring Tom and Hellen. Even Tom jumped. Now, the noise that Hellen caused seemed to literally wake the dead, as the supposedly deceased man suddenly shot to his feet. He would have tipped the table over if it hadn't been bolted to the floor. He looked around in panic, his hands feeling for anything he could use as a weapon as he retreated as far into the corner as he could.

"Who are . . .? Where's . . .? What's . . .?" the Jamaican stammered. He was about sixty-five years old with a scruffy white beard, scarred face, and two friendly eyes that, right now, were filled with fear and confusion.

"Well, he isn't dead," Tom said with a smile, looking over at Hellen, who was breathing heavily and leaning on the counter. Then he turned to the old man, raised his hands to signal that he had no bad intentions, and sat down at the opposite side of the table.

"I'm Tom Wagner. This is my wife, Hellen."

"Hellen *de Mey*," Hellen muttered.

"Who are you? What do you want from me?" the old man finally managed to croak. He lowered himself back onto the bench and straightened his overalls. His eyes continued to scan the room nervously.

"What's your name?" Tom asked.

"Torrente. Ignacio Torrente." With an effort at concentration, Torrente reached for a bottle and raised it in salute, but when he tried to take a drink, he found that it was empty.

"He'd be better off with a bucket of coffee if we want to get any useful information out of him," Hellen whispered to

Tom. Then she turned and spoke to Torrente directly. "Let's go up to the house. You look like you could use some strong coffee and I can take a look at that gash on your head." Hellen gestured invitingly and led the way. The old man dropped the empty bottle on the bench, nodded, and slid out from behind the table.

"Who did that do you?" Tom asked.

Torrente reached up and probed the wound, already dried.

"No idea, man" he said, as he went ahead of Tom up to the deck. "Oh, I remember now. I bashed my head on this door last night." He patted his hand against the low doorframe. "So what do you folks want with an old sea dog like me?" Torrente asked again, his voice gaining assurance as his head cleared.

"We're looking for a friend of ours. We think he was here a few days ago," Tom began.

"A Frenchman," Hellen added.

"That's right," Tom agreed.

"The man with the flask," said the old sailor, and he smiled a little wistfully. "He was a real character, that one." Torrente lowered his eyes and Tom's stomach clenched when the seaman spoke of Cloutard in the past tense.

Tom's "yes" caught in his throat. "What can you tell us about him? Why was he here and where is he now?"

As they returned to the house, the old man began to tell them the story. "He came to me a few days ago. He'd found out that a few years ago I—" Torrente paused and eyed Tom and Hellen again, unsure whether he could reveal everything to this couple.

"You were searching for Anne Bonny's treasure, weren't you?" Hellen said when she saw the old man's uncertainty.

"Yes. We went in search of the treasure. But since my wife died, I . . . well, anyway, your friend showed me a letter and a medallion, and I found a clue in the letter that pointed to a particular island."

They had reached the house now. "Before we go inside," Tom began, "you should know that someone broke in and has gone through everything."

"What?" Torrente brushed past Tom and pushed the door open, then he looked at Tom in surprise. "What makes you think someone broke in?" he asked.

Hellen and Tom cocked their heads in unison. You could almost see the question marks hovering over their heads.

"Well . . ." Hellen said tentatively. "All the mess . . ."

"I spent the last few days on a bender, man. And considering what I've been through, you can't blame me. So I let the housekeeping slide. Give a man a break."

Hellen looked at Tom and rolled her eyes. The man was essentially living in a dumpster. She shook her head but decided to leave it at that.

"Come on, sit." Hellen swiftly pushed all the papers together without looking at them, cleared the empty bottles aside, and pulled a chair out for the old man. "Where do you keep coffee?" she asked when she was done, and Torrente pointed to one of the few cupboards still closed. Hellen found it and started the filter machine. "Do you have a first-aid kit?"

"Oh, forget it. I've bashed my head worse than this."

Tom sat down at the table opposite Torrente.

"What happened next?"

"We sailed out to the island and your friend went ashore. He came back a few hours later. He'd found something, and we started to come back. And then there was the storm and the . . ." Torrente's eyes turned sad. He was struggling. Hellen set a cup of hot coffee on the table in front of him.

"Drink some of this first."

"And th—" But Tom fell silent at a glare from Hellen.

"Let the man collect himself a little."

"Thank you, ma'am. I'm all right now," Torrente said when he'd taken a few sips of the invigorating brew.

"Back to the storm," Tom said. "What happened then?"

"They almost caught up with us . . ." Torrente was still having trouble. ". . . and then there was the shooting and the —" He paused and took a deep breath.

"Shooting?" Hellen repeated in disbelief.

"A boat came out of nowhere and started shooting at us. The Frenchman, I mean Cloutard, was . . ." Hellen and Tom shared a horrified look.

"What about him? Where is he?" Hellen pressed.

"There was an explosion and he . . . he was just gone, man. I couldn't do anything. Thank the Lord they didn't follow me into the storm. But my boat was badly damaged and sank a little later. Lucky for me another fishing boat rescued me in time."

Hellen slumped onto a chair in shock and reached for Tom's hand.

"I do not think your friend is still—"

"No. Don't even say it." Tom jumped to his feet. "François is . . . he can't . . . it's all our fault . . . if only I'd . . ." he stammered. Hellen stood up and put her arms around her husband. For a moment, all they could do was hold onto each other.

"No way, I'm not buying it," Tom said. He broke from their embrace and looked at Torrente. "Is that tub out there seaworthy?"

Torrente nodded.

"Then let's go. Take us out there."

17

LETICIA ORTIZ'S HOUSE, PORTMORE, JAMAICA

There was a knock at the door.

Leticia quickly wiped away her tears. She closed the safe, stood up, smoothed her skirt, and ran her fingers through her shoulder-length black hair.

"Come in," she said as she returned to her desk. She put on her reading glasses, hoping to look a little more businesslike and hide her reddened eyes.

"Good news," said Bradley Shaw, closing the door behind him.

Shaw was from the U.S., where he'd successfully managed a few local election campaigns in the Midwest. He was, Leticia had learned, what they called a campaign manager —or a spin doctor. Leticia knew that Shaw would have had a successful career ahead of him if he hadn't gotten involved with the wife of a gubernatorial candidate in Iowa. After that, Shaw had been unceremoniously fired from the campaign team and his name had become political poison back home. So he'd chosen instead to look for a job outside the States. He'd been living in Jamaica for several years now and had worked in the Caymans before that. But he'd made his name when he had helped Barbados in its transition from British rule to being an independent republic. Leticia knew about the inconsistencies in his résumé. She had done her due diligence on the man after he appeared on her doorstep one day and, unasked, presented her with a series of suggestions for her campaign strategy. His ideas were solid, and Leticia had decided to add him to her team.

"I've got the new poll numbers. We're only about seven points behind," he said, and he held up a handful of printouts covered with bar and pie graphs for Leticia to see.

"But election day keeps getting closer. How are we supposed to pull this off? We're running low on money, and no one wants to get on the wrong side of Graves, even if it's only financial support," Leticia said with a trace of desperation.

"There's still enough time. We just have to find something that will damage Graves' image beyond repair."

"You mean apart from the fact that he's a scumbag manipulating the people with a fake voodoo cult, paying off the cops and bribing half of the West Indies?"

"Sure," Shaw grinned. "Apart from that."

Leticia nodded and looked at Shaw. He seemed to notice that she wasn't having her best day.

"We can do this. I'm still working on arguments we can make to bring the people around to our side. Most of them hate Graves. But they're simply afraid. He's got them wrapped around his little finger with that voodoo schtick."

"Fine, Brad, but please, nothing illegal. I know that's how it works in other campaigns, that candidates just sling mud at each other, but I don't want to win like that. So please, just the truth. I don't want a dirty campaign."

"Nothing dirty at a-a-a-a-ll?" Shaw said, cocking his head to one side. He drew out the word "all" as he moved around the table to Leticia.

She had to smile. She raised her head and looked at him, and he pulled her up from her chair and kissed her. Leticia had known from the very start that this man could be dangerous for her. His reputation as a skirt-chaser had preceded him. But as unlucky in love as she was, she figured she could allow herself a hot affair with her campaign manager. If it helped his motivation and she won the election, that was perfectly fine with her.

Shaw put his hands around her hips, lifted her a little, and pushed her back onto the desk. Writing implements and files fell to the floor. It wasn't the first time they'd made love on her desk, and it certainly wouldn't be the last.

18

CARIBBEAN WATERS, ABOUT TWENTY MILES
SOUTHEAST OF JAMAICA

"How are you feeling?" Tom asked gently. Hellen was standing on the starboard side of the fishing boat, looking out over the calm sea. The old diesel motor chugged away, and wavelets splashed rhythmically against the hull. Torrente was standing on the bridge, steering the old tub. He looked as proud as if he were leading Her Majesty's entire fleet. The old man had transformed completely when they boarded the boat and cast off. He was back in his element.

"I'm all right," Hellen replied. "I just can't stand the thought of losing someone else." She leaned her head on Tom's shoulder.

"Don't worry. Cloutard is a wily old fox. I'm certain he's still alive."

"I know, and I want to believe it, too. But I keep asking myself if it was all worth it. We put our lives on the line for all of those artifacts and treasures, and for what?"

"You don't mean that seriously, do you? We rediscovered knowledge lost for millennia, we solved the secrets of El

Dorado, found the Russian Atlantis, and don't get me started on King Arthur and the Round Table. We even saved your mother's life."

"If we hadn't started poking that hornets' nest, my mother wouldn't have needed saving at all."

"I wouldn't be too sure about that. Absolute Freedom would have made good on their threats. Just imagine if you, Cloutard, and I hadn't stopped them in Barcelona."

Hellen slipped her arm around Tom's waist, cuddled close, and said nothing. For a moment, they enjoyed the fresh sea air.

"I love you, and I love everything you've done for me," Hellen said after a while. "I just feel sorry for you. I know you miss all the adventure, even if you won't admit it right now. That was why you left Cobra in the first place and joined us at Blue Shield."

Tom smiled. He turned Hellen to face him and stroked her hair lovingly.

"I lo—" A loud whistle from above interrupted him. He looked up to Torrente and saw him pointing off to port. The motor fell silent, leaving only the gentle wash of the waves. Torrente grabbed a pair of binoculars and climbed down from the bridge. He dropped anchor and joined Tom and Hellen, who had moved to the port rail. The first bits of floating wreckage were already visible on the calm surface. They'd arrived.

Torrente handed Tom the binoculars, and he searched the waters methodically for Cloutard. Nothing.

"So who were the guys who chased you?" Tom asked.

"I don't know. I don't even know where they suddenly showed up from. Officially, the island's uninhabited."

"Maybe they were treasure hunters themselves?" Hellen suggested.

In the distance, Tom could make out a small, overgrown island. Then he swung the binoculars over the sea again. Apart from a few pieces of flotsam, he saw nothing.

"Shit, shit, shit. Where are you hiding, François?" he muttered.

"Maybe the guys chasing you fished him out of the water?" Hellen said encouragingly.

"I hope so, because if not . . ." Tom couldn't bring himself to finish the sentence. "You said he'd found something on the island."

"Yes. It was a white rod, I think made of ivory. It was about as long as my forearm. But I'm afraid it's as lost as your friend. We left it down in the galley when the first explosion hit us. Everything happened so fast."

When Torrente mentioned the artifact, Tom thought he caught a sparkle in Hellen's eye, despite her concern for Cloutard. He leaned over the railing and gazed down into the clear water.

"How deep is it here?"

"About thirty feet, maybe forty, but the reef ends at a certain point and then it drops off," Torrente said. Tom unbuttoned his Hawaiian shirt, peeled it off, and handed it to Hellen. Then he slipped off his sneakers.

"What are you doing?" Hellen asked.

"What does it look like?"

"But what about Cloutard?"

"You were probably right when you said those guys fished him out of the water."

"But then shouldn't we be checking the island?"

"We're completely unequipped." He turned to Torrente now. "You said they were using automatic weapons and grenade launchers?"

"Oh, yeah," Torrente replied.

"Sorry," he said to Hellen. "You know I'm not shy about confrontation, but I'm not going anywhere near that island without a small army. In the meantime, we can try to find that artifact."

"What? You want to dive down there now?"

"Yes. What did you think I was doing? Mr. Torrente—"

"Call me Ignacio."

"Okay, Ignacio. Do you have a dive mask and maybe a pair of fins?"

"Sure. Come with me. When my wife was still alive, we went snorkeling all the time. We've got some nice reefs around here. But I have to warn you, the gear is old-school."

Torrente led him back quickly to the stern, where he opened an old seaman's chest and pulled out a pair of fins, the kind with a strap that went around the ankle, and an oval-shaped, sky-blue diving mask. He handed the equipment to Tom with a smile.

"Did you steal these from the set of 'Thunderball'? They're practically prehistoric."

"Just like me, man." Torrente smiled. "And if you really want to know, I was seven years old when they filmed 'Dr. No' in Jamaica." He leaned close to Tom as if about to reveal a secret. "I even met Ian Fleming in person, once. He didn't just write about spies. He was a spy himself."

Tom nodded, impressed. He'd heard about that, and in recent years he'd learned often enough that there were more spies and double agents in the world than most people would believe. Tom looked into the chest and saw an old diving knife and a weight belt. He strapped the knife to his right calf and clipped the weight belt around his waist. Then he picked up the fins and mask and went back to Hellen.

"Don't worry," he said, when he saw Hellen's concerned and somewhat reproachful face. "Right now, this is the only clue we have."

He pulled the fins on and adjusted the mask. He drew Hellen close but when he tried to give her a kiss, she suddenly had a laughing fit.

"You look like . . ." She could hardly contain herself. "With those yellow pants and the blue goggles, you look like the one-eyed Minion."

"Banana," said Tom, and smiled. It was nice to see Hellen finally laugh again, wholeheartedly and unrestrained. He climbed onto the railing.

"Be careful down there." Hellen gave him a kiss and Tom swung his legs over the railing and jumped.

For a few seconds, he held onto the anchor chain, ducked his head, and peered down into the water.

"I think I see something. I'll be right back," he called up when he resurfaced a few seconds later. Hellen and Ignacio watched as he took a deep breath and disappeared beneath the surface.

"Should I have warned him about the sharks?" Ignacio murmured. Hellen looked at him in horror.

19

STONY HILL, ON THE NORTHERN OUTSKIRTS OF KINGSTON

Leticia knew the living conditions in Kingston's poorer quarters as well as anybody, but she still found visiting these slums horrifying, every time. Whenever she drove through Trench Town, she felt a rising aggression inside her that frightened even her. The people in Trench Town lived far below the poverty line, and no one had ever done anything to change that. Certainly not Graves. In his years as mayor, he hadn't lifted a finger. If he won Jamaica's highest office, it would spell disaster for her country. Jamaica lived from tourism and, understandably, the bigger cities like Kingston, Portmore and Montego Bay did their best to keep up the image of an island paradise. But the moment you looked behind the scenes, a different, far uglier picture emerged.

She had to topple Graves from his throne and try to help these people.

For this reason, she had stuck to her commitment to visit the SOS Children's Village Kingston, formerly the Children's Village Stony Hill, though Shaw had told her several times that she wouldn't be winning any votes by going there. Most of the time, she took his advice. She trusted him. In fact, she thought she was probably falling in love with the shrewd American. But in this particular case, she had not listened to him. She had personally arranged for television crews and the local press to be there, too. Shaw had turned up his nose.

"You'd be better off using your valuable time somewhere else," he'd said, and although he rarely left her side, he had not accompanied her to the press conference.

In her speech, she had expressed her thanks for the assistance of the Austrian charity organization that ran the facility and promised that, as prime minister, she would make improving the lives of orphans a priority. She had to work hard to maintain her composure when she looked into the eyes of the children—eyes that radiated only misery and hopelessness. It was nothing less than a farce when compared to the umbrellaed cocktails being served at the five-star hotels along the beaches . . . or the luxury in which Graves and his cronies lived just a few miles away.

She had to win this election. She simply had to.

This press conference had taken more out of her than any previous engagement. She needed a shoulder to lean on. She needed Brad—more than she was really comfortable with, she realized. But just then, she didn't care. She wanted to lie in his arms and forget her country's sufferings for a few moments.

"Should I give you a ride back?" Eleasha asked.

"No, thank you. Kian's driving me. He's just getting the car from the mechanic's," Leticia said. "I'll see you back at the office."

Kian Fullwood, her chauffeur and an old family friend, was already waiting for her. She raised her eyebrows in surprise when she saw the car he was standing beside: an ancient VW microbus, mostly held together by rust and mud, by the look of it.

"Your car wasn't ready. You'll have to make do with the Birdmobile," he said with a smile as he opened the door for her.

Leticia had known Kian as long as she could remember. He was an old friend of her father's and had watched her grow up. And he had also seen the role fate had played in her life. Even now, he still felt a little responsible for her. His own history was checkered, certainly. He and Leticia's father had had some wild times, and he hadn't settled down till later in life. When she had asked him to be her chauffeur a year earlier, he had agreed immediately—it wasn't as if he had much else going on in his life.

Kian spent most of his time in the Blue Mountains. The ranges to the northeast of Kingston were where he pursued his hobby: birdwatching. To earn money, he drove tourists, especially fellow birdwatchers, to secret spots around the island. Jamaica was a favorite destination among ornithologists, not least because of the book *The Birds of the West Indies*, which had been authored by a man named James Bond—the name that Ian Fleming had co-opted for his famous spy.

"Where are we off to, Prime Minister?" Kian said with a wink.

"Let's not get ahead of ourselves," she replied archly. "We're going back to my place."

Kian started the motor and they puttered away.

20

AT THE BOTTOM OF THE CARIBBEAN

For a moment, Tom reveled in the absolute silence and the magical seascape around him. The sun's rays danced in the clear water like a curtain of light. Torrente's sunken fishing boat, a similar build to the vessel on which they'd just arrived, lay at the end of the sharply sloping reef. It had come to rest tilted on one side, a short way from where the reef abruptly vanished into the depths. The explosion had damaged the bow badly, and the crane-like mast, originally used to hoist fishing nets on board, had broken free and hung from its ropes over the abyss. Here and there, a few bubbles still rose from the wreck, and Tom felt a little hope.

The diving weights around his waist pulled him mercilessly toward the bottom. He wouldn't be able to stay down without air for more than two minutes, not in his present condition. A year without much exercise had taken its toll. He swam regularly in van Rensburg's pool, and that was helping a little now, but it was clear that his time underwater was limited.

Getting down hadn't taken long. He had reached the boat in fifteen seconds and was now pulling himself hand over hand along the railing to the door that led below deck. It was jammed. He pulled at it with all his strength but slipped. A large splinter pierced his calf and blood welled out from the small wound. *Goddamnit*, he thought, as he pulled it out. He repositioned himself and jerked at the door handle a second time, then a third. Finally, the door gave way, and Tom was able to open a small gap and force his way through. But opening the door had cost him valuable oxygen. He thought momentarily about resurfacing and starting again but decided against it.

Tom had not noticed, however, that opening the door by force had caused the boat to shift position and slip a little closer to the edge of the reef.

He swam inside and looked around. The water here wasn't particularly deep, and with the ship lying on its side, enough light made it through the porthole for him to see. Bits of wreckage, scraps of paper, and other items drifted weightlessly inside the cabin. Fish had already made a new home there. To his left, Tom saw a half-open door. He swam across and pulled it open. The sudden swirl stirred up toilet paper and other muck that floated toward Tom. He drew back in disgust—he'd found the head. He closed the door again and looked around. Up at the cabin ceiling, he saw something that had saved his and Hellen's lives before. He was reminded of the flooded catacombs beneath Valetta. An air pocket sloshed back and forth above him, like a blob of mercury.

Tom quickly pushed his head up into the space and took a deep breath. He estimated he could get another two or three breaths from the air pocket, extending his time inside the boat.

He dived again. For a second, the interior grew darker. What was that? Tom spun around. A large shadow had briefly blocked the sunlight coming in at the porthole. Tom's pulse quickened. He swam to the porthole and looked out but couldn't see anything unusual. Up on the surface, he saw the hull of Torrente's fishing boat. It had probably blocked the sun for a moment. *Calm down*, he chided himself, *or you'll use up the oxygen you have even faster.* He swam away from the porthole and continued his search, the sunlight once again illuminating the cabin interior as brightly as before. Then he saw something glitter.

21

LETICIA ORTIZ'S HOUSE

Returning to her neighborhood always made Leticia feel warm inside. She hadn't lived there very long, but in the suburb of Portmore, in Kingston's southwest, she had found a new home.

Her house was on Lucile Way and looked out over the Dawkins Pond lagoon. They turned from George Lee Boulevard onto North Edgewater Avenue, then into Patricia Avenue. It was a small detour, but Kian knew how much Leticia loved the Edgewater Baptist Church, so he took her past the church whenever he drove her home.

They drove around the church, turned onto Jacqueline Avenue, and continued to the end where it curved left to become Lucile Way.

Leticia looked ahead, along the street toward her house, and was a little surprised to see Brad's car parked out the front. She thought for a moment that he might have come over to surprise her, but then shook her head. No, he had said he had some business to take care of.

"Pull over," she said, thinking quickly, and Kian did as instructed.

"What is it?" he asked. He watched in astonishment as Leticia climbed into the back and hid behind the front seat.

"I don't know," she said softly. "A gut feeling."

That gut feeling became a sad certainty seconds later. Kian and Leticia watched as Shaw hastily left the house, looking around nervously. He went straight to his car. Leticia's heart hammered as she saw him peel off a pair of gloves—and what he was carrying. It was the leather folder from the safe.

She wanted to confront Shaw on the spot, and her hand was already on the door handle. But then she thought better of it. She watched as he climbed into his car and drove away. Without hesitation, she made a fateful decision.

"Follow him, Kian," she said.

The realization struck her like a slap in the face. Again, she was struck by her incredible bad luck with men. She had no idea what Shaw was up to, but it was clear that she'd been wrong about him. She was too angry to be sad. She was completely on her own now. She couldn't trust anyone anymore. Except for Kian, who was doing his level best at the moment to keep his old rattletrap on Shaw's tail. She knew now that she had to win this election by herself. And she hadn't the faintest idea how.

22

ABOARD TORRENTE'S BOAT

"*Sharks?*" Tom had just disappeared under the water. Hellen stood and glared at Torrente.

But Torrente only laughed and fished a cigar out of his pocket. "I didn't mean to alarm you, Mrs. Tom. Don't worry," he said in a placating voice. He made himself comfortable on top of the chest and lit his cigar contentedly.

Hellen paced back and forth, looking out over the sea again and again. Agitated, she took out her phone. On the flight to Jamaica, she'd begun to do a little research on Anne Bonny and the history of pirates in the region. Just out of interest, not because she had any desire to find Anne Bonny's treasure. At least, that's what she told herself. She had been surprised to discover that her old Blue Shield login still worked, which gave her easy access to libraries and archives around the world. She had found out quite a lot. But she didn't have the nerve for it right now.

Every ten seconds, she checked her watch. The more time that passed, the more anxious she became. Two minutes had already gone by, and there was no sign of Tom. *He can't hold his breath this long, can he?* she wondered. Once again, she looked out over the waters. And her breath caught in her throat.

"Sharks," she stammered.

"Mrs. Tom, take it easy."

"No, sharks!" Hellen screamed, pointing out over the sea. Three unmistakable dorsal fins were circling not far from the boat, directly over the wreck. Torrente jumped to his feet and hurried over to Hellen.

"Ignacio, what we can do? We can't just sit here!" Hellen cried, grabbing the old man by the arm.

23

INSIDE THE WRECK, AT THE BOTTOM OF THE SEA

WHAT WAS GLITTERING DOWN THERE? FROM THE CORNER OF his eye, Tom had caught sight of something shiny. He took another breath and pushed away from the ceiling to the cabin floor. There in a corner, he was surprised to discover Cloutard's hip flask. *All hell must have broken loose here*, Tom thought. Cloutard's hip flask meant everything to him, and he would have defended it with his life. He had it on him constantly, keeping a shot of his favorite cognac, Remy Martin Louis XIII, always within reach. Tom picked it up and pushed it into his shorts pocket. He ascended again for air, and that was when he saw it: there on the ceiling, close to the air pocket, floated the ivory rod.

He was already reaching for it when a sudden grating and groaning set his pulse racing again. The boat trembled, slipped a little more, and finally toppled completely onto its side. Tom glanced upward. The air pocket had vanished.

No time to lose. He grabbed the rod, wedged it between the dive knife and his calf, and pulled himself back to the cabin door. With the boat now lying completely on its side, a narrow passage, no more than two feet across, was all that remained between the door and the sea floor. Tom turned to his left, toward the stern, pulling himself carefully but as rapidly as he could through the tight tunnel. He had almost reached the end when the boat began to slip again. Panic rose in him when he realized he was caught. He couldn't move forward. Was this the end? He felt around frantically and discovered that one of the weights on the belt had become wedged behind a wooden spar. *You don't need it anymore*, he thought, quickly unclipping the belt.

He kicked hard with the fins, pushed with both arms, and was free. The wreck groaned and continued to slide. Sand swirled, fish scattered, and the vessel finally tipped over the edge of the reef and sank into the darkness below.

But as Tom turned toward the surface, his heart almost stopped. Circling above him were three sharks.

24

PORTMORE, JAMAICA

Kian hadn't wasted time wondering why Leticia was tailing her own campaign manager.

"Careful he doesn't spot us," she kept saying. Still on the back seat, she peeped forward between the headrests, giving Kian instructions.

They turned toward Bayside and drove along the coast. They stopped briefly at the Port Kingston Causeway toll station, and Leticia held her breath. The two cars had pulled up close beside one another to pay the toll, and Leticia had ducked out of sight, crouching low on the back seat. Then they drove past Freeport Terminal, Kingston's harbor area, before Shaw turned off toward the New Kingston part of the city.

"Are you sure we're not wasting our time here? Maybe he's just going shopping or visiting a friend?" said Kian, turning back to Leticia when they stopped at a traffic light.

"You might be right," she said, although her gut instinct was practically screaming at her. "But something's fishy. Something stinks. I want to know why he broke into my safe."

Her wounded heart needed certainty. She obviously knew far less than she needed to about the man. Sure, the usual background checks and had turned up a little dirty laundry from Shaw's past. She knew that Shaw was a shyster—in fact, that was what had made him so attractive at the start. But even if Kian was right and they were on a wild goose chase, she had to find out what the goose was up to.

At the start of Old Hope Road, Shaw turned into a Pizza Hut parking lot. Quick-thinking Kian slowed and pulled up on the opposite side of the road. From where they stopped, however, they could only see part of the parking lot. Without hesitation, Kian jumped out of the car, crossed Old Hope Road, and headed for the fast-food restaurant.

Leticia's mind was a jumble. She knew that Shaw was a gourmet. He was sophisticated, a bit of a dandy, almost to the point of being a little jaded. Normally, wild horses couldn't drag him anywhere near a fast-food joint. And it didn't seem likely that he'd be meeting an important sponsor for her campaign here . . . so what was he up to? The U.S. embassy was just across the road, she recalled, but what business could he have there? And more importantly, what business could he have there with her leather folder?

No way, she thought. *He opened your safe and stole your most personal papers.* He was definitely up to no good.

She raised her head again to peek through the window but saw neither Kian nor Shaw. A few passing minutes felt like an eternity, but she finally breathed a sigh of relief to see Kian running back across the road.

"He's switched cars. He got into a fancy black limo. They've got a bit of a head start," the old man panted. He started the engine and pulled out onto the road without looking back.

Screeching tires and honking horns followed them as they sped away, but Kian ignored them.

"What happened?" Leticia asked.

"Nothing spectacular," Kian said. He was concentrating hard on keeping the black Lincoln in sight. "Shaw parked his car, and a few seconds later the limo doors opened, and a couple of shady-looking guys came over to him. They talked, but not for long, and it looked pretty heated. Then Shaw climbed into the limo. He didn't look happy at all."

Hope flared in Leticia's mind. "Shaw wasn't happy. Do you mean they forced him to get into the car?"

"That's what it looked like."

Leticia thought about that. Maybe he was being blackmailed? Maybe he was the victim and not the perpetrator? *Maybe he's on my side after all. Maybe he's in trouble, and couldn't bring himself to tell me? But what does he want with my private papers?* She shook her head angrily at her own foolishness. Why should a man confuse her like this? She hated it when her emotions got the better of her and she stopped thinking clearly. Kian interrupted her tangled thoughts.

"Looks to me like they're heading into the Blue Mountains."

Slowly but surely, they had crossed Kingston, leaving behind the suburbs of Liguanea and Mona. At the University of Technology, they turned left. The traffic at Papine Square was terrible, as usual. Cars, buses, bicycles and mopeds pushed their way through. Lane markings and the rules of the road were no more than vague recommendations that no one paid any attention to.

Kian was right. They were driving into the mountains. They crossed the Hope River several times, following the B1 as it wound its way uphill.

Leticia paled as a terrible realization struck her. They were heading for Grayson Graves' estate.

25

ABOARD TORRENTE'S BOAT

"Ignacio, what do we do?" Hellen snapped at the old man. "Tom's been underwater for five minutes already! I don't know how he's holding out so long." She recalled the moment when she herself had almost drowned, when she and Tom had managed to flee the flooded caves on Malta. Recalling the spark of hope she had held onto back then, she was a little surprised at herself. Of course she was afraid for Tom. He was the most important person in her life. But what she felt now was different from before. She wasn't imagining horror scenarios. Instead, a feeling of trust came over her. She knew Tom. She knew how good he was at getting out of dangerous situations in one piece. It was one of the things she found so attractive about him, one of the reasons she loved him.

She had to concede that the adventures they'd been through and the dangers they'd faced together were a big part of what had brought them together. She knew Tom loved adventure. And at that moment, the suspicion dawned on her that she loved it too. After her father's death and the mortal danger her mother had been in, she had talked herself into believing that she no longer wanted any of it. Now she was realizing that it wasn't true. Tom wasn't going to suffocate down there. He wasn't going to be eaten by sharks. He would do what he did best: cheat death, just as he'd done countless times before. And she would be proud of him. Almost angrily, she pushed aside the thought of what would happen if Tom found Cloutard's ivory rod. She had already read about the artifact, and what she had read intrigued her.

"I've got an idea." Ignacio's voice dragged Hellen out of her thoughts. "We'll try to frighten them away." He climbed up to the bridge and started the engine. "Raise the anchor!"

26

ON THE SEA FLOOR

Tom didn't dare to move. The oxygen in his lungs was gradually running out, and he knew he wouldn't be able to hold out much longer. Should he risk it and surface? This wasn't a Steven Spielberg film, after all. Sharks weren't the bloodthirsty monsters Hollywood wanted us to believe, he told himself.

He was drifting over the abyss when one of the sharks caught sight of him and glided slowly down in his direction. What were you supposed to do if a shark attacked? Whack it on the nose, he remembered reading. Human beings are not normal prey for sharks; often the sharks are just curious. Tom lifted his right leg and drew the knife strapped to his calf. Now he saw the wound he'd inflicted on himself when he pulled open the cabin door. A little blood was still oozing from it. Is that what had attracted them? Impossible. If humans aren't on a shark's menu, how would it know what human blood smelled like?

It was getting harder and harder to suppress the urge to breathe. He knew that, at some point, his conscious mind was no longer going to be able to override the needs of his body. His lungs, thirsting for air, would force his mouth to open, would suck in the deadly water, and he would drown.

The shark kept moving closer. The biggest mistake you could make was to try to swim away, Tom knew. No fast movements. Stay completely calm. The large fish turned toward him, sinuous as a snake. It wasn't a great white, at least, but it was still big enough to take a decent-sized bite out of him. A muffled noise made Tom look up for a second. The boat's engine had sprung to life. What was this? Did they think he was dead? Had they decided to leave? No, Hellen wouldn't allow that. Then he saw the anchor start to rise. It was being pulled up. But one problem at a time . . .

The gills, Tom thought. The gills were the most vulnerable part of a shark. Sharks had to be in constant motion to make sure enough water flowed through their gills. A punch there would panic the shark and it would swim away. At least, he hoped it would.

His time was up. He had to act. He slid the knife back into its sheath and got ready. Less than three feet separated Tom and the shark. Its mouth opened, revealing deadly rows of teeth. Tom's pulse was almost bursting his veins when he swung nimbly to one side and slapped the shark's gills with the flat of his hand. The shark whipped around as if struck by lightning and swept away with a strong beat of its tail.

Now or never. With the last of his strength, Tom swam upward, kicking hard with the fins and aiming for the anchor rope. He grabbed it with both hands and let it pull him up the last few feet. To his astonishment, the boat had turned and was heading directly for the other two sharks, which soon took off. At the last possible second, he broke through the surface, and his lungs filled with life-saving air.

27

ABOARD TORRENTE'S BOAT

A relieved smile appeared on Hellen's face when Tom broke the surface. All the concern flowed out of her. Since Tom had dived, her adrenalin level had risen to an all-time high, and she had to admit that she had missed the sensation. It wasn't just her concern for Tom. No, it was the adventure that she missed. That flutter in her belly, the excitement and thrill whenever they went chasing after long-lost artifacts or deciphered ancient myths. She watched with pride as her husband tossed his swim fins over the railing and climbed the rusty ladder at the stern. He had hardly set foot on deck when Hellen threw her arms around him.

"Hellen! Not so—" Tom mumbled among Hellen's passionate kisses. "Look what I found," he said, coming up briefly for air. He reached into the pocket of his shorts and took out the flask he'd discovered inside the wrecked boat.

"François will be jumping for joy, if we ever find him," Hellen said, swallowing the lump that had appeared in her throat.

"Not 'if'," Tom corrected her. "When we find him. I'm not giving up hope." He pulled Hellen close and kissed her forehead. "I brought something for you, too." He smiled mischievously and pulled out the ivory rod still lodged behind the knife on his calf. He presented the artifact to her solemnly and her eyes shifted in disbelief from the rod to Tom's eyes and back. He nodded encouragingly, able to read her thoughts from her face.

"Stop grinning like an idiot," she said, punching him playfully on the arm.

She reached for the rod and began to examine it. Tom couldn't suppress his customary smile. He sensed that something in Hellen had changed. Her scientist's spirit had been reawakened.

"How did you find it?" she asked. "It can't have been easy to spot something that size in a shipwreck."

She hefted the rod in her hands and inspected it closely. It was about eighteen inches long and a little over an inch thick. She turned it around and ran her fingers lightly over every curve and notch of the intertwining designs carved into it.

"It was just floating under the roof," Tom said.

Hellen's expression changed instantly. Creases appeared on her forehead and her eyes narrowed.

"Did you say floating under the roof?" she asked, repeating Tom's words slowly.

Before he could say anything, Hellen gripped the rod with determination in both hands. With a strong twist, she turned the right half of the rod while holding onto the left half tightly. Tom and Torrente flinched at the grating sound as the rod unscrewed in the middle.

Tom's face brightened instantly. Hellen's intuition, as usual, had been on the money. "You've really got a knack for these old things," he said. He watched as Hellen carefully separated the two halves of the hand-carved ivory rod, revealing a roll of parchment in its hollow interior. She took it out and handed Tom the two halves of the rod.

"The air inside the rod made it buoyant," she said. "The screw threading is amazing handiwork. It's completely dry inside."

She pushed past Tom and Torrente and went back to the old equipment chest on the deck. Kneeling in front of it, she carefully unrolled the old document, revealing a kind of map about eighteen by twenty-four inches. All three gazed thoughtfully at the strange lines, symbols, and graphics on the map.

"A treasure map, obviously," she murmured.

"Yes. But without a big red cross to show where the treasure's buried," Tom said. Hellen, as usual, only shook her head and rolled her eyes.

She was engrossed in the map. She held it up to the light, examined the edges, and looked closely at the various lines and symbols on it. Then she suddenly looked up.

"My instinct tells me that something is missing. Like this, the map is completely useless."

Suddenly, they heard a noise to starboard.

28

ABOARD TORRENTE'S BOAT

Water splashed skyward and all three turned in fright. Hellen quickly rolled the map together, slipped it back inside its protective rod, and screwed the two halves together again. They had been so engrossed in the map and their deliberations that they hadn't noticed at all that a small pod of dolphins had joined the slowly chugging boat. Hellen and Tom ran to the bow and watched their graceful new companions as they leaped from the water around the bow and made their typical whistling, clicking sounds.

Hellen leaned her head on Tom's shoulder, the rod held firmly in her hands. "Remember the Jubail Mangrove Park in Abu Dhabi? When we were searching for the Grail?" she asked.

Tom nodded. They rarely got to enjoy nature's spectacles. Their adventuring—or more to the point, their adversaries—never allowed them the time. After a few minutes, Torrente interrupted the idyllic scene.

"I think it's time we were heading back. All right with you?" He had already climbed up to the bridge and, without waiting for an answer, opened the throttle.

An hour later, Torrente's boat cruised past the container terminal and on toward Hunts Bay. In the distance, they could already see his house.

Tom had spent the entire voyage thinking about the treasure, Cloutard, and the men who had attacked him and Torrente, and his discomfort grew. As they chugged slowly into Hunts Bay, Tom picked up the binoculars and trained them on Torrente's house. His fears had been confirmed. He ran to the bridge, Hellen close behind him.

"Ignacio, cut the engine," Tom shouted as he climbed up.

The boat fell silent and immediately began to drift. They had just sailed into the mouth of Hunts Bay, about two hundred yards across, still far enough from Torrente's house to not be noticed. Though he hadn't needed it for almost a year, it seemed Tom's gut instinct was still working.

29

A HOUSE IN THE BLUE MOUNTAINS, ABOVE KINGSTON

IT ALL SEEMED VERY STRANGE TO CLOUTARD. FOR THE LAST few days, he'd been interrogated relentlessly, beaten, and deprived of food and water, all in an attempt to make him compliant. They'd flown him off the island in a helicopter to the filthy hole at Port Royal Harbor. This morning, they had brought him here—obviously the house of whoever was giving the orders.

No expense had been spared. He mentally calculated what the antique furniture just in the entrance hall and on the way to this room must have cost. Even the paintings on the walls were of good quality.

Cloutard made a few mental notes. When all this was over, he would pay another visit to this house. It would definitely be worth it. He recognized a few works by Antoine Watteau and Giovanni Battista Tiepolo, but the really exciting one was the Goya. A rumor had been doing the rounds for many years that "The Naked Maja" hanging in the Prado was a copy. The original was said to have been stolen in the early 2000s, and the Prado had apparently hushed it up. A common practice, as Cloutard knew only too well from other galleries, including the Louvre. And here it was: "The Naked Maja." Unfortunately, Cloutard did not have the opportunity just now to confirm that the painting was genuine. But he would take care of that later.

Now he had other things to think about. The last few days had been painful and exhausting. He certainly hadn't expected things to take the turn they had, but he had to go with it. At some point, he knew, it would all come to an end. And as always, Cloutard had covered his bases.

The strangest part was just how differently he was now being treated. His wounds had been treated and he'd been moved into a luxurious private room. He had finally been able to take a shower and shave, both long overdue. Cloutard hated being unkempt. They had also put out new clothes out for him. Surprisingly, the suit had fit perfectly, and it was a Brioni. Someone had done their homework.

The door opened and Cabrera came in. The show was about to begin.

"Come with me," was all Cabrera said.

Cloutard was led into a library. Now he was absolutely certain he would be coming back. The owner of the house had filled the room with a collection of very interesting items indeed. His affinity for the 18th century was clear.

At the same time, he seemed to have a penchant for the history of piracy, and Cloutard saw a few pieces he could not figure out. There was quite a lot of clichéd junk, for example. Sabers, anchors, a ship's wheel, and a series of old maps on the wall. It looked as if the owner had raided the set of "Pirates of the Caribbean." And among all the kitsch, Cloutard also saw strange-looking statues and figurines, colorful tapestries with strange symbols, headdresses with bright feathers, and a collection of Jolly Rogers, large and small.

A man was waiting for him. Cloutard was not certain, but he suspected he was face to face with Grayson Graves. He'd seen his visage grinning from countless election posters.

Graves stepped toward him with two cognac glasses in his hands.

"Louis XIII, unless I'm mistaken?" Graves said, handing Cloutard one of the crystal snifters—unnecessarily, because Cloutard had already noticed the intoxicating aroma of his beloved beverage the moment he entered the library.

"I must apologize for the rough handling of the last few days, Monsieur Cloutard. I believe a little more respect is called for," said Graves, lifting his glass in a toast.

Cloutard sighed and raised his eyebrows as he clinked glasses with Graves. He saw no reason to start causing problems now. He already had enough of those. He was far more interested in what Graves was planning because, suddenly, it seemed as if he'd decided to bury the hatchet. Cloutard decided to play along.

"Please, Monsieur." Graves indicated one of the plush leather armchairs. "Have a seat and let's talk like civilized men. I think we have more in common than you might realize."

30

TORRENTE'S HOUSE, KINGSTON

THE FISHING BOAT CHUGGED SLOWLY THROUGH THE BAY. Hemmed in on both sides by trees and bushes, the bay ended in a slender river a half-mile farther on.

Tom was still peering through the binoculars.

"Are you expecting anybody?" Tom said, turning to Torrente. "I count three guys. They're just getting out of a big SUV in front of your house."

"What? No, man. Let me see," Torrente said, reaching for the binoculars.

"Any idea who they are?" Hellen asked.

"Ignacio, you said the island was uninhabited, right?" Tom asked, and Torrente nodded. "If everyone thinks the island's uninhabited, and no one wants to go near the place, then it's the perfect hideout. Cloutard might have stumbled onto a drug operation or something when he found the rod. And you're sure he said nothing about it?"

Torrente only shook his head. He kept peering through the binoculars.

"So if we assume that Cloutard isn't dead, and that the guys who followed you fished him out of the drink, then it's not a huge leap to think that they're also after the treasure."

"They might have chased Ignacio and Cloutard because they'd stumbled onto their hideout and wanted them out of the way," Hellen suggested, surprised at herself for voicing such a bleak thought.

"True. But then where's the disc that van Rensburg gave François?"

"It probably went down with the boat."

"No, man. The last time I saw it was when Cloutard showed it to me at my house," Torrente said. "I think he had it on him when he went overboard."

Tom nodded. "I'm telling you, those guys have got Cloutard under lock and key somewhere and now they've got their hands on the disc, too. Why else would they be here?"

"They're here because they traced me from the name of my boat," Torrente said. "Did you already forget that I escaped from them?"

"However they found you, we can't just chug up there and say hi. You wait here. I'll take a closer look," Tom said. "Make sure you hang onto that ivory rod," he said to Hellen, then turned to Torrente. "And you make sure nothing happens to Hellen. Do you have a gun?"

Torrente handed the binoculars to Hellen and immediately began rummaging through a drawer beside the wheel. He dug out a revolver, blew off a thick layer of dust, and held it out to Tom.

"Do you have anything from this century?" Tom said with a grin as he took the gun from Torrente and looked it over. It was at least seventy years old. "A self-cocking, double-action, hammerless Smith and Wesson. This belongs in a museum. Along with this boat." He swung the barrel down. The cylinder was empty.

"You know, 'This belongs in a museum' is actually my line," said Hellen with a smile. She was definitely back to her old self.

"Have you got any ammunition, or am I supposed to beat those guys to death with it?" Tom said, weighing the pistol in his hand. "It's heavy enough."

Torrente dived into the drawer again. "Don't worry, it works," he said, handing Tom a handful of cartridges. Tom loaded five into the cylinder. Swinging the pistol up, he locked the barrel back in place with a click. He rolled the magazine up his forearm and it made a satisfying buzz as it spun. Tom nodded. He put the remaining cartridges in the back pocket of his Bermuda shorts and zipped it closed, then pushed the revolver itself into a front pocket.

"You look like you've handled a few guns," said Torrente, raising his bushy eyebrows.

Tom looked at Hellen, but he could not read her expression very well. Just a little earlier, for the first time in months, she had been afraid for his life. Now here he was, already putting himself in harm's way again—but this time, her fear seemed to have evaporated.

"I'll be back," Tom intoned in a broad Schwarzenegger accent. He pressed a kiss to Hellen's cheek and climbed down to the deck. Seconds later, Hellen and Ignacio saw him swim across the bay and reach the shore in the cover of the trees.

"Your husband's a courageous man, Mrs. Tom," said Torrente with almost fatherly affection.

Tom made his way through the trees. When he spotted the house, he took cover and drew the old pistol. Somewhat out of breath, he peered ahead. *I really gotta exercise a little more*, he thought, massaging away a stitch in his side. The SUV had driven onto the property along the narrow driveway and was parked not far from the house. One of the men was leaning on the hood, smoking a cigarette. He was tattooed and wore jeans and a colorful Hawaiian shirt, open to the chest. A chromed pistol was tucked into his belt at the front. The other two men were already in the house.

Great, thought Tom. *I hate it when I'm right.* He looked around. In the distance, he could hear children laughing—the same children as before, playing soccer tirelessly in the turnaround.

Suddenly, the door to Torrente' house opened. One of the men came out, loaded down with a sizable box, which he shoved into the back of the SUV.

What are they doing? What did the old man have that these guys would be interested in? Tom wondered.

He could take out the guy at the car easily enough, but if one of them suddenly disappeared then his buddies would know that something was up. A little more finesse was called for.

"I need a scalpel, Wagner, not a sledgehammer," his former CO in Cobra, the Austrian anti-terror unit, had put it succinctly after one of the many times that Tom had acted recklessly, leaving chaos in his wake. This time, Tom decided to take the words to heart. Too much was at stake to mess this up. The last thing he wanted was to have to deal with the local cops.

"Okay, Maierhofer, for once let's do it your way," Tom murmured to himself, remembering his old boss. Somehow, he had to lure the guy away from the SUV. He heard the children laughing again and had an idea.

31

GRAYSON GRAVES' ESTATE IN THE BLUE MOUNTAINS

"*Tu en es sûr?* I would not be so certain that we have anything in common," said Cloutard, savoring the flow of his beloved cognac down his throat.

"We both love beautiful things, for instance. Things with history, art from the past. You must have seen the Goya." Graves was practically puffing out his chest with pride. "And like me, you're not always very particular about how you come into possession of these beautiful things, am I right?"

"Monsieur, you are mistaken. I abhor violence. I may be a thief, a swindler, a smuggler . . ." he said, then looked around the room and pointed at one of the paintings, which showed an old three-master, ". . . and yes, maybe even a pirate. But as you no doubt know, pirates had a code of honor. They were more humane than any of the ruling tyrants of their day."

Cloutard got to his feet and set the cognac glass on a small table beside the armchair, briefly matching Grayson's cold stare with one of his own.

"I may have obtained many things in my life by underhanded means, but nobody has ever been harmed in the process. That is certainly where we differ."

Graves' expression grew harder. The conversation was not going as he'd imagined. His contacts had not been reliable. Cloutard had been described to him very differently, as a man who only looked to his own advantage. Instead, he felt as if he was dealing with some kind of modern-day Robin Hood.

"Be that as it may," said Graves. "We are both after the same thing now: the legendary treasure of Anne Bonny. You can't deny that, Monsieur Cloutard."

Cloutard raised his eyebrows in surprise and stroked his mustache thoughtfully. So the truth was out. And the treasure really did exist, that much was now certain. And others were after it, too.

Cloutard nodded. "*Cependant*," he murmured.

"Then I have a proposal: that you and I work together. What do you think? You would even take the lion's share. I only want a small part of the treasure, and you can keep the rest."

Cloutard tilted his head suspiciously. "Really? If I help you find the treasure, you will give most of it to me?"

"All I want is the crown of Baron Samedi. If you help me, everything else is yours."

The strange items and movie props that Cloutard had been unable to make head or tail of suddenly made more sense. Baron Samedi was a voodoo spirit, the Lord of the Dead. Cloutard knew that the religion was widespread and extremely influential in the West Indies, especially in Haiti and Jamaica.

"Baron Samedi's crown?"

"They say it came with slaves from West Africa, then somehow fell into the hands of the pirates," said Graves.

"But what do you want it for?" Cloutard asked, looking at Graves in pretended confusion.

"Let's just say that the crown will help with my candidacy for Prime Minister."

"*Mon dieu!* You want to pass yourself off as Baron Samedi! You plan to use the crown to manipulate the people through their belief in voodoo!" Cloutard burst out. It would not be the first time a populist politician had set himself up as a divine ruler in these latitudes. And he could imagine now that Graves had been the madman on the island—the man who had made the human sacrifice to Baron Samedi.

Graves smiled malevolently. "It's like I just said. You and I think in similar ways. I can certainly make use of your expertise. And I'm about to take a step that will get us a good deal closer to the treasure. I'm expecting a delivery. Very soon I'll have all three medallions in my possession."

Cloutard's expression did not change. He'd dealt with crooks of all kinds for decades, and his poker face had never let him down.

"Now that you've taken mine," he said.

"For which, naturally, I am extremely thankful," Graves said, his words heavy with irony. "And of course, the letter you had in your possession has also been very helpful. Of course, I would appreciate it if you could explain it to me in a little more detail. As I said, I already see us as a team."

Cloutard studied Graves, weighing every word the man spoke, trying to determine whether there was anything to it or if he was just bluffing. He threw back the last of his cognac. "Maybe you are right," he said. "A partnership could benefit both of us."

There was a knock at the door and one of Graves' servants entered.

"Mr. Shaw is here, sir. He says it's urgent." The man's voice trembled. He was clearly terrified of interrupting his boss.

"Perfect timing," said Graves. "That will be the delivery I was just talking about. Take Shaw out to the terrace." He looked at Cloutard. "My library is only for special guests."

"*Alors*, an honor and a privilege. I am truly flattered."

Graves ignored Cloutard's sarcasm. "Come with me," he said, and Cloutard followed him out to the terrace. The view toward Kingston and the Caribbean Sea beyond was impressive.

A moment later, Shaw was led onto the terrace from another entrance.

"Do you have it?" Graves asked, getting straight to the point. Shaw looked first at Graves and then at Cloutard, who glared back.

32

TORRENTE'S HOUSE, KINGSTON

Hellen could not sit still. Tom was out there getting in trouble again, and she was trapped here on this stupid rattletrap of a boat, unable to do anything. She was getting jumpier by the minute. She was surprised at herself. Was she turning into another damned adrenalin junkie, like Tom? Torrente tried to distract her a little, offering her a cup of the coffee he'd just prepared, but she turned it down. She was nervous enough as it was. She had gratefully accepted a bottle of water, however.

When Tom had handed her the 300-year-old rod, Hellen's enthusiasm had returned in a flash. Now she turned the finely worked ivory relic nervously in her hands. It had reawakened her old passion, and she recalled all the excitement she and Tom had been through in the last few years—especially the moments when, after all the tension and danger, she had finally held something that had not seen the light of day for centuries. Several of the artifacts they'd unearthed had been assumed to be purely mythical, and when she had finally had them in her hands, every risk they had taken seemed worth it.

She peered through the binoculars. *What is taking him so long?* she wondered, and she glanced at the time. He'd been gone more than a quarter of an hour, and her apprehension was growing. The black SUV had driven off a few minutes before, but there was no sign of Tom. Then she saw a flash of flame inside the house, and her blood turned cold.

A blinding light shocked her eyes, and she dropped the binoculars. The boat was quite a way from Torrente's house, but she still felt the pressure caused by the deafening explosion. The house had suddenly disintegrated in an enormous fireball.

33

IN THE BLUE MOUNTAINS

"What the hell is Brad doing at Graves' place?"

Leticia snapped the question so loudly that she startled Kian, who turned around angrily.

"Don't do that to an old man. You'll give me a heart attack, scaring me like that."

Leticia laid her hand apologetically on his shoulder, but inside she was seething. What was Shaw doing, bringing her personal papers here? She watched the limo turn onto the property, struggling to keep from storming up to Graves' front door on the spot and confronting Brad. But that would have been foolish, and so far, she hadn't uncovered anything useful at all.

After the limousine turned onto the Graves estate, Kian immediately turned onto a small forestry road that led higher up the mountain.

"Where are we going?" Leticia asked.

"Trust me," Kian said with a knowing smile.

Skillfully, as if he drove through these forests every day, Kian guided the old car through the dense woods. Leticia was bounced roughly on the back seat. At first, she wasn't sure what Kian had in mind, but she found out quickly enough. He pulled to a stop in a high clearing and pointed down over the treetops. Leticia grinned. From here, they had a fine view of Graves' estate.

"You'll have to go on foot from here," Kian said, pointing to a narrow path through the trees. "That's beyond me these days, I'm sad to say," the old man sighed, unhappy that he could no longer hike as he once had. "But you can't miss it. Follow the path for about three minutes. You'll reach a spot where you can see not only the gardens but also into a few of the rooms."

Kian had gone to the back of the car as he spoke and now took a pair of binoculars out of a leather case and handed them to Leticia. "It'll be easier with these," he said, and she nodded.

"Thank you."

She gave the old man a kiss on the cheek and headed down the path. It was soon clear why Kian couldn't go with her. She had to battle through the undergrowth, and fallen trees blocked the path. After a short distance, the route was barely distinguishable from the rest of the forest. But she pushed on, and after a few minutes the dense growth thinned out and she had reached the spot Kian had described. She had a perfect view of the mayor's luxurious estate. The contrast to the children's charity event that morning could not have been greater, and her anger returned. This time, however, it was not directed at Shaw, who was clearly double-crossing her, but at Graves, who had built a paradise for himself at the people's expense. Worse still, he cared nothing for improving the lot of Kingston's poor, though he was constantly making campaign promises to the contrary. If she wanted to change anything for the better she would have to topple the bastard from his throne, whatever the cost—and, as things looked, without Bradley Shaw.

She studied the estate through the binoculars. Kian was right: she really could see into several of the rooms. She saw an office, next to that a kind of library, and a hallway leading out to the terrace, all behind a continuous glass wall. She saw Graves, Shaw, and a man she didn't recognize walk onto the terrace and sit at a table.

Shaw laid the leather folder from her safe, in which she kept not only her private papers but also the medallion that her mother had once found, on the table. There was some discussion about the contents the folder. It looked heated. Unfortunately, from where she was hidden, she could not hear what they were saying, but it didn't look good. She took out her iPhone and began to film the encounter.

Shaw suddenly punched the unknown man, then kicked him as he lay on the terrace. It was an effort for Leticia not to simply turn away in disgust from the man she thought she loved. With trembling hands, she kept the camera trained on the brutal scene, glancing at the screen to be certain it was really recording. It seemed fate had smiled on her: this little outing would give her all the material she needed to put an end to Graves' regime once and for all. A video of Graves sitting and watching a man being beaten was pure gold.

The third man, she assumed, was some kind of criminal, and she was at a point where she would use anything she could to weaken Graves and win the election.

She zoomed in a little on the faces of Graves, Shaw and the unknown man. She wanted to make sure they were easy to recognize.

So Shaw and Graves were in cahoots. She was certain they were hatching some fiendish plot between them.

Suddenly she jumped, as a gunshot shattered the silence.

34

TORRENTE'S HOUSE, KINGSTON

The soccer ball rolled to a stop at the smoker's feet. He was still leaning on the SUV, now into his second cigarette. One of the other men had just stowed a box in the back of the car and returned to the house.

He looked down in surprise, flicked his cigarette aside, and leaned down to pick up the ball. He looked around. No one in sight. The children's laughter had fallen silent. Slowly, he moved in the direction from which the ball had rolled.

Tom's plan worked. He had bought the ball from the kids a few minutes earlier, for what seemed an exorbitant sum, and then sent them away. If things got crazy, as they tended to do when Tom ran into bad guys with guns, he didn't want to risk anything happening to the kids. When the man was far enough from the house, Tom jumped out of hiding, grabbed him from behind, and sent him off to dreamland with a textbook chokehold. He took the man's chromed pistol and dragged his unconscious body into the bushes. Then he crept back toward the house. He hid for a moment behind the SUV and reviewed his options.

With the man's gun at the ready, he crept through the back door. The ancient, heavy revolver was still in his shorts pocket. He moved carefully past the closet, then the stairs and the kitchen door across from them and peeked quickly around the corner. A tall man in cargo shorts and a linen shirt was standing beside the sofa, looking out over the bay. The other guy was frantically stuffing the last of the files and papers into a cardboard box.

"Is that all of it?" Tom heard the man at the window ask without turning around.

"That's all," the other one answered. "What does the boss want with all the old guy's crap?"

"None of your business. Just get it in the car," the man at the window growled.

"Hey, Cabrera," the man with the box said, lowering his voice and moving a few steps closer to his boss. "Is this about that French guy you caught near the island?"

Cabrera just grunted and scowled back over his shoulder.

"Okay, okay, I get it. None of my business," the other guy said, retreating a few steps. He turned on his heel and hurried out through the front door.

"Tell Jarek to get in here and help us," Cabrera shouted after him.

All right, Tom thought. *François is still alive, and these guys are holding him prisoner.* But he also knew he'd be in trouble as soon as they discovered that their friend outside was taking a little nap.

Now or never. Cabrera was alone in the house. Tom left his hiding place and tiptoed down the corridor and into the living room.

"Hands in the air and turn around," Tom said evenly, pistol trained on the man at the window. "Slowly."

But apart from a controlled, casual glance back over his shoulder, Cabrera didn't budge. He made no move at all to raise his hands, but continued staring out the window indifferently.

"Hey! Are you deaf? Turn around, hands in the air!" Tom repeated, getting annoyed. Men with guns pointed at them usually weren't this impassive. Tom kept glancing over at the front entrance. Cabrera's buddy could reappear any time.

"You've lost the element of surprise. You should have used it when you had it," Cabrera said, his voice icy. "You just wasted any chance you had of getting out of here alive." Cabrera now turned around and looked Tom straight in the eye.

"Where's Cloutard?" Tom asked, holding Cabrera's malevolent glare.

"I hope you killed Jarek," Cabrera said, recognizing the pistol in Tom's hand. "For his sake. Because if he's still alive, I'm going to have to have a serious talk with him, and he's not going to like that at all."

Tom's impatience was growing. *The guy must have a death wish*, he thought. He had never run into anybody who stayed this cool with a gun in his face. Admittedly, Tom's soaking yellow shorts, Hawaiian shirt, and sneakers didn't make a particularly fearsome impression. What worried him more, though, was how rusty he was feeling. He hadn't had anything to do with guys like Cabrera in a year, and the last time he had held a gun in his hand was at his own wedding.

Then Tom realized the truth. Cabrera was playing for time. But the realization came too late. "Where's Clou—" he tried to ask again, but he never finished the sentence. He felt only a short, sharp pain at the back of his head before the world turned black.

35

IN THE BLUE MOUNTAINS

Leticia almost dropped the phone with the video evidence. She turned around in fright and slipped the device into her pocket. The shot had come from back where Kian was waiting. She began to run back, though the undergrowth made it difficult. She tore her clothes, scratched herself again and again, even fell a few times, but she got back as quickly as she could. Just before she reached the van, she took cover. Someone else was there.

She peered anxiously through the leaves of a bush. Her hand rose quickly to her mouth to smother her frightened cry, even as tears welled from her eyes. Kian was lying on the ground not moving, and there was a large red patch on his chest. He'd been shot. Executed. Beside Kian's van were three men. One was rummaging around in the back of the VW. She couldn't hear what they were saying, but they seemed to be discussing what to do with the body and the car.

Leticia was stunned. They were Graves' men; she recognized one of his bodyguards. And they had murdered a man, just because he seemed suspicious and had no reason to be where he was.

The sound of the microbus's rear door slamming broke the silence. Leticia flinched. One of the men looked around. His eyes narrowed to slits and he stared in her direction.

Had he spotted her? Was she about to end up like poor Kian?

"Hey, why are you staring into the trees like an idiot?"

"Come on, let's go."

One of the men had climbed into the black Landcruiser in which they'd arrived. Another was behind the wheel of Kian's van. "We gotta go, there's a lot to do. We have to dump this thing and the old bastard in the back," the man in the van said.

But the third man stayed where he was, his eyes locked on the forest. He raised one hand to signal to the others to shut up. For several seconds, no one moved. The only sounds were the twittering of birds and the rustling of the treetops. Leticia tried not to move a muscle, her gaze glued to the man through the foliage. But suddenly, she felt a tickle at her throat. Frozen with fear, holding her breath, she turned only her eyes downward. A spider had crawled across her throat and out onto her shoulder. The man still stood where he was, unmoving. Suddenly, he looked up. In the treetops, a swarm of fruit bats had taken to the wing. He looked away, turned around, and returned to the black SUV. Finally, Leticia could breathe again. She was doubly relieved, in fact. The spider on her shoulder was only a Nephila, a harmless orb weaver. And she had been spared Kian's fate.

The two cars drove away and reality settled over Leticia. Kian was dead, for no reason other than helping her and being in the wrong place at the wrong time. She broke into uncontrolled sobs.

"I am so sorry," she whispered.

Heavy-hearted, after what felt like an eternity, she stood and went up to the clearing where Kian's lifeless body had lain just minutes before. She knew that she, too, was in danger. Graves' threats were more than just hot air.

She had a long walk ahead of her, but she had to get away from there. And she could not allow herself to be seen. Cautiously, constantly on her guard, she set off for Kingston.

36

TORRENTE'S HOUSE, KINGSTON

A WALL OF STAGGERING HEAT SLAMMED INTO TOM AS HE opened his eyes. His head was pounding, but he was wide awake in a second, fighting the panic rising inside him. He was surrounded by a sea of flames. He coughed, lungs burning, and looked around frantically. He was lying on the floor of Torrente's house. Curtains, boxes, the table, the sofa—everything was ablaze. If he didn't want to end up as fuel for the flames himself, he had to act fast.

The back door. He spun around. Not a chance. No way he was getting out that way. He scrambled to his feet and a terrible thought flashed into his mind. That morning, he'd seen dozens of propane bottles in the pantry. It was unlikely that all of them were empty, and he had no desire to find out how many still had gas in them. He had to get out fast.

He slipped off his Hawaiian shirt, still slightly damp, and pressed it over his mouth. He turned in a circle, searching. The sofa was blazing brightly. Flames were climbing hungrily up the curtains and walls, darting across the ceiling, engulfing everything in their path.

The sofa. Tom suddenly realized that the solution was staring him in the face. The trapdoor.

With the shirt over his mouth and one arm held protectively before his face, he moved closer to the sofa. The heat kept driving him back. He needed both hands free, so he tied the shirt around his mouth and nose. Then he reached for the end of the rug and hauled it upward with all his strength, sending the sofa tumbling over backward. Half of the trapdoor appeared underneath it. He retreated a little as the flames from the sofa surged back at him like a wave. Then he slung the rug over the fire and kicked at the sofa as hard as he could. Sparks flew as it crashed into the wall. His escape route, Hellen's discovery, was clear. He pulled the shirt from his head and wrapped it around his hand, then grabbed the red-hot ring on the trapdoor, swung the door up, and threw himself headfirst through the hole in the floor and into the cool water beneath.

And not a second too soon. The surface above him turned a radiant orange as the house exploded in a massive fireball.

37

ON THE TERRACE AT GRAVES' VILLA

"I got everything out of the safe, just like you wanted, but I can't tell if it's what you're looking for. Oh, and Cabrera called; he finished getting the papers out of the old man's house." Shaw paused to add a little drama to his words. "Before he torched the place."

Graves smiles smugly. "One less headache to deal with. Now, would you care to take a look, *mon ami*?" He pushed the leather folder across the table to Cloutard.

Cloutard decided not to tell Graves that a vital part was missing. It was obvious the mayor knew nothing about the ivory rod. He smiled mildly.

"Hey, Pierre. You're not here for your health. Tell us what it says," Shaw spat. Graves' glare was disparaging, but he didn't intervene.

With a sigh, Cloutard sat and began to look through the papers. Graves and Shaw watched impatiently.

"*Très intéressant.* This is a transcript of an interrogation from the year 1720—the same year the British captured the

'Revenge,' Calico Jack's ship, and arrested the entire crew. How much of the story do you know? Anne Bonny was having an affair with Jack at the time. They mutinied against the previous captain, Charles Vane, and left him marooned on an island. Then, with a pirate friend of Anne's named Mary Read, they sailed all over the Caribbean, plundering as they went.

"The Spanish, English, Portuguese . . . everyone was out hunting for the legendary Anne Bonny and her lover. It was a British warship that finally found them, in Jamaican waters just south of Port Royale. The British had an easy time of it, apparently. The crew was dead drunk and put up practically no resistance at all. They said it was like an orgy on board. Now, Calico Jack's ship was not the only pirate vessel that tolerated women on board, but there were a lot of them on the 'Revenge'—many women wanted to be pirates back then, more than most people would imagine today. Anne Bonny was only the most famous of them. She gained acceptance in the most direct manner possible: she rammed a knife into the chest of Charles Vane's helmsman, who had complained about having a woman on board. After that, women on ships were suddenly not a problem anymore. *Le droit de femmes* in the 18th century."

"Well, looks like we have a real expert here," said Graves happily.

"These pages are unfortunately in terrible condition. I can hardly read any of it," Cloutard said. "I doubt they will be of any use to us in our search for the treasure."

Without warning, Shaw's fist slammed into Cloutard's temple. The blow sent him tumbling from his chair, and he found himself lying at Graves' feet.

"He's lying!" Shaw snapped. "This fucking frog is lying through his teeth." He followed up with a kick to Cloutard's gut. Cloutard curled up in pain, unable to catch his breath for a few moments.

Still lying on the floor, he looked up at Graves. "Well, those fine sentiments about respect did not last very long."

Graves nodded. "Respect needs to be earned. Just tell us what the papers say."

Groaning loudly, Cloutard pulled himself back to his feet. He glared at Shaw with blank hatred, sat down again at the table, and scanned the documents again.

"Apparently, Calico Jack became quite talkative after a few days of torture, and he told the British a number of things about the treasure."

Cloutard leaned over the pages, his index finger moving feverishly as he did his best to read the faded, handwritten lines. "It is very difficult to make out, but he describes how to find the treasure. It sounds like quite a complicated process. You need to have three medallions and—"

He paused but realized immediately that it made no sense to keep it a secret—he'd lost it anyway.

"—and an ivory rod. The medallions were apparently distributed among Anne Bonny, Calico Jack, and Mary Read, but Anne's was the only one they captured. The ivory rod is supposed to be a kind of key to the treasure chamber."

"Three medallions and—what? An ivory rod? What the hell is that?" Graves said through gritted teeth. He was visibly torn. The document was further confirmation that the treasure existed, but at the same time, it had thrown up new barriers to finding it.

Graves frowned down at the papers strewn across the table. "So we have the three medallions, but we obviously still need this damned rod." He snatched the transcript from Cloutard's hand and searched for the passage in the text, just to make sure Cloutard wasn't lying to him. However, with the pages in his hand, he noticed one that didn't match the rest. The corner of a whiter sheet of paper was visible among the old documents. It was a letter that Shaw had taken from Leticia's safe, along with everything else.

Cloutard spotted it in the same instant, but he was too slow. Graves already had the page in his hand and was reading it. A broad grin spread across his face.

"Shaw, you're a genius," he said, pointing at the page. "This is the final step, the only piece of the puzzle I didn't have."

He folded the page and put it away inside his jacket. Then he rang a small bell that was standing on the table. Seconds later, the servant appeared, this time with a noticeably more relaxed expression on his face.

"Get me Cabrera! He's got work to do." The servant nodded and vanished.

Cloutard looked first at Graves and then Shaw. He hated being at a disadvantage. Now the three medallions were together, but he'd lost the ivory rod and put the treasure out of reach. His plan had hit a snag.

38

TORRENTE'S HOUSE, KINGSTON

Hellen's scream cut Torrente to the bone, even as the pressure wave from the blast almost knocked him off his feet. He jumped down from the chest, threw his cigar aside, and hurried to Hellen. He reached her just in time—her legs were threatening to give way from the shock.

"I'm all right," she said after a few seconds, more composed. "Can you start the engine?"

For a moment, Torrente stared at the conflagration as it engulfed the remains of his sorry life.

"Ignacio!" Hellen's shout dragged Torrente back to the present. He ran to the bridge and climbed up to the cabin. He started the engine and opened the throttle wide. Black smoke billowed from the stack as the old diesel motor roared. Hellen held tightly to the rail as the boat surged forward.

He isn't dead. He made it out, she kept telling herself.

With shaking hands, she lifted the binoculars and searched the area around the inferno. She scanned the trees lining the bay and the waters around the jetty. Nothing.

Fifty yards from the house, Torrente throttled back the motor and allowed the old boat to drift slowly toward its accustomed mooring, then climbed back down to join Hellen. In disbelief, they stood and stared at the blazing ruin. Hellen was getting ready to jump onto the jetty when a voice from behind stopped her.

"I know I have a reputation for doing stuff like this," said Tom, who'd surfaced a moment before behind the boat and was climbing up the stern ladder. "But that wasn't my fault."

Hellen and Torrente spun around.

"You saved my life. But here's the best part: François is still alive," Tom said, half choked by Hellen's embrace.

"What?" she said. She had smothered Tom's face with kisses and now slowly tore herself away.

"That trapdoor you found? Well, I—"

"Not that. François is alive?"

"Yes. It looks like they really did fish him out of the sea. They're holding him prisoner somewhere."

Hellen laughed with relief and kissed him again before finally letting go. She turned around and noticed Torrente sitting on the anchor winch, staring at the remains of his house in despair.

"I'm sorry," Tom said, turning to the seaman. "Some guy named Cabrera and two others set fire to the place. They knocked me out and expected the fire to finish me off.

"Cabrera? Are you sure?" Torrente asked. "Everyone knows that bastard. He works for the mayor," he murmured in confusion.

Tom and Hellen looked at each other in surprise.

"What does the mayor have to do with this?" Hellen asked, but Torrente waved it off.

"They took a lot of your stuff away with them," said Tom.

Hellen sighed and looked at Tom.

"It's terrible, I know," Hellen said gently. "But I'm sure we can persuade Mr. van Rensburg to help rebuild your house." She laid her hand on the old man's shoulder. "I am so sorry," she whispered.

"They've stolen my life's work, man," Torrente cried, still staring at the flames.

Tom and Hellen shared a look of incomprehension.

"Not to sound heartless, but describing that old shack as your life's work is a bit... exaggerated," Tom said.

Hellen elbowed him in the side. Tom could really be insensitive sometimes.

"Forget the old shack. That's not my life's work. It's the treasure! The treasure of Anne Bonny!"

"Uh... what?" Tom said. Hellen couldn't follow the old man either.

The old man sighed and looked at them. They could see how hard he was struggling.

"Ah, what the hell. I'll tell you the whole story, but I'm going to need a drink first."

"We wanted to check out Cloutard's hotel room anyway. And I assume our favorite Frenchman found himself a place with a decent bar," said Hellen.

Tom smiled and nodded. In the distance they could hear sirens approaching, and a few rubberneckers from the neighborhood were already walking toward the property. Tom jumped onto the jetty and secured the boat. Hellen and Torrente followed him, and they ran to the Mini convertible still parked in the dead end in front of Torrente's house.

39

JAMAICA PEGASUS HOTEL, KINGSTON

"Fancy joint. Five stars. Typical Cloutard," said Tom as they climbed out of the car in front of the hotel.

"True. It's not very pretty to look at, though. It's like a bunker." Hellen replied, gazing up. The hotel had at least fifteen floors. "When you think how poor most of the people in Kingston are, I don't know if I'd feel right about staying in a tourist palace like this. How were we planning to get into Cloutard's room, anyway?"

Torrente smiled. "This is Jamaica. Money opens all doors."

One fat tip later and a maid let them into Cloutard's room.

"Looks like we're too late," Tom said, looking around.

The bed was untouched, but Cloutard's suitcase and duffel bag had been forced open and the contents strewn across the room. The hotel safe in the wardrobe was wide open and —unsurprisingly—empty.

"Whoever this was, they're thorough," said Tom. "First they sink your ship, then they blow up your house, and they've even tossed Cloutard's room."

Hellen sighed. "We're not getting any closer to finding Cloutard by standing around here empty-handed."

"Well, we're not completely empty-handed," said Torrente, with a nod toward the ivory rod Hellen had unconsciously been gripping tightly the whole time. "You're holding something very special, right there."

"What, exactly?" she asked.

"The literal key to the treasure of the pirate Anne Bonny," Torrente whispered, as if he were afraid of being overheard.

"You know a lot more than you've told us so far, don't you?" Tom glowered at the old man. "We're trying to find our best friend and you're keeping information to yourself?" Tom cracked his knuckles and stepped toward Torrente, who raised his hands defensively.

"I don't know anything about your friend, man," he said.

"But you obviously know about the treasure," Hellen added. Even she sounded reproachful.

"Like I said, I need a drink. Let's go to the bar. I'll tell you everything there," Torrente said, already stalking away.

"For once Cloutard isn't around drinking like a fish, and we've already got the next drunk to deal with," Tom sighed.

A few minutes later, Torrente was already knocking back his second rum.

"The legend goes like this: Anne Bonny hid a fantastic treasure, along with her pirate friend Mary Read and her lover Calico Jack Rackham, who had bought her off her husband, James Bonny. And that"—Torrente pointed at the ivory rod—"is the key."

"Uh, what does 'bought her off her husband' mean?" Tom asked

Hellen grinned. "It's true. Divorce was reserved for the rich back then. It didn't exist in the lower classes, so the husband had to be compensated for his loss, so to speak," she explained.

Tom nodded thoughtfully and looked Hellen up and down.

"You're wondering how much I'd bring, aren't you? Admit it!"

"No treasure on this planet—" Tom began, but Hellen smiled and interrupted him with a kiss. Torrente cleared his throat.

"Can we focus, man?" Torrente pointed at the rod. A little abashed, Tom and Hellen returned their attention to Torrente, who continued. "There were even rumors that they had found part of the treasure of 'Black Sam,'—Samuel Bellamy, the richest pirate who ever lived—and added it to their own, then stashed it all somewhere safe."

"You mean the three pirates buried the treasure somewhere and left clues? But why?" Tom asked.

"I guess for the Republic of Pirates—or maybe it's better to say, for their own republic," said Torrente.

"The . . . republic of who, now?" Tom asked.

"The Republic of Pirates," Hellen answered.

"The pirates had a republic?"

Hellen sipped from her White Russian and turned the rod over in her hands.

"The legends surrounding the Republic of Pirates cover the seven seas. In Madagascar, for instance, pirates founded 'Libertalia.' It was a real nation, too, more or less. They governed with their own laws, which guaranteed a new kind of freedom, and everyone followed them. They even say that direct democracy was practiced aboard pirate ships, which was revolutionary at the time. Remember, this was the start of the 18th century. In Europe, you had absolute monarchs like Louis XIV, or Maria Theresia who was a little more moderate. Still, as nice as she may have been personally, rulers back then had no interest in freedom or human rights. Certainly not the Spanish, French or British."

Torrente had listened to Hellen in silence, nodding occasionally. When Hellen paused, he picked up the thread. "It was the same here in the Caribbean," he said. "With the Republic of Pirates. You had the great pirates—people like Blackbeard's mentor, Benjamin Hornigold, and the freebooter Henry Jennings, who taught Calico Jack Rackham and Anne Bonny. They were the first elected representatives of the republic. It was a democracy that welcomed everyone, regardless of the color of your skin or where you came from. The pirates even freed the slaves. Hundreds of thousands of people had been brought from West Africa to these islands to do all the heavy work. That's also how voodoo came to the Caribbean, by the way.

"So the pirates were the first real democrats?" Tom asked.

"And the first feminists. After Anne Bonny got her way, women on ships were treated as equals. That included the right to vote. The French Revolution and the rights enshrined in the U.S. Constitution came much later," Hellen explained.

"Of course, none of that down well with the slave traders and businessmen—and especially not with the nobles," Torrente continued. "No one wanted it, not the Spanish, the British, or the Portuguese. To regain control over the pirates, the British Crown offered them a 'King's pardon.' They promised the pirates clemency and told them they could keep the loot they had if they stopped plundering boats and submitted to Crown rule. That led to the pirates falling out, and finally to the downfall of the republic."

Torrente emptied his glass and raised his hand toward the barkeeper, who hadn't even bothered to put the rum bottle back on the shelf. His well-trained eye had already marked the old boatman as a good customer.

"Anne and her friends wanted nothing to do with the King's pardon; they wanted to keep living in freedom," Hellen added. "They wanted to establish a republic of their own, and the treasure was basically their seed capital."

"That's right. It's a legend they've been telling here in Jamaica for generations. But—"

"That's all well and good," Tom interrupted. "But legends and yarns aren't going to get our friend back. These guys who've got Cloutard, what are they after? Why are they sinking boats and blowing up houses?"

Torrente looked sadly and Tom and Hellen.

"I don't know. And . . ." his voice faltered ". . . and I don't know why I let myself get dragged into it again. My family's been searching for the treasure for generations. It was a kind of family tradition, but not a very happy one."

He paused. They could see he was struggling to get the words out.

"My beloved Lucia died while she was chasing a clue, and I swore I'd never talk about the treasure again—and never go looking for it again, either."

Tom's and Hellen's expressions changed. They knew what Torrente was going through. Both had lost people close to them on quests of their own.

"Lucia was your wife?" Hellen asked cautiously.

Torrente nodded, and a tear trickled down his cheek. "She was following up one of the many clues we'd collected. There's no way her death was an accident."

Tom wanted to say something, but Hellen laid a hand on his arm, and he held his tongue. Now was not the right moment to go poking around in the old man's past.

"But I couldn't bring myself to destroy all the documents my family had gathered over the years," Torrente said, after another swallow of rum.

"What documents?" Hellen asked.

"All little pieces of the puzzle surrounding the Republic of Pirates and Anne Bonny and her legendary treasure. But it never led us to anything. All it ever brought us was misery."

"Maybe this is the missing piece of the puzzle?" Hellen said, holding up the rod.

"It's the puzzle pieces that are actually missing," Torrente replied.

"You're getting on my nerves again," said Tom, emptying his glass. "Getting information out of you is like pulling teeth."

"The legend says that to find the treasure and open the door that leads to it, you need the ivory rod and three medallions.

The medallions are the puzzle pieces. Anne Bonny had one, and Mary Read and Calico Jack probably had the others."

"You mean one of the medallions that van Rensburg gave Cloutard?" Hellen asked.

"Exactly."

"There are three of them?" asked Tom.

"And if you have the medallions, you can decipher the map in the rod and find the way to the treasure," Hellen guessed.

Torrente nodded.

"Which means that the people who are holding Cloutard were really after the medallions?" Tom was getting excited. "I've got a feeling that if we go looking for the treasure, we'll also find Cloutard."

Hellen nodded. She was as excited as Tom. "Do you know who has the other two medallions?"

Torrente let out a deep sigh. Slowly, he nodded. He began softly. "If we . . ." He swallowed, and his voice grew stronger. "If we really want to find the treasure—and your friend of course—then there's only one person who can help us."

Hellen and Tom looked at the old man in surprise. Torrente looked as if he had spoken almost against his will. Whatever his suggestion was, he didn't seem comfortable with the idea at all.

40

PORTMORE, JAMAICA

"Come on, Ignacio, enough with the suspense."

With Tom at the wheel, Torrente had navigated them to the suburb of Portmore. After a twenty-minute drive, they had just pulled over and parked.

"What are we doing here? Who's this mysterious person who can help us?"

Torrente gazed pensively out the window. His gaze was fixed on a house at which a taxi had just pulled up. A woman climbed out. Torrente's expression softened and a sad smile spread across his face.

"Is that her?" Tom asked. Torrente only nodded.

Tom didn't hesitate for a second. Hellen wanted to stop him —she sensed that something unusual was going on here— but it was too late. Tom was already out of the car and approaching the woman. But when he got within a few steps of her, he stopped in his tracks and looked at her. She seemed terribly distraught. Her hands were shaking, she was as pale as death, and her eyes were red and swollen from crying. When she saw Tom, she also stopped.

Tom didn't know what to do. His enthusiasm had vanished. But before he could say anything, he saw her face change. She stared past him as if she were looking at a ghost, and the lines of her face hardened. Tom turned around and saw that Torrente had also gotten out of the car. The woman's eyes met Torrente's, and for a few seconds the world stood still. Hellen was there now, too, and went to Tom, who looked at her, puzzled.

"What's going on here?" he whispered. Hellen shrugged.

"What are you doing here?" the woman asked, her voice like ice. Her eyes were still on Torrente. The old man did not move from where he stood but stayed silent. After a few seconds he looked down at the ground.

"Now I recognize her. That's Leticia Ortiz," Hellen whispered.

"Should I know who that is?" Tom asked. He was looking back and forth between Leticia and Torrente.

"Do you have eyes in your head? Half the city is plastered with her election posters. She's running for prime minister."

Torrente still had not responded to Leticia's question. On leaden legs, he moved toward her slowly. The atmosphere was strange.

Tom and Hellen were standing a little to one side, watching the uncomfortable silence between the two. Tom stepped forward and cleared his throat.

"Excuse me, but a friend of ours has disappeared, and Ignacio, I mean Mr. Torrente here, says you might be able to help."

Leticia ignored Tom's bumbling explanation and kept her eyes on Torrente. Then she began to cry, at first reticently and softly, but after a few seconds she could no longer contain herself and broke down into miserable sobbing.

Tom frowned and looked at Hellen, who seemed to have a better idea of what was going on. Tom knew that look only too well.

"Kian is dead," Leticia finally sobbed. "Everyone is dying. Everyone who has even the slightest connection to this fucking treasure is dying."

Torrente had approached to within a few feet of Leticia and looked at her sadly.

"What are you doing here? Why now? Today of all days?" Leticia cried, as she fell into Torrente's arms.

Hellen nodded. She knew what Leticia was going through.

41

LETICIA'S HOUSE, PORTMORE, JAMAICA

The four of them sat around the table on Leticia's terrace. A few minutes had passed since Leticia had recovered her composure and asked them to join her in the house. Hellen didn't seem particularly surprised.

"How did you know? Are you psychic?" Tom whispered to her.

"I didn't *know*, but I *suspected*," Hellen answered, and she smiled at Tom. "I have a sense for these things. You're more attuned to . . . rougher things, let's say. I'm more sensitive to delicate situations like this."

"Still, I never would have guessed that Torrente was Leticia's father," Tom murmured.

"What happened? You said Kian was dead?" Torrente said.

It was terrible to talk about, but at least it allowed Leticia to put her family problems aside for a little while. She told them about Graves and his maneuverings, about her traitorous campaign manager and the unknown man in Graves' villa, and about Kian's murder.

Torrente's eyes soon filled with tears, too. Leticia knew how close Kian and her father had been. She had had a falling out with her father after her mother's death, but she still felt his pain.

"As soon as the treasure gets involved, people start to die," Leticia said. She was on her feet now, pacing back and forth across the small terrace.

"The treasure? What makes you think the treasure is involved?" Tom asked.

"Shaw stole Mama's medallion from my safe." She faltered, her voice breaking. "And her letter."

Torrente took her in his arms when she began to cry again. For a few minutes, no one spoke. Sobbing, Leticia looked up at her father. Torrente smiled back lovingly and wiped a tear from her cheek.

"You have your mother's eyes," he said softly.

"Yes. And her horrible birthmarks."

"Oh, nonsense. I always loved those about her."

Leticia smiled through her sobs. Finally, she freed herself from their embrace, wiped her eyes, and sat down again. A moment later, Hellen moved to sit beside her.

"I understand what you're going through. My family suffered terribly, all because of lost treasures and precious artifacts. My father is dead, and I almost lost my mother, too," Hellen said in a sympathetic voice.

Leticia looked Hellen in the eyes, and it was clear that the two women empathized with each other. They had shared a similar fate; Hellen made Leticia feel that she wasn't alone. Suddenly, the ice seemed to be broken and a bond was forged between them. Leticia smiled tentatively at Hellen and nodded in gratitude.

"You spoke about a man in Graves' house," said Tom. "What did he look like? Can you describe him?"

"I don't need to. I have the whole thing on video," Leticia said. She rummaged around in her handbag. Seconds later, all four were looking at the small screen.

"It's François. He's alive!" Tom and Hellen said at the same time, with obvious relief.

"Your missing friend?" said Leticia.

Tom nodded.

"Let me guess. He came to the island for Anne Bonny's treasure?"

Tom nodded again, but more hesitantly. Hellen laid a hand on Leticia's shoulder.

"My family has been hunting the treasure for generations," Leticia said bitterly. "We moved from Cuba to Jamaica decades ago in search of it."

"I know exactly what that's like," Hellen replied. She gulped but stayed focused and resolute.

"We're going to free François, and we're going to put an end to Graves' scheming while we're at it," said Tom. "The guy is pretty clearly a bad enough mayor as it is and definitely not what you want in a future prime minister."

"To say the least," Leticia said. "The man's a criminal, and I'm pretty sure he's got half the Caribbean in his pocket already. There are rumors that he's using the voodoo religion, that he sees himself as the reincarnation of Baron Samedi."

"Baron who?" Tom asked, frowning at Hellen.

"Baron Samedi is one of the voodoo spirits—the Lord of the Dead," Torrente explained.

"Yes, and he's terrorizing thousands with it. Voodoo is still an important religion in Jamaica and Haiti, and Graves is exploiting it shamelessly," Leticia continued. "But you won't be able to get your friend back so easily. Graves has a small army guarding his house."

"We've dealt with all kinds of situations," said Hellen. "Believe me, Leticia, if anyone can do this, then it's Tom." Hellen's voice betrayed no doubt at all.

Tom was a little less confident than his wife. He was feeling rusty, and Graves seemed prepared for almost anything.

"Then you can bring back my mother's letter, too. It was the last one she wrote to me, and I want it back. It came the day she died," Leticia said sadly. She looked at Torrente. "You remember. It was the day she was in Charleston, all because of that damned treasure." A tear ran down her cheek, but she quickly composed herself again. "I don't care about the stupid medallion. You can keep it. The treasure story is nothing but a myth anyway. It leads nowhere."

"I'll bring back your letter," Tom said with resolve. "I know this is hard for you, but we have to get a better look at the house and the property before we can work out a plan."

Leticia nodded. She looked at her father.

"We'll go together," he said. "We've been fighting about the treasure long enough. It's torn us apart. At least it might be good for something."

Leticia nodded and laid her head on her father's shoulder.

"If it's okay with you, Ms. Ortiz, we'd like to get moving. The sun's already going down and I don't want to lose any time. Our friend is in a tight spot and Graves could do anything."

"Call me Leticia, please," she said. "And yes, let's go. I'd like to see you give Graves and his men a good thrashing. He's earned it."

42

"We're nearly there," Leticia whispered as they pushed cautiously through the dense undergrowth. They had parked the Mini out of sight among the trees. Leticia was now leading the group along same the narrow path she had followed just a few hours before. In the moonlight, the Blue Mountains did justice to their name.

Tom, Hellen, and Ignacio followed close at the heels of the young politician. Once their eyes adjusted to the darkness, they could get by without using their flashlights. They did not want to alert the patrolling guards, who already had Kian on their conscience—especially when they were seriously outgunned. Torrente's antique revolver and the ten cartridges still in his pocket were their only defense.

"There it is," said Leticia. Tom signaled to the others to take cover. They crept forward on all fours until, protected by bushes, they had a good view of the property. Tom crouched beside Leticia and looked down over Grayson Graves' sprawling estate. The view was breathtaking. In the background, the lights of Kingston and the moon shimmered across the waters of the Caribbean.

"Typical," Hellen sniffed when she saw the villa. Before them lay a sprawling, two-story wooden structure with numerous terraces, a separate garage, and a private access road. A pool in the center of the H-shaped main building completed the luxurious estate. "Of course a pompous scumbag like Graves would camp out up here. He must think he's some kind of Bond supervillain."

Leticia nodded in agreement. The villa was perched high in the mountains like a fortress overlooking the realm Graves ruled.

"The terrace where Bradley beat up your poor friend is over there." She pointed to the left side of the villa. Tom took out a small device he'd bought at a RadioShack along the way and attached it to the bottom of his iPhone.

"What's that for?" asked Torrente softly.

"That, my friend, is something from *this* century," Tom replied with a grin. He turned the phone with the device attached toward the property, and a moment later its function became clear. "It's a thermal imaging camera, with a range of more than a thousand feet. We can see everyone on the property, even inside the buildings."

Hellen, Leticia, and Ignacio crowded close and gazed excitedly over Tom's shoulder at the screen. Tom cleared his throat softly. "People, please. I can't breathe when you're all over me like that." All three moved back a little.

He swung the device slowly across the estate. Everyone inside and outside the house appeared on the screen like fiery ghosts. They could also make out the basic layout inside.

"There's a small army down there," Tom whispered. He counted at least fifteen guards patrolling the grounds with automatic weapons. Inside the house, he added five more.

"That must be Cloutard," Tom said after a while, pointing to a person sitting at a table on the upper floor.

"How can you be sure? I can't make out anything," said Hellen. "It looks to me like the ultrasound from a pregnancy examination."

"It's the only room with guards outside," Tom whispered, turning the phone a little to the right. He pointed at two unmoving orange blobs by the door.

"And where's Graves?"

"I'm not sure. Maybe he's not even here," said Leticia.

"Shh!" Torrente suddenly hissed. "I heard something." Tom quickly covered the phone's screen and ducked low. The others followed his example. A branch snapped, and they heard rustling, footsteps. All of them lay flat on the ground in their hiding place, hardly daring to breathe. Hellen could sense Leticia's rising panic. She had been in the exact same situation just hours before. Torrente put a protective arm around his daughter. She looked into her father's eyes and didn't push him away.

As if in slow motion, Tom's hand closed around the grip of the old revolver. He raised his phone carefully to check what was moving out there.

We're screwed, he thought. A half dozen men in tactical gear and armed with silenced assault rifles were creeping through the underbrush toward the villa.

43

GRAVES' VILLA

Their relief was great, but the astonishment was greater still. The soldiers, armed to the teeth, took no notice of them at all. They simply crept on toward Graves' villa. Tom raised his head, careful not to make a noise. He quickly scanned the property with the thermal imaging camera and saw more men approaching the villa from the other side. He counted twelve in total. Tom realized that all hell was about to break loose. This was a tactical assault, executed by professionals.

"Who are these guys?" Hellen whispered. She was kneeling beside Tom, studying the screen.

"Don't ask me. A man like Graves obviously has at least twelve enemies." Tom smiled and pointed at the screen, but his little joke was lost on Hellen.

"There are twelve . . . ah, forget it," he muttered to himself.

"Maybe it's a raid?"

"Unlikely," whispered Leticia. She and her father had also raised their heads and risked a look. "Graves has the police in his pocket. They would never do anything against him."

They were taken aback to see how easily the first unsuspecting guard was taken out by one of the attackers. A stealthy rush from behind, a stab to the throat, and the man collapsed, dead. With military precision, the twelve-man team moved in on the house. Anyone standing in their way was taken out without hesitation.

Tom turned away. He'd been ready for just about anything, but not this. He tried to analyze the attackers' goal. Was it Graves? Or could they be there for Cloutard?

"What are you going to do now?" Torrente asked.

Tom weighed his options for a moment. A man like Graves, despite having an iron grip on Kingston—and soon, perhaps, all of Jamaica—must have no shortage of enemies. Was it a coup attempt? A power grab? It seemed unlikely. So, maybe it was someone looking for Cloutard? He, too, had made plenty of enemies over the course of his career. But it didn't matter who was after whom. He couldn't sit by and watch Cloutard get caught in the crossfire.

"Easy. I'll just go down—" But that was as far as he got.

"Like hell you will," Hellen snapped. "You want to take on two armies at once?"

"But if we don't do something fast, Cloutard's dead. We'll never see him again." He took Hellen by the shoulders and looked at her intently. "Don't worry. I won't let myself get caught. Besides, those guys have already taken out most of the resistance. It'll be a piece of cake. I won't do anything reckless, I promise. I just want to make sure nothing happens to Cloutard."

"Fine. If it's going to be a piece of cake, I'll come too," Hellen snapped back.

"No. No way, it's far too—" Tom faltered. The look in Hellen's eyes made the blood freeze in his veins.

"Too dangerous after all, is it? And another thing: who suddenly died and made you the boss of me?" Hellen said, glaring at Tom. He sighed and nodded. Then he turned to Leticia.

"Here, take this," he said, and he pressed the ancient revolver into her hand. "Make sure you get back to the city in one piece."

Without waiting for Leticia or Torrente to reply, Tom slipped into the bushes, closely followed by Hellen, and they disappeared into the undergrowth.

44

GRAVES' VILLA

They had dragged the fallen sentry behind a bush just seconds before, and Tom now knelt beside the lifeless body, put his phone aside, and searched the man. He wore a shoulder holster with a pistol on one side, balanced by two spare magazines on the other. Beside him lay a Heckler and Koch MP5, a compact submachine gun. Tom took the man's holster and put it on, then went on patting him down. Both he and Hellen kept scanning in all directions for unwanted company. In the meantime, the attackers had forced their way into the house, and the estate lay in silence. Graves' men had been taken completely by surprise. They had had no chance against the tactical assault.

"What is it with gangsters and chromed pistols?" Tom murmured as he held up a Colt Government .45 that glittered in the moonlight. On the iridescent blue grip, an image of a cobra had been engraved. Tom smiled and shook his head, then pushed the pistol back into its holster. He swung the submachine gun over his shoulder and picked up his phone.

"What now?" asked Hellen.

"Now we try to find Cloutard."

From where they hid, Tom turned his improvised night-vision device toward the building. The man he thought had to be Cloutard was no longer sitting at the table. He had noticed the unrest outside and was on his feet, pacing the room.

"That has to be him. Up there," Tom whispered. He pointed at the display, then up to the terrace overhead. "I have to find a way up there."

He passed the phone to Hellen and looked down at himself. He still wasn't exactly a fearsome sight. The only change to his tourist outfit was the fact that now he was reasonably well armed. He looked around.

"Let's go."

Keeping low, they ran across the grounds to the main house. The attackers had done their job well. All around them lay dead and unconscious guards. Tom and Hellen pressed close to the wall beside a palm growing at the corner of the house. A quick glance left and right: no one was in sight. Above them and to one side was the terrace outside Cloutard's room.

"I know you're not crazy about guns, but this isn't the time to protest." Tom slipped the belt of the MP5 over his head, pulled back the bolt, and turned off the safety. He handed it to Hellen. "Careful, the safety's off. It's point and shoot." Hellen looked at him anxiously but nodded. "Don't look at me like that. You're the one who wanted to come. I'll be right back."

Tom took a few steps back. With a short run-up, he jumped, pushing off first from the trunk of the palm, then from the house wall, and got a hand onto the bottom edge of the balcony. He pulled himself up and swung himself over the railing, drawing the chromed pistol even before he landed softly on the terrace floorboards. *Not rusted solid yet*, he thought. He crept along the wall until he reached the large glass windows fronting the room and risked a quick look. There he was! Cloutard was alive, standing only a few yards from him in the center of the room. He was stuffing a few things wildly into a satchel, which he threw around his neck. He looked panicked and kept glancing back over his shoulder at the double doors that led to the library. Tom saw the numerous injuries on his face and for a moment felt a pang of guilt, thinking of the life of ease he'd been living while his best friend was going through hell. Just as Tom went to knock on the window, the double doors opened. Tom pulled back, concealing himself behind a lounge chair.

Two men moved into the room, wearing tactical uniforms with night-vision goggles turned up on their helmets and armed with pistols, knives, and assault rifles. For a moment, Tom considered taking them on, but decided against it. Cloutard retreated when he saw the men, but they grabbed him and dragged him, protesting wildly, out of the room. Tom pushed his pistol back into its holster, climbed over the railing, and jumped across to the palm, catching the trunk and swinging nimbly to the ground.

"What's going on? Where's Cloutard?" Hellen asked in a whisper.

"I was too late. They've taken him."

They checked that the coast was clear, then ran around the corner and along the wall to the front of the villa.

A loud crash made Tom stop. He grabbed Hellen and dropped with her to the ground behind a bush. The noise came from the direction of the main gate. The assault team had reassembled in front of the villa. Still on full alert, they secured the entrance area. Three black SUVs raced up the winding gravel road to the villa and came to a stop on the front plaza in a cloud of dust. At the same time, the two men and four others exited the villa with Cloutard. Not very gently, they dragged their prisoner to the newly arrived vehicles, stuffed him into the back seat of one, and climbed in. Even before the last door closed, the three SUVs were already roaring away.

"What now?"

Tom looked around. He pointed to the garage building.

"We need transportation."

When he was sure the departing soldiers could no longer see them, they ran across the courtyard to the garage. Tom's face lit up when the automatic lamp in the garage came on. Even Hellen's expression brightened.

"Come on, we're in a hurry," she said. "No time for sightseeing."

They were standing in a room packed with four-wheeled masterpieces. Tom, who had a weakness for fast cars and owned a mint-condition 1967 Shelby Mustang GT500 and a 1970 Dodge Challenger R/T convertible, was more than impressed by the mayor's fleet. There were four cars in front of him, and one empty space—presumably because Graves was away from the villa just then. *You're a bastard, a crook, and a killer, but when it comes to cars, you've got good taste*, thought Tom. Before him stood a Ferrari 275 GTB rally car, an original 1964 Aston Martin DB5, a 1955 Porsche 550

Spyder, and a flame-red, fully restored AC Shelby Cobra MkIII.

"Man, this is a tough decision," Tom said with a smile. "But I think we have a winner."

He took a key from the box beside the entrance and jumped over the door of the low-slung Shelby. Hellen ran to the other side, opened the door, and slid into the passenger seat. She put the submachine gun on the floor between her feet.

Tom looked at Hellen, leaned across, and slid his hand along her leg.

"There's no time for that now!" she said and went to push his hand away. But she stopped herself when she saw what Tom really had in mind. He clicked on the MP5's safety and smiled mischievously at Hellen.

"Buckle up, please. Safety first."

Hellen shook her head.

The Cobra's motor howled to life when Tom turned the key in the ignition. For a moment, he sat, soaking up the roar and the vibrations coursing through the 500+ horsepower motor. Then he pressed the garage door opener and eased the machine outside.

Once they were past the main entrance gate—the assault team had simply crashed through it in their powerful SUVs—it wasn't long before they caught up with the convoy. They followed cautiously, keeping a safe distance between them.

45

IAN FLEMING INTERNATIONAL AIRPORT, BOSCOBEL, ST. MARY, JAMAICA

It took the small fleet of SUVs almost two hours to reach its destination. At first, they had driven back into Kingston before turning onto the A1 highway toward Jamaica's north coast. Finally, they followed the coast for a few miles to Boscobel, in the St. Mary district. Along the way, Hellen had nodded off.

Tom saw the SUVs' destination ahead. The convoy slowed and turned onto the expanse of Ian Fleming International Airport. Parallel to the north coast, the airport was named after the creator of James Bond, the world's most famous secret agent. But in spite of the prestigious name, it was a very small airport, with a low terminal building and three small hangars beside a single runway. Now it was clear to Tom why the team had driven for two hours to reach the north coast. At small airports like this—unlike Norman Manley Airport, just outside Port Royal—if you had enough cash on hand, few questions were asked.

Tom drove past the entrance and pulled up on the right after about a hundred yards, in time to watch as the three SUVs disappeared into a hangar a few seconds later. Tom checked the time. It was after midnight. The road was empty. He looked around, then leaned across to Hellen and kissed her carefully.

"Sweetheart, we're here."

"What? Who? Where are we?" Hellen woke with a start and looked around. She stretched.

"North coast. St. Mary," Tom said with military brevity. "They drove into that hangar over there." He pointed across the tarmac. "Let's go."

There was no obvious video surveillance, but a hurricane fence eight feet high enclosed the airport. It was angled outward at the top and crowned with barbed wire. Here and there, a few trees and bushes also grew around the perimeter of the property. Tom went back to the trunk and rummaged around inside. "Graves, you old romantic," he said, taking out a picnic blanket and holding it up to show Hellen.

"Are we having a picnic now?" she said drily.

"No. Have you got the MP5?"

Still sleepy, Hellen held the gun up high. Tom nodded with satisfaction and, taking cover behind some bushes, crept to the fence. He looked left and right a final time, then swung the blanket over the barbed wire and began to climb.

"Clever," Hellen murmured. She slipped the submachine gun's strap over her shoulder and followed Tom.

A few minutes later, they had reached the rear of the hangar and stopped outside the back entrance. Tom took out his pistol and pressed his ear to the door, but what he heard surprised him. He narrowed his eyes.

"What is it? What can you hear?"

"If I didn't know better, I'd say a horde of Italians were partying in there."

The door missed him by a hair's breadth as it was pushed open from inside. Tom had heard the footsteps at the last second and managed to jump out of the way. He and Hellen pressed against the wall behind the open door.

One of the soldiers had stepped outside. He took three steps, stopped, unzipped, and with a loud groan proceeded to relieve himself. Tom and Hellen looked at each other, neither daring to breathe. An eternity seemed to pass before the soldier disappeared back into the hangar. Slowly, the door swung shut behind him, but Tom stopped it from closing completely just in time. He pulled it open carefully and signaled to Hellen to follow him. They moved quietly, keeping low.

A narrow corridor led past two small storerooms before reaching the main hangar.

The distinctive sound of a pistol being cocked made them freeze. A moment later, Tom heard a muffled squeak from Hellen and felt the cold steel of a gun barrel at the back of his neck.

"*Forza, gettate le armi.* Drop your guns, now," he heard a stony voice behind him say. As if in slow motion, they did as they were commanded. The voice didn't sound like it would put up with any delay. Hellen eased the strap of the MP5 over her head and Tom laid the chromed .45 on the floor. Slowly, they straightened up again and raised their hands. A push with the gun against the back of his head told him to walk.

"*Avanti. Forza*," the voice barked.

When they stepped into the large hangar, Tom couldn't believe his eyes. He had to blink several times to process what he was seeing.

A white Gulfstream jet stood in the brightly lit hangar. Behind it was an old helicopter. Nothing unusual about any of that. It was what you'd expect inside a hangar. But the rest of the scene was surreal.

A long table covered with a white tablecloth and opulently set with antipasti, pasta, wine, and other delicacies had been set up at the foot of the Gulfstream's steps. Among the soldiers, now divested of their tactical gear and shoveling down platefuls of pasta, sat Cloutard and his friends, Fabio and Adalgisa. Everyone was enjoying the banquet as if it were the most natural thing in the world.

"What the—" Tom muttered.

"Tom! Hellen! *Mes amis!*" Cloutard's voice rang joyfully through the hangar when he noticed the newcomers' arrival. The soldier holding them at gunpoint instantly holstered his pistol. Tom and Hellen lowered their hands.

"What the hell is this, François?" said Tom, going over to his friend.

"You came to save me! And here was I, thinking you and your irresistible wife had forgotten your old Frenchman," Cloutard said, but Tom stepped back when Cloutard tried to embrace him.

"What's going on?"

"I can explain everything, but before we—"

"Francesco, cos'è questo rombo?" a woman's voice suddenly interrupted him. It came from inside the plane and rang through the hangar. The party instantly fell silent, and everyone looked up at the old woman who had appeared in the airplane's doorway. Tom knew of only one person in the world who used the Italian version of Cloutard's first name, and before whom the Frenchman invariably showed respect, if not fear: his foster mother, Giuseppina, the widow of one of Italy's most feared mafia bosses.

46

HANGAR, IAN FLEMING INTERNATIONAL AIRPORT

"*Mes amis*, I think it is time for us to go and find a treasure, *n'est-ce pas?*"

Cloutard was on his feet. He had dropped his satchel onto the table with a bang that made Tom and Hellen jump.

"While you two lovely people were living the good life in van Rensburg's villa on the Caymans, I was jetting halfway around the world doing your job for you. On top of which, may I add, I got my ass severely kicked for it."

Tom and Hellen gulped. They were not used to hearing these kinds of things from the Frenchman. They'd been blaming themselves enough as it was.

"All right, *Francesco*, let's see what you've got," said Tom, knowing full well that Cloutard was not particularly fond of the Italian version of his name. Normally, only his adoptive mother was allowed to use it. Tom had had to put up with his family name being mispronounced often enough himself. Cloutard shot him a glare, but his smile returned almost instantly.

"After I saw the second medallion when that voodoo-psycho guy was, shall we say, interviewing me, I knew Jamaica was the right place to be. By the way, remind to tell that old sea dog what I think about him withholding the third medallion from me. All we are missing now is the—"

But that was as far as Cloutard got. A tidal wave of Italian curses came from inside the plane, and Tom, Hellen, Cloutard, Fabio, and Adalgisa all ducked at once.

"*Oui Maman. Je suis désolé, maman*," Cloutard called back. "La Mamma wants to sleep," he said, whispering guiltily.

The entire situation was more than embarrassing for Cloutard. After "La Mamma" had had to rescue him from several sticky situations, she'd made him promise that he would check in with her regularly. When his call was overdue, and when she had heard from her sources that another family had put a bounty on him, she had made up her mind to act.

And Graves had drawn attention to himself. Apparently, he'd been greedy enough not only to use Cloutard to find the treasure but had also planned to hand him over to the mafia afterward. But La Mamma had managed to find out where Cloutard was being held. She had then flown to Jamaica with her men to rescue her beloved "Francesco" before Don Ernesto got his hands on him.

"I will never hear the end of it. Yet again, she has had to save my backside," murmured Cloutard. He was sitting next to Tom and drained the last of a glass of red wine. He screwed up his face.

"You mean like the time she sprung you from jail after we crashed the helicopter just outside Rome?" Tom asked.

Hellen chimed in, too. "Or when she got us out of prison in Geneva after we visited the Spanish king, who'd been living there in exile because of his money laundering?"

"Oh, yes, rub it in. Keep reminding me of what a mommy's boy I am." Cloutard refilled his glass and pouted.

"Yes—a mommy's boy who can't look after his own things. You shouldn't leave your stuff lying all over the place. I'm tired of cleaning up after you," said Tom, and he grinned broadly as he held an object under Cloutard's nose. Cloutard's eyes widened.

"*Mon ami*, you are the best!" he said as Tom proudly presented him with the flask he'd rescued from the wreck of Torrente's ship at the bottom of the sea.

"But . . . but where . . ." Cloutard stammered, accepting the flask and putting it away in his breast pocket.

"From the same place I found another little trinket," Tom replied.

Hellen retrieved the ivory rod from her backpack and laid it on the table. Cloutard, Fabio, and Adalgisa drew a sharp breath and their eyes widened.

"*Merveilleux*. I thought I would never see it again. But then, I thought the same thing about my bosom companion here." Cloutard smiled at Tom and patted his breast pocket.

"I pulled both of them out of Torrente's sunken boat and had a little run-in with some sharks while I was at it. After that, Graves' men tried to burn me alive. So no more complaints about how hard you've been working, François, please."

Tom's tone was more sardonic than serious, and everybody grinned. It felt good to be working as a team again.

"Well, we have the three medallions and we are fortunate enough to have the rod, too. But we still have no plan about where we are supposed to search," Cloutard said.

"I can help with that," said Hellen. "But first, another question. Wasn't there a letter with the last medallion? Not an old document, but something more recent?"

"Indeed," Cloutard said, nodding. "Graves got his hands on it before I saw it."

Hellen looked at Tom. "We promised Leticia that we'd bring back the letter."

Tom nodded. "We will when we can. Now don't keep François in suspense like this."

The Frenchman looked up curiously. Hellen smiled spiritedly, lifted the ivory rod, and carefully began to unscrew it, revealing the rolled parchment inside. "You said something about a plan?"

"I knew there had to be something else," Cloutard said. "The cleverest key in the world is useless if you do not know where the lock is."

Tom cleared away part of the table while Hellen withdrew the parchment from the hollow tube, unrolled it carefully, and spread it before them on the table.

47

AFRICAN VILLAGE, TREASURE BEACH, JAMAICA

It was the middle of the night, but the shop still opened for Graves. It was a shop that sold all kinds of African souvenirs, ostensibly for the tourist trade. But only ostensibly.

In the 17th and 18th centuries, an estimated half a million slaves were transported from Africa to the Caribbean as cheap labor, mainly for the British. The lords and ladies of the empire didn't like the idea of getting their own hands dirty. Even today, the wounds are still open. Even today, Jamaican hostility toward Great Britain runs deep.

So it was even more absurd that many on the island earned a living from African curios and slavery souvenirs, but also from voodoo.

Graves had known voodoo all his life. His own mother had been a priestess in the religion, though she had secretly told him many times that she didn't think much of all the hocus-pocus. Little Grayson, however, had realized early on how easy it was to manipulate people through voodoo. And his mother had been the one who planted the seed of the idea in his head.

"Baron Samedi ought to rule this island himself. Then there wouldn't be any problems anymore," she had said casually one day.

Graves had taken it to heart. Politics and religion had always been a powerful force in human history, when they were exploited correctly. But he had quickly realized that there was only one way to exercise unlimited power: by uniting the power of government and of religion in a single person.

A plan had germinated in his mind, a plan to revive voodoo in its most extreme form, shying away from nothing—not even human sacrifice. Of course, that would have to be kept secret. The masses weren't ready for that, not yet.

The first victim had been an effort of will, but he told himself that the end justified the means. Since then, he had come to enjoy it, and his success had proved him right. The superstitious population was terrified of the Lord of the Dead, terrified of Baron Samedi, terrified of him.

And when he had the Baron's legendary crown in his hands, his plan would be complete. According to legend, the crown had come to the island from West Africa with slave traders, from the holy city of Ile-Ife, where voodoo had its roots. Anne Bonny had taken it during one of her plundering raids.

Beyond that, her treasure didn't interest him in the slightest. He didn't need money. He had more than enough of that. In the Caribbean, in his position, it was easy to make money. What mattered to him was the power he would have when he had the crown—when he became Baron Samedi. The last doubters would fall silent, and he could begin conquering the entire archipelago. On the other islands, too, especially Haiti, the cult of voodoo held enormous sway.

"I've taken delivery of a few new items from the old homeland," said Jamaal Ratcliffe, the owner of the store. Most of the time, the old man sold cheap junk, but for Graves he always put aside a few special pieces.

Graves' experienced eye wandered over the skulls, ancient-looking voodoo dolls, skinned chameleons, animal heads reworked as headdresses, stuffed bats, and all the rest. Jamaal was counting on Graves taking all of it, as usual.

But not tonight.

The shop door opened, and Graves turned around in surprise. Shaw and Cabrera came in.

"We're closed," said Jamaal, annoyed.

"They're with me. Leave us alone," Graves said, without even a glance back at Jamaal. The frail-looking old man quickly retreated to the back of the shop.

"What is it?" Grayson snapped at his men. "I left my phone behind because I needed a few hours of peace and quiet. Is it really so important?"

Shaw and Cabrera looked at one another and gulped. Then they told Graves about what had just happened—that Cloutard had been freed from the villa by some kind of military team, and that he'd taken the medallions and all the papers with him.

Graves was furious. The veins in his temples were pounding and his face turned purple.

"You must be the biggest idiots in the Caribbean. I put a private army at your disposal, I have high-end security installed—at great expense, mind you—only to leave the house for a few hours and see the work of years destroyed!"

He swept his arm across the counter, sending all of the artifacts Jamaal had set out for him flying through the store. The diminutive shopkeeper peeked anxiously from the back room between a pair of tapestries. He could not bring himself to protest, although Graves was demolishing his shop.

"I hope you two geniuses have come up with a plan."

Cabrera nodded eagerly. As tough as he was, he hardly dared to meet his boss's eye. Shoulders slumped and staring at the floor, he began to speak. "I went through the security camera footage and spoke to a few of our contacts in the United States. One of the men was a guy named—" He paused dramatically "—Tom Wagner."

Grayson looked at him and Shaw and waited. For a few seconds, there was no sound at all.

"And? Who the hell is that?" Grayson finally bellowed. "One of the Expendables? Chuck Norris's son? Stallone's nephew? Schwarzenegger's second cousin?"

"You're not so far off with Schwarzenegger," said Cabrera. "Wagner's also from Austria. He's the guy who derailed the nuclear attack in Barcelona a few years ago and saved the Pope."

"And he and his wife, Hellen de Mey, and that Frenchman, took down the Absolute Freedom organization," Shaw added.

"Am I supposed to gape in awe or something? So what? It's not like they're the Avengers! Or maybe they didn't need to be. Maybe you—" he pointed accusingly at Cabrera "—put together a gang of cripples and cretins for my security team."

Cabrera swallowed. "Wagner and his people are real pros, especially when it comes to tracking down old things. Our contact told me they even found the Library of Alexandria."

"I don't care if they found the Holy fucking Grail."

"Er . . . they did," Shaw said, clearing his throat meekly.

Graves raised his eyebrows. "Really?"

"Sir, with all due respect, these people need to be taken seriously," Cabrera said. "But they have a weakness. They're 'good guys.'" He accompanied "good guys" with air quotes.

Graves understood what Cabrera was trying to say to him. "And 'good guys' always have weaknesses. Do you have a suggestion for what we can do against this Justice League?"

"Of course, sir."

"Then let's hear it."

Cabrera could breathe again. His boss had calmed down.

"As we know, Miss Ortiz is old Torrente's daughter. We knew that from the background checks we did before the election began."

"So . . . ?" Graves asked, already getting impatient.

"We found Miss Ortiz's chauffeur sniffing around on our property yesterday. Don't worry, sir, we've taken care of that problem—but it looks as if Torrente, Ortiz, and Wagner and his people are in this together."

Graves frowned. His mouth curled into a crooked smile. He began to see where Cabrera was going. He silenced him with a wave and turned to Shaw.

"You're back in the game, Casanova. Let's assume your cover is still intact and that you and Ortiz can still break a bedspring or two. If yes, then you know what to do."

Shaw looked at Graves in confusion. "Uh . . ."

Graves shook his head. "How is it possible for an election strategist like you to be so smart and calculating in so many ways, and then so thick-headed in others? All right, let me spell it out for you."

48

HANGAR, IAN FLEMING INTERNATIONAL AIRPORT

Before them lay a beautifully hand-painted map more than three hundred years old. At the top right was a richly embellished compass rose. At first glance, the map looked completely normal. It showed both land and sea and included parts of both the Caribbean and North America. Lines of latitude and longitude, coastal outlines, trade routes, depths, and the biggest towns of the day were marked on the map.

"Out with the medallions," said Tom.

Cloutard nodded and opened his satchel. "*Mesdames et messieurs,* may I present . . ."

One by one, he laid out the letter from Anne Bonny, the interrogation record of Calico Jack, and the three medallions. Tom immediately picked up one of the golden discs, each of which was about four inches across and a quarter of an inch thick, with a hole in the middle. He weighed the metal in his hands.

"Is it real gold?" he asked.

"No, it's brass," Fabio replied. He and Adalgisa were examining another of the medallions.

"Gold would weigh more than twice as much," Adalgisa added.

"And the gold by itself would be worth more than thirty thousand dollars, quite apart from the historical value," said Cloutard.

Tom whistled softly through his teeth.

Cloutard continued, "The brass, however, is not even worth fifty dollars."

"Quite apart from the historical value," said Tom drily.

Hellen had taken the letter from Anne Bonny and the interrogation report and was reading and rereading them. Tom turned the medallion over in his hands and studied it intently. He picked up a second one and looked at the engravings and recesses they all exhibited.

"Hey, check this out. They fit together," said Tom. He had jumped up from his chair excitedly and was pointing at his handiwork: two of the medallions were now joined together like jigsaw puzzle pieces.

"Give me the third one," he said to Fabio. He took it, rotated it and flipped it in his hands until the recesses aligned and the discs slid together. Five pairs of eager, astonished eyes stared down at the joined medallions.

"They fit perfectly," said Hellen, pulling them over to her.

"*Non, ma chère*, not completely," Cloutard said, and he pointed to the small triangular hole at the intersection of the three discs.

"It reminds me of a flower, in a way," Adalgisa suggested.

"To me, it looks more like Mickey Mouse," Tom said. He was right, and Hellen laughed. The three conjoined discs certainly did look like the Mickey Mouse logo.

"But hold on. Maybe Adalgisa's right," Hellen said. "I read something about a flower and the way to freedom here in Anne's letter." She quickly scanned the document again.

Cloutard looked up.

"Yes," Hellen confirmed. "She writes about a 'Blossom of Prosperity.'"

"I found the ivory rod in Blossom Bay. It was buried on an island in a field of flowers that grow nowhere else—the 'Blossoms of Prosperity.' Incidentally, it was also where a mob of crazies were carrying out a voodoo ritual."

"A voodoo ritual?" Hellen asked.

"Yes. And Graves, whose hospitality I briefly enjoyed, was the leader of the crazies."

Tom and Hellen looked at each other.

"Leticia said the same thing. Graves is trying to use voodoo superstition to manipulate the people and keep them under his control."

"That explains a few things. He does not want the treasure at all. He actually offered it to me. He only wants it because it contains the crown of Baron Samedi," Hellen reasoned.

"So Graves isn't after the whole treasure? He only wants the crown?" said Tom, confused.

"Well . . ." Hellen's voice grew serious. "If you recall, a lot more fuss was made about an antique sword just a few years ago. It doesn't surprise me to find the same thing happening here with a crown."

"Look at this. The engravings on the medallion form some kind of picture," Tom said. He pulled the Mickey Mouse-shaped assembly closer and traced the lines on the three medallions with his finger. Each line leading to the edge of one disc aligned perfectly with a line on the next, and again with the next. He turned the construction in a circle and looked at it from all angles. "There's a notch here shaped like an arrow," he said.

"Yes, like on the compass rose."

"That must be north."

"Okay," said Hellen, and she turned the three medallions so that the arrow pointed away from her, to north on the map.

"Here. Doesn't that look like the east coast of Florida?" Tom pointed at the lines engraved on the bottom medallion.

"You're right," Hellen cried, louder than intended. All five froze for a moment when a man grunted in his sleep. They had completely forgotten the soldiers, who were sleeping on their camp beds just a few yards away.

Hellen pulled the medallion back across the map. Everyone held their breath. Slowly, she positioned them so that the engraved lines on the medallion matched the Florida coast on the map. They fit perfectly. All of them had come to their feet, and five heads leaned together over the map and stared into the small triangle formed where the medallions met.

"Charles Town" was written in small letters beside the dot in the center of the triangle.

49

CHARLESTON, SOUTH CAROLINA

"Be sure to thank your mother again for letting us borrow her plane," said Tom.

After the previous night's stunning discovery, the team had treated themselves to a little rest. The next morning, they had been able to persuade Giuseppina to grant her brave soldiers some beach vacation time and to lend them her jet for the trip to Charleston. Tom has spent the flight relaxing in one of the leather seats with his feet up.

"So, what do we know about Charleston, and what's the connection to Anne Bonny?" Tom asked. They were on their way from the airport toward downtown Charleston in a rental car.

"Charleston, or Charles Town, as it was called when it was founded in 1670, is one of North America's oldest coastal towns," said Cloutard. "Named for King Charles II of England, the young city quickly established itself as the center of the slave trade in the 18th century. Almost half of all the slaves in America came into the country through

Charles Town. It was also a hotspot for pirates. The notorious Edward Teach, better known as Blackbeard, occupied Charles Town for a time in May 1718. He only released it and withdrew when the governor bribed him with a chest full of medicines," he lectured.

"Blackbeard . . . wasn't he the guy with the burning beard?" Tom asked.

"*Oui*. He was plagued by syphilis and was slowly losing his mind. He was finally hunted down by Robert Maynard, a lieutenant in the Royal Navy. His beard didn't actually burn, though—he simply wove fuses into his beard and lit them. That, and the ludicrous number of weapons he carried, made him an imposing sight, and time and legend has made him into the fearsome cult figure he is today."

"Charleston is also the city where Anne Bonny grew up," Hellen added. "After her father bought her freedom from prison, some people believe it's where she spent the last years of her life, as well."

"Correct," Cloutard confirmed. "Although Anne Bonny—or McCormac, which was her family name—was actually born in Ireland. Her father was a lawyer who got his maid pregnant and, after a career-destroying scandal, emigrated with her and their illegitimate child, Anne, to the New World. To Charles Town, in fact, where he worked his way up to become a respected plantation owner."

For the first time in their years together, Hellen was feeling a little useless. She had done some research on the flight to Jamaica, but Cloutard knew far more about Anne's history than she did.

"At the tender age of sixteen, Anne met the young seaman and rogue James Bonny and married him. Her father was not happy about that at all and disowned his young daughter," Cloutard went on.

"Sounds like a real soap opera," Tom said. "Rich guy's daughter falls for a rock star and goes on tour with him. Father disinherits daughter."

Hellen laughed. "You're not far off. Back then, the pirates, with their political views and love of freedom, were certainly comparable with the romanticized image of certain rock stars today."

"Unfortunately, that is about all that anyone knows about the most famous female pirate ever," Cloutard said. "And there is little documentary evidence even for that. There are countless theories about when, where, and how she died. Until recently, most assumed that after her ship, the 'Revenge,' was captured by the British, she was arrested along with Calico Jack and Mary Read and died with them on the gallows. Another story says that Anne lived until 1782, at the age of 84, here in Charles Town."

Tom's head was buzzing with all the information.

"History can be tricky. It's not always cut-and-dried," Hellen said to Tom.

"But we've got the letter, the medallions, and the map. Shouldn't we be able to use them to find some clue to where exactly in Charleston the treasure's buried?"

"One would think so, of course. But even though I've been combing through everything I could find on the subject, the real breakthrough only came last night."

"Obviously," Tom said triumphantly. "Now that the team's together again, everything's running like clockwork."

"But the clockwork seems to have gotten jammed," said Cloutard, nipping at his flask. Happily, his mother had brought along a few bottles of his beloved Louis XIII.

"Couldn't you find anything at all in Torrente's or Leticia's papers?" Hellen asked.

"*J'ai bien peur que non.* Nothing useful," Cloutard said resignedly. "There was only one thing that stood out. In Torrente's papers, I found a handwritten note. 'WWW Bermuda S., Mulatto Alley.' But I have no idea what it means."

"A website for the Bermudas? Street names, maybe? The S could stand for street. Bermuda Street?" Tom suggested.

"I tried everything I could. There is no Mulatto Alley in the Bermudas, and there never has been."

"And Bermuda Street?"

"There is one in Charleston, but I found no connection. However, there used to be a Mulatto Alley in old Charles Town. Today it is called Chalmers Street. It is in the French Quarter. In Anne Bonny's day, it was a street of taverns and brothels," Cloutard said.

"That's it," Hellen cried. She took her iPad out of her backpack and tapped a few search terms into the browser: WWW, Bermuda, Charles Town, Mulatto Alley, pirates, Anne Bonny. Within seconds, she had it.

"Didn't Leticia say that her mother was in Charleston when she had her accident?" Tom asked.

"Yes. And I'm starting to realize why she was there. I've got it. Here it is," Hellen said happily. "Originally used as ship's ballast, coral stone or 'Bermuda Stone'—there's your 'S'—was also used as a building material. The second-oldest home in Charleston is built of West Indies coral stone, and still survives today."

"Which house is it?" Tom asked.

"The Pink House," said Cloutard, shaking his head. Of course. It was suddenly clear to him.

"Correct. The Pink House. It was once a tavern named for the pink-colored stone it was built with. It was a popular port of call for seamen and pirates in search of the three W's," Hellen read.

"Three W's?"

"Whisky, wenches and 'wittles,' meaning vittles, or food. Not unlike the more modern 'wine, women, and song,'" Hellen explained.

"So Anne Bonny buried her treasure in the basement of a former bordello?"

"Which more recently became a tourist attraction and an art gallery," Hellen confirmed.

"The dates fit, at least. The house was built at the end of the 17th century," Cloutard said.

"Yes, and that handwritten note you found definitely points to the place, too. And it gets better. Listen to this: to this day, the Pink House is supposedly haunted by the ghost of Anne Bonny."

"A haunted house with a pirate treasure in the basement. You couldn't make this stuff up."

"It would be the last place anyone would think of searching. It looks as if it's still in its original condition," Hellen said.

"Okay, it's certainly worth a try. What's the worst that can happen? We show up three hundred years too late and find nothing but an empty treasure chest," Tom joked.

"Agreed – off to the Pink House we go!"

50

PINK HOUSE, CHARLESTON, SOUTH CAROLINA

"This is another reminder of just how young this country is. The house is only three hundred years old, but it's one of the oldest in the entire country. It even predates the 'united' part of 'United States,'" Hellen said, looking out the side window of the rental car at the tiny house.

"Sure, but most of the buildings in Vienna aren't much older, are they? I mean, apart from a church or two and all the imperial stuff," said Tom.

"You're right. But our history and culture go back a lot further, to the Roman Empire and even beyond. Vienna is mentioned by name in the Salzburg Annals, from the year 881, and an earlier version of the name, Vindobona, dates from much further back."

"Okay. Time to go."

Hellen grabbed her backpack, which contained the medallion and the ivory rod. The trio climbed out of the car and looked across the road at the pink, two-story house.

"It's still an impressive little place," Hellen said. "In its three hundred years, it's survived more than thirty hurricanes, two huge earthquakes, two wars, snowstorms, and countless fires."

"Fascinating," said Tom. "But shouldn't we be thinking about how we're going to get inside?"

"I thought the house was a gallery now?" Cloutard said in surprise.

"It *was* a gallery, but in 2019 it became a private house again."

"*Formidable*. Now you've jinxed it," Cloutard said. He flicked his hand dismissively, leaned on the hood of the car, and pulled out his little flask.

"What? How?"

"I don't think so," said Hellen. "From what I've read, everything inside is still original. The architects who did the renovations apparently made sure of that."

"So who lives here now? Apart from the ghost of Anne Bonny."

"No idea. But we could try knocking and asking nicely," Hellen suggested.

Tom nodded. "What are we waiting for?" he said, and he strode across the street toward the Pink House.

"It's amazing, isn't it? These are the exact same stones that Anne Bonny, Blackbeard, and all the other great pirates walked on," Hellen said, looking down at the cobblestoned street, which had been built at the same time as the house. For a moment, Hellen imagined what the street must have been like in the 18th century, with all the smells, the people, and the miserable conditions that prevailed in the French Quarter. But she also imagined happy people, parties and singing, and she smiled.

Just four blocks from the Waterfront Park Pier, the former Mulatto Alley was now a charming little avenue lined with palms, blossoming trees, and gardens with manicured hedges.

"Let me do the talking," said Hellen when they were standing at the front door. The house was hardly more than twelve feet wide. She searched through her wallet and took out her old Blue Shield ID card. Tom looked at her curiously.

"Not now," Hellen said, knowing what Tom was about to say. She knocked.

A moment later, a man opened the door, dressed like a lawyer or banker. With a briefcase in his hand, he was obviously just on his way out.

"Sorry, I'm not buying anything," said the man, not really taking any notice of them. He pushed past them, closing the door behind him.

"My name is Dr. Hellen de Mey, from Blue Shield. We'd like to ask you a few questions." She took a step back and held up her ID card for him to see. He took a step sideways and kept going.

"Lady, I don't care who you are or who you work for, I'm late for a meeting," he said, pushing past the three newcomers.

"We're from UNESCO," Hellen lied. "We're responsible for the protection of cultural heritage and historical artifacts. We have a few questions about the Pink House," she explained, following the indifferent man.

"I don't want to hear it. Go away," the man said more gruffly. Then he climbed into a car and drove away.

"*Quelle impolitesse*," Cloutard snorted. "What now?"

"Asshole," Hellen muttered. Then she shrugged and returned to the house. She cupped her hands on the window and peered inside. "Wow. The house is really tiny. We have to find a way inside."

Tom looked around. It was a look Hellen knew. She was about to say something, but Tom disappeared around the corner of the house without a word, striding through the parking lot next door to the back of the house.

"What are you planning?" Hellen said, hurrying after him. Cloutard followed.

The Pink House itself was only about twelve feet square. Attached to it was a high wall that ran alongside the parking lot toward the back, ending in a brick wall at chest height. Tom hopped onto the brick wall and peeked over the higher wall into the backyard of the Pink House.

"There's a small garden and a back door. Wait here."

Before Hellen could say anything, Tom had already vaulted over the wall and vanished into the garden. Hellen looked around anxiously, afraid that someone might have seen him.

"He has not changed a bit," said Cloutard with a grin.

Hellen and Cloutard hurried back to the street and stood nervously at the corner of the house.

"Come on in," said Tom less than a minute later, standing in the open doorway of the house.

"Are you crazy?" Hellen's eyes were still darting up and down the street.

"Oh, come on. Or do you want to wait out here for the next Instagrammer to come along and add the Pink House to their selfie collection?"

Another quick look around, and Hellen and Cloutard scurried inside.

"This is breaking and entering. You can get ten years for that here," Hellen said, punching Tom on the arm.

"Relax. No one saw us—and how do you even know that?" said Tom, rubbing the spot Hellen had just whacked.

"What if the owner comes back? What then?" said Hellen, arms crossed and looking angrily at Tom.

"He's not coming back. 'Lady, I'm late for a meeting,' remember?" Tom said, mimicking the man's voice.

Cloutard, in the meantime, had made himself comfortable on the sofa. He was watching Tom and Hellen and sipping from his flask.

"Maybe he forgot something. He could come back any second."

"Oh, come off it . . ." Tom stopped and turned to Cloutard. "Can I get you some popcorn or something?" he said, noticing Cloutard's amusement at their little tiff.

Cloutard just shook his head and lifted his flask in the air, grinning. "*Merci beaucoup*, I have all I need."

Tom and Hellen both glared at him. Hellen was about to say something, but she suddenly realized where she was. Her anger and fear evaporated. She looked around. Dark-brown wood paneling covered the low walls. Next to the huge fireplace, a set of stairs no wider than her shoulders led to the upper floor.

"All right, we've got no time to waste. Look around," Hellen said, her voice assuming an unaccustomed note of command.

Cloutard put his flask away and stood up. Just then, a rattling sound made them stop and turn. A key had been inserted into the front door.

51

PINK HOUSE, CHARLESTON, SOUTH CAROLINA

No one dared to breathe. They looked around in panic. The room was too small to hide in. The backyard was a dead end, and they had no time to make it outside anyway. They were trapped.

Thinking on his feet, Tom quickly stepped toward the front door and pressed against the wall behind it. Hellen and Cloutard had nowhere to go. They stood in the middle of the room as if rooted to the spot.

The door swung open and the man they had spoken to just a few minutes before stepped inside. Digging through his briefcase and cursing to himself, he did not immediately register that an older man in a beige Brioni suit and a woman in shorts and tank top were standing in his living room. Slowly, Tom pushed the door closed behind him. The man yelled, and his briefcase and keys flew through the air. He stared in panic at two sheepishly smiling faces. He had not noticed Tom behind him.

"Don't worry. We're not going to hurt you," Hellen said, hands raised, in an attempt to calm him down. He stumbled backward, ran into a chest of drawers beside the entrance, and looked around in fear. Tom took a step to the side, blocking the door.

"Who are you? What do you want?"

Without warning, the man spun around, jerked open the top drawer, and fumbled out a revolver. But before he could even get a decent grip on it, Tom had disarmed him. The man threw his hands in the air, seeming to wither, and squeezed his eyes shut.

"Please, please don't kill me," he whimpered. "Take whatever you want."

"What was that about not jinxing it again?" Tom said, looking at Cloutard and Hellen.

"Our prison term just doubled," Hellen whispered.

"Don't piss yourself, mister. We don't want anything from you and we're not going to hurt you," Tom said to the terrified, sobbing man. He held up the revolver, tipped the magazine out sideways, and dumped the cartridges into the palm of his hand. Then he replaced both in the drawer and pushed it closed. "Sit," he told the man, who had watched Tom's movements in amazement. His swift work with the pistol and his commanding tone made the man cower. He did as he was told and sank meekly onto the sofa.

"What do you want from me?"

"If you hadn't ignored my wife so rudely earlier, this conversation could have gone very differently," Tom said.

All three stood in front of the seated man, looked at each other questioningly, and finally nodded. There was only one way they were getting out of here without the police after them: the truth.

"Let me," said Hellen.

She put her backpack on the floor and sat on the coffee table in front of the man.

"Hi. I'm Hellen. What's your name?"

"I . . ." Hellen smiled and nodded to allay the man's fears. "I'm Christopher," he stammered softly.

"Okay. Christopher. Now, I know this is all going to sound insane, but we're here because we believe the treasure of the pirate Anne Bonny is hidden here in the Pink House," Hellen began. As briefly as possible, she told him everything. While she talked, Cloutard went around the inside of the house and examined everything closely. He rapped on the walls and inspected the large fireplace that, in earlier times, had been used both for heating and cooking. Wide-eyed but obviously skeptical, the man listened to Hellen's account, though he was constantly distracted trying to keep an eye on what Cloutard was doing in his house. Tom stood behind his wife with his arms crossed, gazing expressionlessly at the man. When Hellen finished, the man looked from one of them to the other, uncertain what to think of the whole story, and whether he was allowed to speak.

"Go ahead, let's hear what you think," said Hellen.

"But . . ." Christopher began, barely audibly. He cleared his throat, and his voice grew stronger. "But the . . . the Pink House doesn't have a cellar," he managed to stammer.

Tom's hands sank to his sides. Hellen was perplexed. She looked first at Christopher, then to Tom, and finally at Cloutard. Had they been wrong about everything?

"That's impossible. It has to be here," Hellen said, standing up and pacing the room. "All of the clues point to this house."

Christopher looked past Hellen at Cloutard, who was just examining the fireplace.

"Excuse me, but what are you doing there?" Christopher asked, a little more loudly. He got to his feet, but a stern shake of Tom's head made him sink back onto the sofa.

"What *are* you up to?" Tom asked, joining Cloutard at the fireplace.

"I think there's something here," the Frenchman said as he lifted pieces of wood and the iron grate out of the fireplace. "Oh, *mon dieu*."

"What?" Hellen said, and she also moved close behind Cloutard and peered over his shoulder into the now empty fireplace.

Now she saw it. In the back wall of the fireplace, about a foot above the base, was a small circular relief emblazoned with a skull. Hellen pushed Cloutard a little aside, crouched beside him, and ran her fingers over the engraving.

"This must be it," she breathed.

52

PINK HOUSE, CHARLESTON, SOUTH CAROLINA

"Have we found the keyhole?"

"I don't know. But there is definitely a hole here."

With one finger, Hellen probed the inside of the skull's wide-open jaw. "Give me the ivory rod," she said, pointing to her backpack, which was standing beside the coffee table. Tom grabbed the pack, unzipped it, and handed Hellen the rod.

"What's the plan?" he asked.

"It feels like this is threaded," Hellen said. She took the rod from Tom and looked at it more closely. "See the grooves?" she said, pointing out a deep furrow that spiraled from one end of the rod down two thirds of its length—a thread, but it was interrupted in three places. "At first I thought it was just decorative, but it looks as if it also has a function."

She placed the rod carefully into the skull's mouth and turned it.

Christopher, completely forgotten, watched what was happening from the sofa. His eyes wandered from the fireplace to the chest of drawers where his revolver lay, and then to the front door. Slowly and silently, he stood up, but halfway to the door, he stopped. His curiosity was too great. He shook his head, turned back, and joined them.

"I always thought that was just ornamental," he said, looking at the skull. Hellen, Tom, and Cloutard all jumped. "Sorry, but if a pirate's treasure is hidden in my house, I want to know about it."

"This treasure is going into a museum," Hellen said. She continued to turn the ivory rod carefully.

Cloutard rolled his eyes.

"Fine with me. The value of my house will go through the roof if you really find something," Christopher said with a grin.

"It's jammed," Hellen said. "I can't turn it any further."

"Let me try," said Tom. Hellen moved aside, and Tom crouched and took hold of the rod with both hands. He turned it with all his strength. They heard a crunching sound, and dust trickled from the edge of the circular relief.

"Something's moving," Tom said.

He kept turning. The crunching and grating grew louder.

"It isn't a relief at all. It's a round stone set into the wall," Hellen said excitedly.

Gradually, like the cork from a wine bottle, a stone cylinder moved outward. Two more turns and Tom had done it. He twisted the rod out again and laid the cylinder, about four inches in diameter, to one side.

Hellen drew a sharp breath.

"*Incroyable*," Cloutard gasped.

"No one's going to believe this," said Christopher.

Tom took out his Surefire flashlight and shone it into the hole.

"Whew. No bugs, thank God," he said. "But there's definitely some kind of mechanism." He handed the flashlight to Hellen, reached for the backpack, and took out the medallions.

"Torrente said that the ivory rod was the key to the treasure. But I think he meant more than just the rod."

Tom looked more closely at the medallions, realizing that furrows also lined the holes in the middle of each.

"The thread on the rod is broken in three places, and we have three medallions. The holes in them look like they'll fit the gaps in the thread." He fitted the rod to the hole in one of the medallions and turned it. Like a nut being screwed onto a bolt, the medallion rotated onto the rod, but seized up at the first gap in the thread.

"Maybe they have to be screwed on in a certain order," said Cloutard.

Tom screwed the first medallion off again and picked up the second.

"You guys are unbelievable. Do you do this often?" said Christopher, pushing closer, not wanting to miss a thing.

Tom gave him a stony glare. "I didn't know Stockholm Syndrome only takes ten minutes to kick in. Sit your ass back on that couch and let us work," Tom ordered, with a wink at Cloutard.

Cloutard laughed, but grew instantly serious again. "Normally, we do not leave any witnesses behind," he said.

Christopher's eyes widened and he raised his hands apologetically as he sat back on the couch.

"Nice one," Tom whispered, and he and Cloutard chuckled.

"I've got it," Hellen cried. She had taken over from Tom and now had the three medallions screwed on in the right order. With the discs evenly spaced on the ivory rod; it looked like an oversized honey dipper.

For a moment, no one said a word. Tom, Hellen and Cloutard shared a look.

"The moment of truth," Hellen said, and she carefully inserted the freshly assembled key into the hole. She turned it slowly, until the recesses in the first medallion snapped into place with a *click*.

She turned the rod to the right. Behind the wall, they heard mechanical noises. Suddenly, there was a jerk, and the rod was pulled farther into the hole. It locked in place again.

"One down, two to go," said Tom.

Hellen repeated the operation twice more.

Silence. Hellen released the rod and waited. All three stared tensely into the fireplace. Even Christopher was back on his feet, although he stayed near the sofa.

Rumbling and vibrations underfoot made them move back. Grinding and chafing, the base of the huge fireplace slid to one side, revealing a staircase leading down.

53

BASEMENT OF THE PINK HOUSE, SOUTH CAROLINA

A PUNGENT ODOR OF MOLD AND DECAY ROSE FROM THE HOLE in the floor. Tom, Hellen and Cloutard looked at each other, stepped forward without a word, and crouched slowly. They craned their necks, peering down into the newly opened hole. A steep stairway, barely as wide as a man's shoulders, disappeared into the darkness. Tom turned on his flashlight and shone it into the hole, but they could not see the bottom.

Christopher had found the courage to join them again and gazed down over their shoulders.

"There really is a basement!" he exclaimed, but he let out a high-pitched yelp when Tom suddenly sprang up and glared at him.

"Man, you're a nervous one," Tom said, his glare transforming into a smile. "Don't worry, the French guy was just making a joke earlier. But you could do us a huge favor." Tom put a friendly arm around Christopher's shoulders and stepped with him to one side.

"What?"

"We're going to go down there now. If we're not back in thirty minutes, or if you hear any noises that sound like something's collapsed or anything like that, call this number." He handed Christopher a business card. "Don't even think about calling the police. This is our boss. He'll know what to do. Just tell him exactly what happened."

Christopher took the business card and nodded.

"And, hey, no offense. We didn't mean to scare you or hurt you." Tom gave him a chummy punch on the upper harm, perhaps a touch too hard. "Sorry about the back door, too. You can send the bill to this address." He pointed to the card, then returned to the others, leaving Christopher bewildered.

Step by cautious step, Tom led the way down the steep stairway. Cobwebs and mold covered the moist walls.

"In spite of everything, I have to say: God, how I've missed all this," Hellen whispered. Tom smiled. Now it was official. The team was back, united, and hunting for treasure.

"Van Rensburg will be happy to hear it," said Tom.

"*Oui*, but could you not have had this epiphany a week earlier?" Cloutard looked at Hellen rather forlornly.

"I'm so sorry, François. I'll make it up to you, I promise," she said, with real regret. After all, she was the one who had wanted nothing more to do with ventures like this until recently. It was because of her, at least in part, that Cloutard had gone in search of Anny Bonny's treasure by himself.

"It is all right, *ma chère*. Nothing that won't heal," he said, to ease her conscience.

The stairs took a ninety-degree turn, and after a few more steps they finally reached the bottom. Tom twisted the front of his flashlight to widen the beam.

They could hardly believe their eyes. All three stared around the small room in confusion.

"What the fuck?" Tom sputtered.

"*Putain de merde*," Cloutard agreed.

"You said it," said Hellen.

They were standing in a room with the same dimensions as the house above. Torches hung in iron holders on two of the walls. Tom lit both of them and switched his flashlight off.

"Not as exciting as I had hoped, this treasure chamber," said Cloutard.

"I'm with you," said Tom. "I'd been picturing a mountain of doubloons, pearls, gold plates, goblets, candelabras . . . the whole works."

"This isn't 'Pirates of the Caribbean,' and you're not Jack Sparrow," said Hellen. Tom forced a smile.

Opposite the stairs, at the end of the room, stood a single, ancient sea chest. Apart from that, the room was completely empty.

"That chest had better be filled with gold doubloons."

They went over and crouched beside it.

"Great. Locked," said Tom, lifting the rusted padlock dangling from the clasp. "And I don't think this is going to fit." He grinned wryly and pointed at the ivory rod with the brass medallions in Hellen's hand.

"We probably don't need this anymore," she said, stowing it in her backpack. "Any ideas, apart from brute force?"

"Oui, laissez le maître s'en occupier," said Cloutard, elbowing Hellen and Tom aside.

"My French is a little rusty," Hellen said.

"Let the master work," Cloutard repeated, patting his jacket pockets and taking out a small case. He opened it and produced two lock picks.

"You had that on you all this time? Why the hell did I climb over the damned wall and kick the back door in?"

"Because you're an impatient, hotheaded blunt instrument," Hellen said, blowing Tom a kiss.

"I love you, too," he replied.

A loud click resonated through the room.

"Done," said Cloutard. He put the opened lock aside and slipped his tool case back into his pocket.

"On three?" said Cloutard.

"Do you mean one, two, three, and then open? Or one, two, and open?" Hellen asked.

"Now she has started with the silly film quotes," Cloutard said with a sigh.

"One, two, three," Tom said quickly, and he lifted the lid.

Tom, Hellen, and Cloutard gasped as one.

"Enough twists already," said Tom. "I imagined a search for pirate treasure very differently."

Inside the chest, in two rows, stood eight large bottles sealed with wax. The glass shimmered a fiery red in the torchlight. On top of the bottles lay an envelope with a red seal.

Hellen and Tom looked doubtfully at Cloutard.

"Why are you looking at me like that?"

"Are you running out of Louis XIII? Have you got us chasing really old booze for you now?"

"I . . . ask van Rensburg. He's the one who sent us on this mission."

Hellen picked up the letter and looked at the wax seal, which showed two snakes coiled around a rainbow. She took out her phone and photographed it. Then she opened the letter, taking care to do as little damage as possible to the seal.

Folding the parchment envelope open, she removed a folded sheet of paper and quickly read through the hand-written lines.

"Listen, you're not going to believe this," said Hellen. Aloud, she read:

To whom it may concern.

Then the Lord answered Job out of the whirlwind, and said, who shut up the sea with doors, when it brake forth, as if it had issued out of the womb? When I made the cloud the garment thereof, and thick darkness a swaddling band for it, and brake up for it my decreed place, and set bars and doors, and said, Hitherto shalt thou come, but no further: and here shall thy proud waves be stayed?

Job 38, 8-11

You have solved my riddle. For that, my congratulations.

You have found the legendary treasure of the dreaded Anne Bonny.

Have a drink to me, to freedom, and to love!

Anne Bonny

Hellen stared at the letter in disbelief, turned it over, and studied it from all sides. She picked up the envelope and scrutinized that, too.

"Nothing." Subdued, she let her hands fall in her lap.

"What does it mean? Was this all a joke? Did she blow all the gold herself?" said Tom.

"I guess so," said Hellen. "It looks as if she publicized the legend herself and got half the world searching for her treasure..."

"... while she sat on a beach somewhere, slurping down Mai Tais," Tom finished her sentence. "Great. Are you seriously telling me that we risked our lives for a few lousy bottles of hooch?"

Hellen shrugged.

"All I can say is, this is a very unsatisfying conclusion," Tom added.

"At least one of us is happy. Look," said Hellen, and she nodded in Cloutard's direction.

Cloutard had lifted one of the bottles carefully out of the chest. He was holding it in front of him in the flickering torchlight, as gently as if he were holding a baby, studying it from all sides. "I do not know about you, but right now I could use a drink," he said.

54

LETICIA ORTIZ'S HOUSE, PORTMORE, JAMAICA

Leticia sat on her terrace and replayed the events of the last twenty-four hours in her mind. In recent years, her life had been suddenly turned upside down more than once. But the previous afternoon and night's events far exceeded the usual.

She had discovered that Bradley Shaw, her lover and campaign manager, was colluding with her rival. Shaw had not only double-crossed her, but he had also stolen the medallions and her dead mother's letter. Kian, her chauffeur and a family friend for decades, had been killed by the same people. And to top things off, her father, with whom she had fallen out over the senseless search for the treasure, had come back into her life. Finally, she had seen Graves' house stormed in a military-style assault—while helping people she hardly knew try to save a man she didn't know at all.

It was a lot to digest. And although she didn't normally drink before noon—she had seen what it had done to her father—after everything that had happened, a glass of Jamaica rum for breakfast seemed appropriate.

She was dragged rudely from her musings, however, by the sound of the front door and a familiar, cheery voice. "Hey, it's me."

Shaw. In all the turmoil, she hadn't really thought about how to deal with him. Should she confront him with everything she knew and demand an explanation? Or was it better to put on a poker face, play things tactically, and see where they led?

She made a gut decision for the latter, hoping to get some useful information out of him. Maybe she could turn the tables. But she did not know how long she would be able to keep up the pretense.

Shaw came out on the terrace. He looked—she hated to admit it—as good as ever, and he had put on his best smile. She would have liked nothing more than to get up and slap his face, but she swallowed her anger. He leaned down and kissed her.

"Wow. Hard night?" he asked, nodding at the glass of rum. "Didn't things go well at the charity village? Don't worry. I've got good news. As of this morning, we're one step closer to victory–you're just a few percentage points behind Graves."

He smiled, took one of the croissants that lay on the breakfast table, and took a bite as he sat down. Leticia wanted to hurl the scalding coffee in his face but managed once again to subdue her natural urges. She hoped he could not see how brittle her smile was.

"That's great," she said, playfully taking the croissant back and taking a bite herself. Their eyes met. Leticia was boiling inside. *You bastard*, she thought.

"We should go through your appointments for the next few days," Shaw said, chewing. "You've got a lot going on, and these next meetings could make all the difference. This afternoon you've got the workers at the cruise ship marina in Montego Bay, and tomorrow you're meeting with the tourism union reps in Ochos Rios, followed by a visit to Black River High School."

Shaw had taken out his phone and was scrolling through the appointment calendar when Leticia heard a noise inside her house.

Shit, she thought. *I completely forgot about Papa*.

After the eventful night, father and daughter had sat out on the terrace for quite a while, looking out over the sea and talking things through. Everything that had been bottled up during their separation had finally come out, and they were on a good path to reconciliation. Torrente had even promised to stop drinking. It was late—or rather, very early —and Leticia had offered him the small guest room to sleep in, not least because he had just lost his house to Graves' thugs.

Now he was standing at the terrace door in boxer shorts, his face still rumpled with sleep and his hair sticking out in all directions, trying to process the scene in front of him. Leticia realized instantly that her father was not nearly the actor that she was.

His expression took seconds to change from surprise to anger, and from there it was only a short jump to full-blown rage. With astounding agility for his age, he leaped on Shaw and grabbed him by the throat. Shaw crashed backward in the chair and landed on his back on the floor, Torrente bearing down on top of him.

"You bastard," he said, voicing Leticia's thought, his face purple with fury.

So much for my plan to mislead Shaw, Leticia thought, but she made no move to help him. It was only after Shaw and Torrente had wrangled for a while that she realized how damaging this could be for her image. She was in the middle of an election campaign, and her father, a well-known boozer, beating up her campaign manager on her terrace was not going to look good. Shaw deserved no better, but it wouldn't make for flattering headlines.

She leaned down to her father and tried to pull him away but was astonished at how strong the old man was. Neither Shaw nor she was able to break his grip. And Shaw was already turning blue.

"Let him go, Papa! This isn't helping," Leticia screamed, tearing at her father's hands. But he kept the pressure on Shaw's throat with the strength of his rage. Shaw wasn't looking good at all. His tongue was protruding from his mouth, and he was struggling to breathe.

"Papa, please!" Leticia screamed again. "You're ruining everything. I have an election to win!"

That got through. Torrente, suddenly breathing hard himself, backed away from Shaw and stood up. Shaw sucked in a lungful of air and fell into a fit of coughing. He sat up and rubbed his throat, still panting.

In the tumult, no one had noticed that a third man had entered the house. Leticia recognized Cabrera instantly, but she was too slow. The baseball bat slammed into her father's head, and he crashed to the floor like a felled tree.

55

NATIONAL POLICE COLLEGE OF JAMAICA, SPANISH TOWN, WEST OF KINGSTON

"IT IS NOT USUALLY MY STYLE TO ENGAGE IN POLITICAL mudslinging. I would rather leave that to others. But that does not absolve me of my duty to inform the people of Jamaica."

Graves stood at a podium on the parade grounds of the Police College of Jamaica. In a sense, it was a home game for him, considering that he had almost the entire police force of the island on his payroll. He had invested early in the training of cadets, ensuring that new police recruits were on his side from the start.

The rear of the stage on which Graves was standing was filled with dignitaries from the upper echelons of the police,. In fact, the whole event seemed more like some kind of police event than the press conference it really was—organized, of course, by Graves himself. He loved this image. He knew how intimidating it looked when literally every police chief on the island was sitting behind him. He could not imagine a more compelling projection of power.

The event had attracted not only representatives of the local news outlets, but also journalists from CNN, the BBC, Fox News, Reuters, even the New York Times. And while he couldn't bribe any of them, it made no difference. The media, as usual, were only interested in one thing: sensation. And he would deliver. It was like being in a marketplace: the press wanted scandals, and he had scandals to sell. But of course, only the ones in which he was not personally involved.

"Last night, my house was the target of an insidious terrorist attack," said Graves, putting on an excellent show of dismay. Beside him, a flat-screen TV had been set up, on which scenes from the previous night were playing.

"It is almost a miracle that I was away from home and escaped this dastardly assault—there's no question that it was an attempt not only on my life, but also an attack on the freedom of our beautiful island."

Pictures of Kian and Torrente had been intercut with the video footage.

"This man . . ." he pointed to an old image that showed Kian and Torrente together ". . . was discovered yesterday afternoon on my property, spying on me and no doubt scouting the terrain. My security detail attempted to intervene and escort him off the grounds. He resisted and began to shoot wildly at them. My people returned fire and were able to neutralize the threat."

He looked at Kingston's chief of police, who nodded readily.

"The man beside him is Ignacio Torrente. Last night, together with the terrorists, he stormed my house. My security cameras prove this."

The journalists looked at the TV screen but saw only a series of blurry photos that showed nothing even close to a recognizable face. But that didn't seem to matter to Graves.

"The spy who died was Leticia Ortiz's chauffeur," said Graves, and he allowed a long pause to add weight to his words.

A murmur ran through the journalists. The revelation meant little to the hard-boiled reporters from CNN and Fox, but the local press representatives, who clearly sympathized with Graves' opponent, looked at each other in confusion.

"The other man . . ." The image of Kian and Torrente reappeared on the screen, and Graves pointed at Torrente, ". . . is Miss Ortiz's father."

Another pause. The broadside hit its target. Even the international pros were dumbfounded. They smelled a sensation.

"I am obviously the victim of a terrible conspiracy, and its objective is no less than clearing me out of their way."

Graves' voice had become more urgent as he spoke, his body language more aggressive. He puffed himself up and straightened his back, seeming to grow two inches taller. His gestures were expansive, his expression resolute.

"But do not fear. I will not let them intimidate me. I, Grayson Graves, will fight without cease for the well-being of our island. No terrorist attack, no attempt on my life can keep me from that."

Journalists' hands shot up. Questions were fired at Graves. He was in his element: basking in the attention of a horde of journalists hanging on his every word—it was his greatest strength. He raised his hands for calm and signaled that he had more to add.

"The police and the district attorney's office, of course, immediately tried to approach Miss Ortiz for a statement about these events, especially given the grievous evidence already collected."

Graves paused for a moment, and his face suddenly grew concerned. He had spent hours in front of a mirror practicing these changes in his facial expression.

"Unfortunately, Miss Ortiz has disappeared without a trace. And while I hope for the best, I suspect her criminal connections have spelled her own doom."

He turned away from the journalists with supreme confidence, ignoring the hundred questions they shouted after him. He smiled as he settled into the back seat of his limousine and left the pack of journalists to their wild speculations.

56

TWELVE HOURS LATER, KINGSTON, JAMAICA

Tom and Cloutard heaved the heavy chest out of the trunk of the car and carried it toward Leticia's house.

"They're going to be so disappointed," said Hellen.

"I'm pretty sure they had a mountain of gold coins in mind, and not a miserable case of rum, or whatever that stuff is."

"But if we were to get decently drunk on 'whatever that stuff is,' then at least the disappointment would not be so great," Cloutard joked. Wearily, they set the chest down beside the front door. "Careful. Even if it is not gold, those bottles are extremely valuable."

"For who? For you? Can you even still drink three-hundred-year-old booze?" Tom asked, wiping the sweat from his brow. "We had to cart this stuff halfway round the world just because you're such a connoisseur."

"And I believe I have honestly earned it."

"Yes, you have," Hellen agreed, clapping Cloutard on the shoulder. "You really have."

"Let's get this stuff inside and give them the bad news," said Tom, his hand ready to knock.

But the door was ajar. He pulled up short.

"What are you—"

Tom raised his index finger to his lips. He drew the pistol that Cloutard's mother—fortunately—had given him after their return to Ian Fleming Airport.

"You two wait here," he whispered. Cautiously, he pushed the door open and entered the house, slipping from room to room, pistol held at the ready, as he'd learned in antiterror training. He saw clear signs of a struggle, and his worst suspicions were sadly confirmed as soon as he entered the living room.

"Hellen, François, get in here!" he shouted toward the front door. He replaced his pistol in its holster and knelt beside the unmoving body that lay on the living room floor. It was Torrente, badly injured. Tom placed two fingers to the old man's neck and, to his relief, found a faint pulse. From the traces in the living room, he could see that Torrente had crawled from the terrace into the house and lost consciousness here.

"Oh my God! What happened?" Hellen cried as she and Cloutard came in.

"Oh, *mon dieu*," said Cloutard.

"He's still alive. Quick, help me get him onto the couch," said Tom.

"No. Don't move him. We don't know where he's injured."

"You're right. Call an ambulance and call the police." Tom pushed the couch aside to make a little room. Hellen took out her phone and began to dial.

"No," Torrente coughed, taking Tom's hand in a weak grip. "No police." Hellen paused.

"What happened?"

"They've . . ." Torrente began to cough and tried to sit up. With Tom's help, he was able to lean back against the couch. "Leticia," he said weakly. "They've taken my daughter."

Hellen put her phone away, ran into the bathroom, and returned with a first-aid kit. "Who did this to you?" she asked, as she began to disinfect his ugly head wound.

Torrente twisted his face up in pain but did not try to stop her. "Thank you, my dear," he said.

"*Putain de merde*, is it not obvious?" Cloutard growled. "I know this signature only too well. It was Cabrera, Graves' personal thug."

Torrente nodded. "Could I get something to drink?" he said weakly.

Cloutard instantly produced his flask. He went to give it to the old man, but Hellen stopped him. "Nothing like that," she snapped, and she jumped up and hurried into the kitchen, returning a moment later with a glass of water. She handed it to Tom. "Put that away," she said sharply to Cloutard.

"Here, drink this." Tom passed the glass of water to Torrente and stood up. Torrente looked at the glass a little sadly, but he drank.

"The man is completely insane if he thinks he can kidnap his opponent for prime minister," Hellen said.

"What does he think he'll gain? This can't end well," said Tom.

"He still wants the treasure, man, I'm sure of it," Torrente said. "He must have found out who you are somehow and that we're working together. That's probably why he took Leticia. He wants the medallion and the rod back."

Tom, Hellen and Cloutard looked at each other.

"Please help my daughter. I can't lose her, too." A sob escaped the old man. "That damned treasure . . ."

"Speaking of which . . ." Tom said and swallowed. But he said no more when he noticed Hellen shake her head slightly. He understood.

"Don't worry, we'll take care of your daughter. But right now, we need to get you to a hospital," Hellen said. Tom nodded.

"No, I'm all right. I want to help you."

The trio moved a few steps away. Torrente was still sitting on the floor. He held a compress to his injured head and sipped at the glass of water.

"Where do we go from here?" Cloutard asked.

"We don't even know what he wants with her," said Tom.

"Torrente's probably right, though. Graves wants to swap Leticia for the medallions," Hellen said.

Cloutard gulped. A terrible thought occurred to him. "We cannot sit around here and wait for him to call. What if he has something completely different in mind?" he said.

"What about the island where they were holding you?" Tom said. "That seems like a good hideout to me."

"Yes. Graves has a kind of guerrilla camp there. And he—"

"Okay," Tom interrupted him. "Let's give your mother a call. We need her help again."

57

IAN FLEMING INTERNATIONAL AIRPORT, BOSCOBEL, ST. MARY, JAMAICA. THREE HOURS LATER.

"The best defense is a good offense," said Tom. "We can't wait any longer. We're running out of time. More to the point, Leticia is running out of time."

Tom, Hellen and Cloutard were standing with Giuseppina's soldiers in the hangar. Fabio and Adalgisa were elsewhere, with Cloutard's mother. They wouldn't be able to help in this situation, anyway. They were not fighters, and right now, fighters were needed.

Tom turned to the leader of the mercenary team, Gabriele Rossi. "The island's a fortress," Rossi said, "surrounded by impassable rocks. We can't get to it from the water." He was holding up a military map of the area, depicting the sea and coastline in far more detail than a normal map would. He threw it back on the table in irritation.

Rossi was the leader of the twelve-man mercenary team employed by Cloutard's mother. He was also the man who had led the raid on Graves' villa. He was tall and nondescript, but his face showed the marks of a hard life. And he was deadly. He had once been part of the 9th Paratroopers

Assault Regiment known as "Col Moschin," a special unit of the Italian army similar to the British SAS, but after dedicating twenty years of his life to the service, he had resigned from active duty—he'd had enough of putting his life on the line for spineless politicians and their dubious interests—and had worked for Giuseppina ever since. She had literally made him an offer he couldn't refuse, allowing him to continue his calling and paying him handsomely for it. Being on the other side of the law didn't bother him. He had committed more cruel and illegal acts in the service of his homeland than Giuseppina would ever ask of him.

"Actually, that is not correct," said Cloutard. "I was on that island myself a few days ago."

"Then tell us how you got there."

"In my boat," Torrente croaked. The elderly seaman had refused to be taken to a hospital. He wanted to help in any way he could. The mercenaries' medic had examined him thoroughly and patched him up as well as any doctor could. He had come through his encounter with Cabrera's baseball bat extraordinarily well, but he was in no condition to actively help. What he needed most of all was rest.

"Getting onto the island is not our only problem. We don't know what defenses Graves has. We can't just waltz in there without a plan. He'd see us coming a mile off," Rossi said.

"Then we have to make sure he's looking the other way at the right moment," said Tom.

Rossi laughed, shook his head, and looked coldly at Tom. "Where's his camp? How many men does he have? How well armed are they? What kind of terrain is it? Does he have an alarm system?"

"I saw no more than a dozen men with AK-47s guarding a handful of barracks. But there could be more," said Cloutard.

"Oh, please. That doesn't sound so bad. I could almost handle that myself," Tom joked.

That made Rossi really angry. "Is he always like this?" he asked

Hellen and Cloutard nodded emphatically. "You have no idea," Hellen said, sighing heavily. Then she smiled at Tom and blew him a kiss.

"The problem is not just the guards," Cloutard said, "but the many civilians who also took part in his ritual there. And he is holding several innocent young women, too."

"Potential collateral damage. This gets better and better," said Rossi.

"So it would help if we knew exactly what's happening on the island and where," said Tom, stroking three days' growth of stubble and looking fixedly at Rossi.

"Of course. Reconnaissance is indispensable for a mission like this. You're a soldier too, right?"

"I'll give you that. But reconnaissance can also be done from a distance."

Hellen's iPad chimed loudly.

"Perfect timing," said Tom. He reached for the iPad and pulled up a file that had just arrived via email. He pushed the tablet across the table that stood between him and Rossi.

"What's—" But Rossi fell silent when he saw what was on the screen.

"These pictures are less than five hours old," said Tom.

"How did you get these?" Rossi asked, impressed.

"I could tell you, but then I'd have to kill you."

Rossi looked at him darkly, tossed the iPad onto the table and turned away in irritation. "Can't this guy stay serious for one second?"

"Okay, fine. I have a few contacts in the Pentagon. My uncle was pretty high up in the CIA. I made a few calls on the way here and a friend of his sent me the satellite pictures."

Rossi returned to the table and studied the various images. Infrared and topographical images were also included.

"These are good. Now all we need to do is figure out how to get onto the island unseen."

Tom smiled. "François, I hope you haven't gotten too rusty," said Tom. He looked at Cloutard and pointed to the old Bell UH-1H helicopter—a Huey—standing behind the jet in the hangar.

58

LAKE DELTON, DELTON POINT, WISCONSIN, USA

THE LINCOLN NAVIGATOR TURNED IN AT THE ENTRANCE TO Delton Point, Wisconsin's most exclusive residential address. Like Miami's Star Island, the only way in was to live there or be invited.

Eon van Rensburg looked at his wife, Kiara, in surprise. The houses were luxurious, certainly, but they were well on the way to becoming multibillionaires, able to afford entire island groups in the South Pacific if they wanted to. Living by a small lake in Wisconsin seemed somehow ... wrong.

"How much do we actually know about this guy?" Kiara asked, fumbling with her husband's fly as if it were the most natural thing in the world.

Eon, distracted, stammered, "Roland Tassilo, Baron von Hohenfeldt, comes from old German nobility, from a family that was one of the few to turn all of the crises of the 19th and 20th centuries to their advantage. I've known him for a long time, but I don't know much more than that. They say he's one of the few non-American members of Skull & Bones, and that he's a regular at the Bilderberg Conference."

He let out a groan when his wife succeeded in opening his zipper and began massaging him. In the rearview mirror she locked eyes unashamedly with de Waal, at the wheel of the Lincoln. De Waal, used to the couple's escapades, stoically ignored the show.

"And he has the—"

"Please, baby, not now. I have to focus. If you're going to be so poorly behaved, I'll have to punish you back at the hotel."

Kiara purred like a cat, slid her hand out of her husband's pants, and zipped him up, not without disappointment.

"We've arrived, sir, madam," they heard de Waal's slightly bored-sounding voice from the front.

De Waal jumped out of the driver's seat and opened the back door. Kiara climbed out. Eon looked down at himself to be sure there were no visible bulges in his pants and climbed out after her.

They were shown inside by a servant. The interior was exceedingly plain. Von Hohenfeldt seemed to have read their minds. "You are doubtless wondering why I am meeting you in such modest surroundings," he said, appearing from another room. He feathered a kiss on the back of Kiara's hand, then turned to shake Eon's. "Welcome. I like to live a little below the radar. I have my peace and quiet here. I have no interest in Bel Air, Monte Carlo, or any of those other shallow pseudo-hotspots."

The baron led them out to his terrace, which offered a gorgeous view over Lake Delton.

Eon walked ahead, and Kiara took the opportunity to pinch her husband's behind. He let out a sharp "Ouch!" and batted away his wife's wandering hands.

The baron, studiously ignoring Eon's outburst, turned to him for a moment. "It was important to me that we meet in person. This business is too important to be conducted at a distance."

Another servant brought coffee and the three fell into the kind of small talk only wealthy people can make. After a few minutes, the baron cleared his throat, a clear sign that it was time to get down to business.

"I would like to make one thing clear straight away," said the baron. "I am not at all interested in the treasure of Anne Bonny in its entirety. To be sure, it has a certain value as a curiosity—apart from the actual value of the gold and jewels it contains—but that is of no importance to me." He took a sip of coffee, his little finger extended, as was undoubtedly common in his circles. It would have looked absurd on most people, but it matched von Hohenfeldt's slim, ascetic appearance, graying temples, aristocratic nose, blasé expression, and slightly adenoidal voice. It all formed a consummate total image.

"I don't understand," said Eon in confusion. Even Kiara was so taken aback that she briefly left off pawing her husband. They looked at the baron in bewilderment.

"I am only interested in part of the treasure. An important item was stolen by Anne Bonny and her crew, and that is all I want. Not until you bring me this item will I hand over the artifact you crave so dearly."

Van Rensburg's breathing grew faster. He felt a flush of anger that the object of his desire was in the possession of this man, who unfortunately held all the cards.

The baron picked up a small bell standing on the arm of his chair. Seconds after he rang it, a third servant appeared.

"The papers," said the baron. The man exited, only to return moments later carrying a framed picture. "This is the manifest from one of the ships captured by Anne Bonny."

Von Hohenfeldt proffered the glass-fronted parchment and indicated one line on the list.

"That is what matters to me. Only when you hand that over to me do we have a deal."

Eon and Kiara looked at the line, then looked at each other in astonishment.

59

AN ISLAND, THIRTY MILES EAST OF JAMAICA, LATE EVENING

SHAW, IN HIS THREE-PIECE SUIT, PACED BACK AND FORTH across the dusty yard in front of the barracks. He kept pausing and looking at the guard, who was sitting on a bench beside the door, chain-smoking cigarettes with obvious pleasure. Shaw reached a decision and abruptly stopped. Taking out his cellphone, he searched through the address book, and found the contact he wanted. His finger hovered over the call button. Should he risk it? He ran through the possibilities in his head. Angry at his own indecision, he punched the phone's sleep button and put it away. He took a few steps, then turned back and repeated the process. What should he do? For a moment, he stopped and stared at the guarded door. Then he made up his mind. He marched toward the barracks, went up the three steps, and reached for the door. But to his amazement, the guard stood and blocked his path.

"What the hell is this?" he snarled at the man.

"My instructions are to let no one in," said the man, who stank of sweat. Shaw looked him up and down. He had to admit, he was a fearsome sight. It wasn't the AK-47 slung over his shoulder, nor was it the machete dangling from his belt or the chromed pistol in its holster. It was his eyes. A dark-tanned, deeply creased face with eyes that had seen all kinds of cruelty, and which nothing could frighten anymore.

"I have to talk to him," Shaw said.

The sentry's expression didn't change. He simply stood and stared back at Shaw, took a drag on his cigarette, and blew the smoke in his face. Shaw stared back, but he had to cough when he breathed in the smoke.

"If you don't want Cabrera to use you as a guinea pig to test how sharp his boss's knives are, then I suggest you—"

The door flew open, and Cabrera emerged. The sentry stepped aside, and Shaw took a step back. Cabrera glared menacingly at Shaw.

"Sir, I have to speak with him. It's important," Shaw stammered, and he tried to look past Cabrera and into the room behind him.

"Bring him in," Graves' voice said from inside the gloomy shack.

The corner of Cabrera's mouth twisted up and he grunted softly. Then he grabbed Shaw by the collar, dragged him inside, and threw him to the floor. Shaw stood up, brushed the dirt from his suit and raised his head. He was about to protest, but the words stuck in his throat. An icy shudder ran down his spine as he tried to process the eerie sight before him.

The weak glow of candlelight reinforced the nightmarish atmosphere. He was looking at a kind of altar covered with bones, skulls, small totems, jars with unidentifiable contents, a bowl of blood, and many candles. Above the altar the torso of a skeleton had been suspended, hung with countless strings of animal bones, nutshells, and feathers. A red cloth had been slung around the ribcage like a sash, and dried plants completed the ghastly spectacle. A black top hat crowned the skull of the huge totem.

To the left and right of the altar cowered two young women, shackled by their ankles to a wooden post. They did not dare to raise their heads. Two African priestesses in colorful robes stood to Graves' left and right, making final adjustments to his outfit.

Shaw gulped. Graves stood before him in a black-leather, floor-length overcoat. Around his neck were countless strange necklaces. His black-and-white makeup made his face look skull-like, and on his head he also wore a top hat, the hatband made of small bones pinned with countless feathers. From the center of the brim snarled the skull of a small animal.

Shaw was speechless. He knew Graves was a devotee of voodoo, and he had heard about the rituals that took place here, but nothing could have prepared him for this. He stood in front of him and stared, his mouth hanging open, unable to utter a word. Graves leaned on his walking stick and stared back.

"What is it? You look as if you've seen a ghost," Graves said. His diabolical grin was accentuated a hundredfold by the skull makeup he wore.

"I, I . . ." Shaw stammered.

"Spit it out, man. I don't have much time."

Shaw took a deep breath and finally found his voice. "She's worth more alive than dead, sir."

"Are we talking about your little girlfriend? Don't tell me you've actually grown fond of her."

"No, of course not," Shaw said more quietly. "I just think that we can use her to—"

He fell silent. Graves indicated to the two priestesses to leave him alone, and he stepped toward Shaw. Shaw tried to step back, but Cabrera was standing at his back.

"Listen, Shaw, I don't have the slightest interest in trading Miss Ortiz for the artifacts," Graves said. "If Wagner and his friends have found the treasure, then we'll simply go and take it from them. I don't have the time for these games anymore, and if I don't have to do any digging myself to get what I want, all the better."

Shaw looked at him in horror. Cabrera grinned.

"But sir, Miss Ortiz is a prime ministerial candidate. You can't just kill her. Her disappearance will be investigated."

Graves laughed. He stepped beside Shaw and put his arm around him. His fingers clawed into Shaw's shoulder, and he leaned close and spoke directly into his ear. "Have you already forgotten our press conference? Miss Ortiz and her father have been officially branded as criminals. They are on the run, and my police will soon have evidence of their guilt."

Repulsed, Shaw turned his head aside as Graves hissed into his ear: "Mr. Cabrera here has instructions to let me know if Wagner finds the treasure. He will then bring me what I want. And your little girlfriend will be useful to me in other ways. She will take me one step closer to my goal, the last sacrifice before I can complete the final coronation ritual."

Shaw was frozen with fear. Graves stepped back and pushed him away.

"Now get out of my sight. I have to prepare."

Without warning, there was a deafening roar overhead, followed by the rattle of machine-gun fire.

60

AN ISLAND, THIRTY MILES EAST OF JAMAICA

Cabrera stepped out of the barracks into the middle of a battle. Several men lay dead on the ground. Others fired wildly into the night sky. He jumped down the three steps and looked up, turning in a circle as he tried to pinpoint the receding sound of the engine. Then he saw it. Against the moon, he made out the silhouette of a helicopter turning in a wide arc over the treetops, coming back for a second attack on the camp.

He jumped back up to the sentry by the door, grabbed his AK-47, and ran out onto the open space. "Make sure the boss is okay," he shouted back at the guard. Then he opened fire on the approaching chopper.

The helicopter flew in a curve around the central yard. In the open side door, behind a blaze of muzzle flash, Cabrera saw a man with a machine gun. Like laser beams, tracer rounds slammed into the ground, each one lighting the yard brightly for a fraction of a second.

Cabrera didn't move an inch. He fired until the magazine was empty. Then he tossed the gun aside and ran, diving for cover behind the nearest barracks at the last second. Bullets missed him by a whisker, slamming instead into the timber of the barracks beside him.

As the helicopter turned again above the trees on the other side of the camp, he broke cover and ran across the yard to the building opposite. He swung the door wide, re-emerging a moment later with a boxy, rectangular object about two feet long.

Wild cries, deafening gunfire, and the roar of the helicopter overhead had instantly transformed the quiet island into a war zone. Cabrera's men fired unremittingly at the chopper. Unfazed, Cabrera himself moved to the center of the yard. Keeping his eye on his target, he knelt in the dust. He tugged a handle on one end of the box, pulling out four tubes from inside it. Then he opened a cover on the other end and squared the weapon on his shoulder. The M-202 Flash, as it was known, was a leftover from past conflicts. Officially not in use since the end of the Vietnam War, rumors continued to circulate that the rocket launcher was still used today in Afghanistan. It was not a standard rocket launcher, but more a type of flamethrower. The projectiles it fired were filled with aluminum phosphate, which burned on impact at almost 3000°. Accuracy was around fifty percent.

Cabrera grasped the pistol grip on the underside of the box, put his eye to the sighting mechanism, and took aim at the helicopter as it came in for its next pass. He fired.

A projectile hissed from one of the four tubes and roared toward the helicopter. A miss. Cabrera fired again and a rocket shot from the second tube. This time he was on target. A brilliant flash lit the sky as the projectile hit the tail of the chopper. Flames and clouds of dark smoke billowed from the engine, and the helicopter spiraled down out of sight behind the trees.

Cabrera's men stopped firing. Silence. There was no explosion, but the sky in the east glowed red-orange. The men's cheering broke the silence. Satisfied, Cabrera laid the M-202 on the ground and called his men to him.

"Give me the radio," he ordered. "Camp to Crow's Nest," he barked into the handset.

"Yes, sir," a voice answered immediately.

"What's going on out there?"

"Sorry, sir. I only saw the chopper at the last second. It must have been flying close to the water. When it came over the cliffs, it was already too late."

"is there anything else coming?"

"No, sir. Nothing. Sea is calm, no vessels in sight."

"Send Malik and the other guy to the crash site. Check for survivors. If yes, keep it that way. I want them alive. I want to talk to them."

"Yes, sir," the man responded.

"And keep your damned eyes open. I don't want any more surprises."

Cabrera did not wait for a reply. He tossed the radio back to the man he'd gotten it from and returned to his boss's barracks.

61

WEST SIDE OF THE ISLAND, AT THE SAME TIME

Tom jumped from one of the black inflatable rafts. Hellen, Rossi and another of the mercenaries followed him. Under cover of the darkness, they waded through the knee-deep water and pulled the boat ashore. Four more mercenaries pulled the second boat up the beach a few yards away.

Each member of the landing squad wore a black wetsuit and a tactical vest with spare magazines; each was armed with a pistol in a thigh holster, a Wasp Injection Knife and a Heckler & Koch G36 assault rifle.

The six-man team, led by Rossi, ran across the narrow strip of beach, took cover on the edge of the forest, secured the area, and hid the inflatables among the bushes. Tom and Hellen wore the same outfits, though Hellen had turned down the offer of a rifle.

Tom adjusted his throat mike. When he and Hellen reached the trees, he pressed the push-to-talk button, which he wore as a ring on one finger.

"Landing squad to decoy," he whispered, and released the button. All he heard was radio static in his waterproof earbuds. "Couldn't we have come up with more original call signs?"

He repeated the call. Again, nothing but white noise. Hellen looked at him anxiously.

"François, come in," Tom said more insistently, pressing the talk button again.

"Landing squad to decoy, status report," they heard Rossi say, a trace of nervousness in his voice. La Mamma would personally rip his heart out if he didn't return her beloved Francesco unscathed.

Cloutard was supposed to draw the guerrillas' attention, giving the inflatable boats enough time to make landfall unseen. Thirty minutes earlier, at a safe distance from the island, he had steadied the helicopter just above the water. Rossi had pulled back the sliding door, heaved two large parcels into the water, and jumped out after them. One after the other, five of the six mercenaries had followed him. One of the soldiers had remained behind to help Cloutard. In seconds, the two parcels had inflated into small boats. The sea, whipped up by the helicopter's rotors, lashed Tom and Hellen mercilessly in the face when they positioned themselves at the side door.

"You don't have to do this," Tom bellowed over the deafening roar of the rotors.

"I know, but I want to. Leticia needs our help. Besides, someone has to make sure you don't do anything reckless," she yelled back, with a smile at Tom.

"Then jump! Just like I told you."

Hellen nodded and looked down. The mercenaries were already in the inflatables, waiting for them. Rossi waved to her to jump. Cloutard kept looking back from the cockpit and did his best to keep the helicopter as steady as possible.

"This is what I get for marrying an adrenaline junkie," Hellen said to herself, and she took a deep breath. Eyes closed, with her arms folded over her chest, she dropped into the water. Tom jumped after her and Rossi and his men pulled them on board. The remaining soldier slid the side door closed.

They looked up one last time as Cloutard swung the helicopter away in a wide curve to the other side of the island, staying close to the water.

"I hope he'll be all right," Hellen said.

"Cloutard knows what he's doing. He's a good pilot."

The small outboard motors were nearly silent, but they were powerful and got them to the beach quickly. The sea was calm, and thanks to Torrente's instructions, they were able to approach the island without issue. He was in no condition to accompany them, but he had been able to help them with everything he knew about the island. For his own well-being, they had left him in the capable hands of the medic and La Mamma.

Hellen was clearly uncomfortable with all the tactical gear. She plucked at her vest and the wetsuit as they waited for some sign of life from Cloutard.

"How do you stand these things?" she whispered. "I feel like a dominatrix in a latex suit."

Tom's eyes widened.

"How would you know . . .?" Tom began, but he didn't finish the question. He just shook his head, trying to get rid of the mental image. Hellen grinned mischievously.

"Landing squad to decoy, come in please," Rossi repeated.

"We can't wait any longer," Tom said. "There are all kinds of possible reasons why his radio isn't working."

"But—" Hellen said.

"There's nothing we can do right now. François is on his own for a while. But I'm sure he'll be okay. He's resourceful."

"You're right. We should get to our rendezvous point," said Rossi.

Tom nodded.

Rossi looked left and right to his men, and circled one hand over his head. The men stood, and Rossi jabbed his open hand twice toward the forest. A few yards apart, with rifles raised, the men disappeared among the trees.

"Shall we?" Hellen said, heading off after the men. Seeing Hellen from behind in the tight wetsuit, Tom had to smile, and for a second, the mental image of her in a dominatrix outfit returned.

Focus, he chided himself, following her.

They pushed through the underbrush in silence. Rossi kept an eye on his compass to make sure they were going the right way. It was practically impossible to travel in a straight line—one reason why people got lost in forests all the time. Without even realizing it, people naturally tended to move in a circle.

After about twenty minutes, they had almost reached their goal. Rossi's fist shot into the air. Immediately, his men stopped and crouched. Tom also followed the instruction. Only Hellen still stood upright, taken by surprise. Tom grabbed her by her bulletproof vest and pulled her down. Keeping low, he went to Rossi, who was peering through a small monocular. He passed it to Tom and pointed ahead. Tom lifted the cigar-sized telescope to his eye, and his heart skipped a beat.

62

IN THE HELICOPTER

Alarms screamed in Cloutard's ears. The soldier was hanging onto the cargo net in the main bay of the helicopter as hard as he could. Searing flames from the burning tail section were licking through the open side door.

Cloutard struggled to keep the helicopter in the air. They were spinning like a carousel and rapidly losing height.

"Are you all right?" he shouted to the man in the back. "Strap in!"

But there was no response. There was too much noise. Cloutard risked a backward glance and saw the man being tossed around helplessly, his eyes squeezed shut.

He turned forward again. *Can we make it out over the sea?* he wondered. A water landing seemed to him to be the better choice, especially when your aircraft was on fire. But the decision was snatched from him in the same moment. The helicopter suddenly dropped, crashing through the treetops and tearing the skids off, which only accelerated the spin. Working the stick as hard as he could, Cloutard was able to stop the rotation and aimed for the one open space he could see among the trees.

"Hold on!" he bellowed, knowing this was not going to end well.

The chopper crash-landed hard and skidded over the uneven terrain. It turned, and the tail boom slammed into a boulder. Although he was strapped into his seat, Cloutard was tossed around wildly. His helmet struck the side window several times. The man in the back screamed. Sparks flew as the tail rotor scraped over rock, the force of the impact breaking away the boom completely. The cockpit windows shattered. Flames were everywhere. The main rotor blades snapped like twigs as the machine rolled down the steeply sloping clearing in a ball of fire. After fifty yards, the cockpit came to rest upside down.

Cloutard opened his eyes. A wave of heat hit him from the rear of the chopper. He looked back to see a terrible sight. The soldier in the cargo area hadn't stood a chance. His clothes were on fire, but he made no sound. Cloutard guessed that he'd been thrown halfway out of the open door, then crushed by the rolling cabin before the flames reached him. The man was dead.

Cloutard swiftly unbuckled his harness and fell hard onto the cockpit ceiling. He curled onto his back with an effort and kicked at the cockpit door with both legs. After several kicks, it flew open, and he crawled outside. He tore off his helmet and ran as fast as he could away from the stricken aircraft. A moment later, it exploded in a massive fireball. The shock wave threw Cloutard off his feet. He knocked his head hard against the ground and lost consciousness.

63

A LIGHTHOUSE ON THE ISLAND

Two men armed with AK-47s were dragging an unconscious body across the clearing in the direction of an old lighthouse. Through the little scope, Tom could see who the men had captured. "They've got Cloutard," he said.

"What? We have to help him," Hellen whispered.

Tom nodded and stood up.

"Wait," said Rossi, and he turned to his men. He signaled to them to take out the two men dragging Cloutard. Two of the mercenaries nodded and raised their silenced assault rifles.

"What is it? What are you waiting for?" Rossi whispered, when his order was not immediately carried out. One of his men nodded toward the lighthouse. Rossi turned back and saw what had made his men hesitate.

"What the hell are you doing?" Rossi hissed through the radio in Tom's ear. Tom was creeping toward the lighthouse —directly in the line of fire of Rossi's men.

"What does it look like? I'm helping my friend," Tom replied.

When he reached the edge of the forest, he stood up, drew his silenced pistol, and, keeping low, crept across the small clearing toward the lighthouse. He took in every detail of his surroundings, but he saw no one else except the silhouette of a man up on the lighthouse gallery, moving on the far side of the tower.

"Idiot! Get out of the firing—" Rossi's voice buzzed again in Tom's headset. Irritated, Tom turned it off. Rossi's tirade would only distract him.

Tom saw the two men start dragging Cloutard through a door in the side of the lighthouse. They had no idea that Tom was only five yards behind them.

He took aim at one of the men, but a split second later he froze. He felt bullets buzz past his head, left and right, and slam into the two men lugging Cloutard, strewing the contents of their heads over the crumbling lighthouse wall. Like a marionette with its strings cut, Cloutard slumped to the ground. Tom hurried over to him and checked his pulse. He was still alive. Then he checked the two men lying beside him. Their faces had been blown off completely.

Tom stepped over Cloutard, raised his pistol again, and cautiously opened the lighthouse door. He looked up. A dilapidated stairway wound up the inside of the stone wall to the lantern room at the top. Step by step, his back to the wall and pistol pointed upward, Tom ascended.

"Malik, is that you?" a voice called down.

Tom paused and pressed against the wall, trying to stay out of sight.

"Malik?" the voice called again.

Tom made a grunting noise and waited.

"What's going on down there?"

The man couldn't see him. Then Tom heard the guard move back out onto the gallery. He ran higher.

"Crow's Nest to camp, come in."

Tom's eyes widened. The man was calling his base.

"Crow's Nest to camp, come in," the man repeated.

Tom cleared the final steps and was now standing in the drafty lantern room. When the man heard him, he spun around and reached for his gun.

"I wouldn't do that. I'm way ahead of you," said Tom, panting a little from the climb, his pistol aiming directly at the man's head. "Slowly," he said, watching carefully as the man withdrew his chromed pistol from its holster and placed it on the floor.

"Camp to Crow's Nest," the man's radio crackled. Both men looked at it.

"One wrong word and you're dead," Tom said, and he stepped out of the lantern room onto the gallery circling the tower. "All good, all quiet, no vessels. Do you understand what I'm telling you?"

The man nodded.

"Camp to Crow's Nest, come in. Why did you call?" the radio crackled again.

"Nothing. Everything's okay. Malik was just fooling around. All quiet here," the man said into the radio as he stared down the barrel of Tom's gun.

"Good. Now give me the radio." Tom reached out his hand.

"No problem," said the man. And he flung the radio at Tom and leaped after it, taking him by surprise. He grabbed Tom and dragged him down, the two men landing back inside the lantern room. The man straightened up and began swinging at him.

―――

Moments later, Rossi and Hellen ran from the forest. Hellen ran straight to Cloutard, who sat up groaning and looked around. In a second, he was wide awake, as the sight of the two dead men beside him sent his adrenaline soaring. Hellen held him under his arms and helped him up. Cloutard raised his hands to his head.

"*Putain de merde*, what happened?" He looked down at his clothes, spattered with gray matter and bone fragments, and flicked them off in disgust.

"Where's Alessandro?" Rossi whispered.

Cloutard looked gravely at Rossi and shook his head.

Rossi's mouthed a "fuck." Then, aloud, he said, "Where's Wagner?"

"I don't know. I was—" But without warning, a body slammed into the ground a few feet away. Hellen let out a sharp cry, but instantly pressed the flat of her hand over her mouth to muffle the sound.

Cloutard, Hellen, and Rossi looked up to see Tom leaning over the gallery railing. He gave them an exhausted thumbs-up.

Still wobbly on his legs, Cloutard leaned against the lighthouse wall. With trembling hands, he took out his flask and drank a large mouthful of revitalizing Louis XIII.

"Your husband is completely insane," Rossi snapped at Hellen.

"Maybe. He does have his own unique way of solving problems," Hellen grated. She looked up fearlessly into his icy glare. "But if you put him in danger one more time,"—she pressed the blade of her Wasp knife almost casually into Rossi's crotch—"then you'll be singing soprano for the rest of your life."

Cloutard spat out his second mouthful of cognac, coughed, and smiled.

Rossi looked down. "Careful with that. There's a CO_2 cartridge in the handle," he said with a grin. Hellen did not look away.

The lighthouse door flew open, and Tom came out. Hellen and Rossi both spun toward him.

Rossi cleared his throat and stepped to one side. Hellen quickly replaced the knife in the sheath on her vest. Tom looked first at her, then Cloutard, and finally at Rossi. He frowned, and his eyes narrowed.

"Did I miss something?"

"Not a thing. All good here," Rossi said.

Cloutard grinned. Hellen shook her head innocently.

"Okay. Then come with me," said Tom, and he disappeared back into the lighthouse. He climbed the spiral staircase, Rossi close behind. At the top, Tom returned the small telescope and pointed into the distance. Rossi lifted the scope to his eye.

"We'll have to split up," said Tom. "I'll take care of Graves. You free the women."

Rossi lowered the telescope. He looked at Tom and nodded. "Let's hope we're not too late."

64

AN AMPHITHEATER ON THE ISLAND

The narrow track was lined with flaming torches set high overhead. Two African priestesses in colorful costumes and turbans led the small procession. They carried bowls filled with blood and murmured unintelligible words, sprinkling the path with blood as they walked. The beat of drums pulsed through the forest.

Graves, wearing his Baron Samedi outfit and carrying a skull-topped walking stick, followed close behind the priestesses. After him came Cabrera and one of his men, hauling a writhing woman along the gravel path. Shaw brought up the rear.

"You'll never get away with this," Leticia cried, as the two men dragged her along. "And neither will you!" She turned her head back toward Shaw. "How can you collaborate with a psychopath like this?" she screamed at him. He swallowed and looked at the ground.

Graves laughed.

"My dear, you should simply try to accept that I'm going to win," said Graves, and he lifted his arms toward the sky. "The gods are on my side."

"You're a madman, no more."

"Ah, just like your mother." Leticia fell silent. The mention of her dead mother hit her like a punch to the gut. "She didn't know her place either," continued Graves. "So I had to teach her a lesson."

Leticia, wearing a plain white dress, fought with all her strength against the iron grip of the two men. "You . . ." she struggled to find words. "You killed my mother?"

Graves laughed viciously. "Not personally, of course. But yes, I couldn't allow that little slut to destroy everything I'd built."

"You miserable bastard," Leticia screamed. Tears of rage and sadness poured down her cheeks.

"Now, now. Don't fret. In a few minutes, you'll be joining her."

Despite Graves' cruel words, Leticia felt a sudden calm and stopped struggling against the men holding her. She stared forward, eyes wide, as a small clearing opened ahead of them.

The two priestesses moved off to the left and right, and Graves descended a series of steps carved into the rocks around them.

Before Leticia was a kind of amphitheater ringed by wooden poles and torches. Half-naked men with white-painted faces drummed and danced around a stone altar in the center of the pit. The stench of death filled Leticia's nose, making her shudder. Her legs gave way, but Cabrera and the second man held onto her tightly. Impaled on each of the wooden poles was the partially decomposed body of a young woman, each one decorated with trinkets of every description, like life-sized totems. One pole was still free.

The knowledge of what was about to happen was too much. Her limbs failed, tears ran down her face, and an indescribable panic rose inside her.

"Let us begin," Graves called, raising his arms again.

The two men dragged Leticia, now apathetic, down the steps. They lifted her onto the table-high altar and bound her tightly by her hands and feet. Graves was standing at the head of the altar, and Shaw positioned himself behind him and to one side. He could not bring himself to look directly at Leticia. Cabrera and the other man moved to the foot of the altar. The drums boomed monotonously into the night.

With rhythmic, dancing movements, the two priestesses crept around the altar, murmuring incomprehensible magic spells. They grasped Leticia by her head and poured a green substance from a small bottle into her unresisting mouth. She began to thrash madly and screamed. Moments later, her body convulsed and went slack. She lay in a daze. They cut away her dress and poured the blood of the women sacrificed days before over her body. The drumming grew faster and more intense.

The priestesses snarled and screeched and sang. With their fingers, they outlined symbols on Leticia's blood-soaked, naked body.

Graves, dressed as Baron Samedi, approached the altar slowly and withdrew a small dagger from his walking stick. He leaned back, threw his arms high, and screamed incoherent words in the old language. As if suffering an epileptic fit, his body began to twitch and quake. His eyes rolled up in their sockets. The drum beat accelerated and became louder still. The priestesses danced ecstatically beside the altar and screamed to the skies. Graves stepped up to the altar as if in a trance, his hands high in the air and his head thrown back.

A shot cut through the night. Cabrera spun around as the man beside him fell to the ground, dead. The drumming and screaming fell silent.

"Hey, asshole. Halloween's not till October," Tom shouted, the still-smoking gun in his hand.

65

ON THE ISLAND

Rossi peered through his rifle scope at the open space in front of the barracks. Hidden in the bushes, blending invisibly into the forest, he lay just a few short yards away. He and his men had encircled the camp and were ready to attack. Tom, Hellen and Cloutard would free Leticia and take care of Graves while and his men freed the captive women.

"I count ten hostiles, maximum," he whispered.

"Yes, ten," a voice sounded in his headset.

"Ditto," said another.

"Awaiting your command," said a third.

One by one, his men responded.

Rossi swung his rifle left and right, checking everything. The guerrillas were doing clean-up, dragging away the dead and tending to their injured comrades after the Cloutard's lethal air attack. This was their chance, while they were distracted.

"Cover me," said Rossi. Holding his rifle in front of him, he crawled toward one of the barracks. When he reached the building, he got to his feet and pressed himself against the back wall. He screwed up his nose. A glance at the ground behind the building told him where the stench was coming from. The barracks were built on low stilts, and beneath each one ran a single trench filled with rubbish and shit. He turned away in disgust and crept along the side wall to the front of the building.

A peek around the corner revealed a man leaning next to the door, playing a game on his phone. Across the open space, Rossi saw two men loading a body onto the back of a jeep, and to their left, two more were carrying an injured man into a building. The rest of the guards were sitting on the steps of the wooden structures, leaning on walls, or patrolling between the buildings.

"Wait for my signal," Rossi said, barely audible, but the throat mike allowed his men to understand him perfectly.

He slung his rifle onto his back and drew his knife. Crouched, his eyes shifting between his surroundings and his target, he crept toward the man from behind.

The men in the yard tossed the last body onto the jeep. Then they went to the others and began talking to them.

Now, Rossi thought. As if in slow motion, he raised his left arm. Focused on his game, the man had no idea that Rossi was barely two feet behind him and about to take his life.

Everything happened fast. Rossi's left hand came down over the man's head and closed over his mouth, simultaneously pulling him backward. With his other hand, lightning fast, he rammed his knife three times into the man's kidneys. The man collapsed without a sound.

Rossi pushed open the barracks door with his back and dragged the dead man inside.

"You finally finish that game?" Rossi heard a voice behind him. He dropped the man, his knife still in the lifeless body. He drew his silenced pistol as he turned, and before the man farther back even knew what was happening, Rossi had fired two bullets into him.

He stood for a moment without moving and scanned the barracks. Then he took a step back, pushed the dead man's legs aside, and shut the door.

He smelled the same stench inside as outside, but stronger still. Added to it was the reek of decomposition. Flies buzzed through the room.

He peered down a long, dimly lit corridor. In the middle of it lay the man he'd shot. On both sides were narrow wooden cells, one after another. They were no bigger than telephone booths. He listened: breathing, groans, whimpering, wailing. Returning his pistol to its holster, he pressed a handkerchief over his mouth and turned on his flashlight.

He moved slowly down the corridor and shone his flashlight through the small, barred hatches in the padlocked doors. He had seen a lot in the course of his career, but this sight would stay with him for the rest of his life. In several of the cells, cowering on the floor, were young girls, none older than seventeen.

A thin arm suddenly pushed through the bars of a door and reached for him pleadingly. At first, he recoiled, but then he took the hand in his and looked into the desperate eyes of the girl inside the cell.

"Please help us," she said in a weak voice.

"You're safe now. You're all safe. We're getting you out of here," Rossi whispered. Then he released her hand, hurried back to the entrance, and vomited in a corner of the room. Still doubled over, he pressed the transmit button on his radio.

"Wagner, do you read?" he said. He straightened up and wiped his mouth.

"Yes."

"The girls are safe. Finish off that piece of shit."

"My pleasure," Tom replied.

Rossi spoke again, this time to his men. "Go. No survivors. Send them all to hell," he said.

He listened. A barrage of shots followed. His men, like him, were using silencers, and the shots were barely audible. Almost simultaneously, he heard the muffled sounds of falling bodies. It was over in seconds.

His radio crackled. "Mission complete."

Rossi smiled, satisfied. He returned to the cells and, one after another, began breaking the locks.

66

THE AMPHITHEATER

No one moved.

Tom was standing at the edge of the amphitheater, his rifle trained on Graves' head. Cabrera had frozen a few steps away, his hand hovering over his pistol.

"One move and your boss is dead," Tom said.

Behind him, Hellen and Cloutard emerged from hiding, each with a pistol in their hand. Hellen instantly aimed hers at Shaw.

The half-naked men dropped their drums and jumped back in fright. The drums clattered down the stone steps. The priestesses cowered beside the altar, hissing like cats. Shaw stood with his hands in the air just a few steps behind Graves.

"Mr. Wagner," said Graves. "Surprise, surprise. Did you bring me something?"

Tom looked at the man in surprise. Then he laughed. "Oh, you mean the treasure. I'm afraid I have to disappoint you. There is no treasure. The hiding place was empty."

Graves froze. "I don't believe you."

"Believe whatever you want. Oh, wait, you already do, judging by what's going on here."

"So you've come to free Miss Ortiz. Noble indeed. But also very, very stupid," Graves said. "Look around you. We outnumber you easily," Graves said, unperturbed.

Cabrera laughed. "What do the three of you think you can do?" he growled.

"Who says there's only three of us?" said Tom, and he looked quickly left and right, into the forest.

Cabrera and Graves looked at one another as if either their own men or Tom's would appear at any moment.

Without warning, one of the drummers, screaming like a wild beast, charged straight at Tom. Quick as lightning and before anyone else could react, Tom fired into the ground at the man's feet, then immediately returned his aim to Graves. The drummer froze. Cloutard turned his gun toward him, and the other drummers screamed and vanished into the forest.

"Count again," Tom goaded, then his voice turned serious. "Here's how we're going to do this. You two witches are going to cut Leticia free, and Hellen will get her away from here. The rest of you are then going to form one line and march back to camp like good little schoolkids. And I guarantee that if even one of you tries anything, there'll be a bloodbath." He paused for a second. "Although, that's what you're here for, isn't it? So if that's what you want, go for it. And one last thing, just in case it wasn't clear: you're all under arrest."

Cabrera, Graves, and the priestesses exchanged glances.

"Get on with it," said Hellen. "Cut her loose." She switched her aim from Shaw to one of the women.

The priestesses looked quickly toward Graves, then stood up and cut Leticia's bonds.

Hellen slowly descended the steps, her pistol swinging nervously left and right.

"Careful. Those two are wild," said Tom.

Leticia was moving now, but not yet fully in control of her body. The two priestesses retreated. Hellen reached for Leticia's hand.

Suddenly, one of the two colorfully dressed women jumped forward with a scream and hurled a small container at the ground. There was a blinding flash of light. White smoke rose. The second priestess screeched and leaped at Hellen, dragging her to the ground. The pistol slipped from Hellen's hand and skittered across the ground toward Shaw.

The blinding light sent a piercing spasm through Tom's head. He pulled the trigger, but his aim was off. He missed Graves by a hair's breadth, putting a bullet through his top hat instead.

Cabrera, who had evidently known what was about to happen, now had his pistol in his hand. He fired at Tom, the shot grazing Tom's arm. Before Tom could react, Cabrera was on him. Tom dropped his rifle as both men slammed into the ground.

Cloutard, also blinded, was taken off balance by the last remaining drummer. He had put his hands up to cover his eyes, and the drummer tackled him and began swinging at him. Cloutard, at least two heads taller than the man, quickly managed to shake him off: he simply lifted him into the air and threw him away.

Cabrera had gained the upper hand with Tom. He was straddling him, one hand crushing Tom's throat and the other punching him in the face. "Not quite the Superman you thought you were, are you?" Cabrera snarled, his eyes manic as his fist pounded Tom's face again. "You not going to squirm your way out of this so easily."

Tom only gurgled and twisted. At least he could finally see again. He grabbed hold of the hand at his throat with one hand and tried to twist it away. With the other he fumbled on the ground beside him, got hold of a rock, and bashed it into the side of Cabrera's head. He pushed the dazed Cabrera off and drew his Wasp knife.

Hellen was pinned down, lying on her back. Hissing and snarling, the priestess pressed Hellen to the ground and spat incoherent words at her. She pulled a long needle from her turban and raised her hand high to stab Hellen. Still half-blinded, Hellen saw the attack coming just in time. She grabbed the woman's arm at the last second and stopped the needle an inch from her throat. She pushed hard against the arm with one hand and fumbled for her gun with the other. It was lying on the ground, but out of reach. The priestess was raging now. She threw all her weight onto the arm holding the needle. Hellen gave up on the pistol and brought her second hand up to block the lethal needle.

"Help me," Hellen croaked, when she saw Shaw edging closer. He looked at her, crouched for the gun, and picked it up.

The half-naked drummer was on his feet again. Cloutard was leaning over, searching for the pistol he had dropped when the flash blinded him. The drummer jumped onto his back.

"*Petite fouine*," Cloutard bellowed, rearing up as the man, hanging onto his back, got him in a headlock.

Cabrera and Tom stood face to face, both crouching low. Cabrera had drawn a switchblade and was tossing it from one hand to the other. He stabbed forward, and Tom dodged back.

"Come on! Let's finish this," Cabrera hissed, slashing wildly. But Tom was too fast.

"I'm all in. You just gotta stand still for one second. I'll make it quick."

Cabrera laughed. "You'd love that, wouldn't you?"

"Everyone makes mistakes. And when you do, you're mine," said Tom.

"What makes you think—"

"Enough!" Graves roared. For a moment, everyone froze. A silence settled.

Tom risked a glance at Graves. He had pulled Leticia, who was still hardly able to stand by herself, in front of him and was pressing his dagger to her throat.

"Drop your weapons or I'll stab this bitch—"

It was the last word he spoke.

A shot cut him off mid-rant. His head jerked sideways, a puff of red mist spurting from his temple. Jaws dropped in disbelief all around. Graves toppled to one side, dragging Leticia down with him. Shaw threw his pistol aside, darted forward, and freed Leticia from her tormentor's grasp. Then he sank with her to the ground and held her tightly in his arms.

Cabrera let out a furious cry, but it stuck in his throat. Literally. Tom saw what happened faster and took his opportunity. He sprang forward and rammed his knife upward through Cabrera's jaw and into his head. For a moment, the two men stood eye to eye.

"I may not be Superman, but I do keep my word," Tom said. Cabrera's face was a mix of incomprehension and surprise. Blood streamed from his mouth. He gurgled. "Now go to hell." Tom pressed a small button on the knife shaft and turned away as the CO_2 cartridge in the knife handle emptied through the channel in the blade. Cabrera's head exploded like a balloon, and his headless body slumped sideways. Tom instantly drew his pistol and took aim at Shaw, who had Leticia in his arms and was wiping the blood from her face.

"Take your filthy hands off her or you'll end up like Cabrera," Tom growled. Shaw quickly raised his hands. "Hellen? Are you all right?"

The priestess had quickly realized that it was over and had retreated.

"I'm fine. I had her right where I wanted her," Hellen said with a dry smile, getting to her feet.

Cloutard had finally managed to shake the little man off. He ran to Tom and pushed his pistol arm down. "Leave him, Tom," Cloutard said earnestly. "Shaw is with me."

67

LETICIA'S HOUSE, PORTMORE, JAMAICA

The next day started late. The previous night had left its traces on all of them. Tom and Hellen had spent the night in Leticia's guest room, Cloutard had slept on the couch in her living room, and Shaw had spent the night with Leticia. They had a lot to talk through.

Of all of them, Tom was hurt the worst, but he was also the first one back on his feet. A lot of what he'd suffered was because he'd been neglecting his fitness regime, plain and simple. But starting today, that was going to change. He wasn't going on any more quests in this condition.

When he stepped into Leticia's kitchen to make the first coffee of the day, he was momentarily startled to find someone already there.

"Ignacio! Good morning. Shouldn't you be taking it easy?"

"Hell, no. It's going to take more than a knock on the head to finish me off, man," Torrente said. And it was true; he was actually looking very good.

"So you're feeling better?"

"Yes. La Mamma took good care of me. She was a bit strict, though . . . she didn't even let me have a taste of that fantastic cognac."

Tom smiled. "There's no messing around with her. I'm scared to death of the old lady. She sleeps with a gun under her pillow, you can bet on it."

Torrente nodded and leaned close to Tom. "I would have preferred my nurse a little younger. Then she could be as strict as she wanted," he whispered. He took a mouthful of coffee and winked at Tom over the rim of his cup. Tom grinned. Torrente set his cup down again, picked up the pot, and poured some for Tom.

"I guess you heard what happened?" Tom asked, and Torrente nodded.

"My daughter told me everything," he said. "And by the way, I wanted to say thank you for rescuing her."

Tom accepted Torrente's thanks with a nod.

Hellen came in, followed a second later by Cloutard. Both looked worn out and rumpled, but also happy.

"*Mes amis*, we have done it again," Cloutard said. Torrente handed him a cup of coffee, and Cloutard poured a shot of cognac into it.

Tom pointed to the hip flask. "I don't like to be nosy, François, but . . . isn't it a bit early for that?"

Cloutard just gave him an uncomprehending look, as if he had no idea what Tom was talking about.

Hellen smiled, kissed Tom on the cheek, and took the cup of coffee Torrente had poured for her. "Explain the whole thing with Shaw," she said to Cloutard.

"Please. I'm dying to hear this one," Tom said. He and Hellen sat at the kitchen counter and looked expectantly at Cloutard.

"*Mes amis*, you know me. I do not even go to the bathroom without a Plan B. I am surprised that you did not think that I might still have an ace up my sleeve. Do you really believe I am crazy enough to go treasure hunting without backup?" He clucked his tongue and shook his head, looking at them reproachfully.

They had to admit that he had a point. In the past, Cloutard had had a small army of allies. His contacts had included smugglers, thieves, graverobbers and plenty of other shady individuals. His "business dealings" had taken him all over the world for years. And like a sailor with a girl in every port, Cloutard had friends wherever he went.

"One point for you, François," said Hellen, dropping four slices of bread into the toaster.

"I have known Shaw since we did a small job together in Marrakesh, quite a long time ago. After that, we completed a couple of, shall we say, joint ventures in the United States. He is a first-rate con artist, able to slip into all kinds of roles. He is exceptionally good at deceiving people—usually those who deserve it."

"So he's not a campaign manager at all?" Hellen asked. The toaster suddenly clacked and popped the four slices back up, making her jump.

"Oh, he is. But he switched from campaign manager to con artist. The two jobs are related, after all," Cloutard said with a grin. "Neither one has much to do with the truth."

Hellen nodded. Tom, meanwhile, had begun searching through Leticia's refrigerator. He took out everything even vaguely breakfast-related. Torrente clattered around in a drawer and came up with a large pan, which he put on the stove.

Tom counted the eggs he'd found in the refrigerator. "Eight eggs," he said. "What are the rest of you eating?"

"You should watch your waistline," said Cloutard, pointing at Tom's midriff. "You used to have a six-pack, but now it is more of a keg."

"I'm working on it," Tom said a little petulantly. He smoothed his hand over his belly, as if to try to reduce it.

"Step aside," Cloutard said, "and let the master go to work."

"So many things you're a master of," said Tom.

"Back to the Shaw story, please," said Hellen.

"Well, Shaw had had a little tryst that ended in a scandal. I knew that he had retreated to the Caribbean afterwards. It was pure luck that he was living in Jamaica and that he was already in contact with Grayson Graves. But sometimes, a little luck is all you need."

He bit proudly into a slice of toast.

"We had no real plan. I mean, nothing worked out in detail. We did not know each other well enough for that, and we did not have time to put a real plan together. But he owed me a favor, and we agreed that he would help if things really turned ugly."

"And that was yesterday."

Four heads turned toward the door. Shaw and Leticia had just come into the kitchen. Leticia looked contented; it seemed she and Shaw had cleared up their differences.

Good-mornings were exchanged, and Leticia gave her father a hug. Tom kissed Hellen on the cheek and used the opportunity to whisper in her ear. "She looks okay, considering what she went through yesterday. Shaw must have worked overtime in the bedroom. She looks pretty relaxed."

Hellen grinned and jabbed Tom playfully in the side. Cloutard, meanwhile, had taken charge of the ingredients from the refrigerator and begun to conjure dishes worthy of a Michelin-starred Paris restaurant.

Leticia looked over his shoulder as he moved adroitly between stovetop and oven. "If you ever find yourself in financial trouble, you can have a job as personal chef to the prime minister whenever you want," she said with a smile.

"Cloutard and financial trouble? There's no such thing," said Shaw, and everyone grinned and nodded. They all took seats at the table and waited eagerly for Cloutard's creations.

"Now that Graves is out of the way, you practically have the election sewn up," said Tom.

Shaw nodded. "Absolutely. We've done it."

Leticia nodded, too. But despite the smile on her face, a darker thought was clouding her mood.

68

LETICIA'S KITCHEN

Hellen noticed right away that not everything was right with Leticia. While the men continued joking loudly in the kitchen, she drew Leticia aside. The two women went out onto the terrace.

"Is everything all right? Yesterday was pretty tough, I know."

Leticia nodded, but she was trying desperately to hold back her tears. "That isn't it. Yes, things could have ended horribly yesterday, but that's not what's bothering me. Mama's been gone a long time, and this is one of the times that I . . . just miss her."

Hellen knew exactly how she felt. Her feelings for her own father were far from simple after all that had happened, and she still missed him sometimes, too. Leticia must have shared a very close bond with her mother. Hellen could imagine how hard it was for her.

Hellen opened her arms and Leticia leaned gratefully into her embrace. For a few minutes, the two women simply stood and hugged. It was a deeply consoling moment for Hellen, but for Leticia it was far more.

"I have to read Mama's last letter. It always gives me strength," she said, wiping the tears from her eyes. After shooting Graves, Shaw had retrieved the message that meant so much to Leticia, and she had held it close and hugged it in her joy. No money in the world, no pirate treasure, however valuable, could have made up for losing it. Now she sat and took it out.

Hellen nodded sympathetically. "Should I leave you alone?" she asked, already getting up.

"No, Hellen. Please stay," Leticia said. She unfolded the sheet of paper and began to read. Hellen sat beside her, knowing that the strength and comfort of her mother's final written lines would help her to recover.

"Mama would have been proud of me," Leticia said. "It's a shame she can't be here to see me win the election and finally do some good for our country."

"She would have been very happy to know that you're finishing what she began," Hellen said, a hand on Leticia's shoulder.

For a few seconds, they simply listened to the wash of the sea. Then their moment of intimacy was interrupted by Cloutard's call: "Breakfast is ready!" Smiling, still a little tired, the two women stood and went back inside to find places at the already crowded table.

As usual, Cloutard had outdone himself. Everyone began to eat, and he was showered with compliments from all sides.

"What about a toast, to celebrate the day?" Cloutard suggested.

"That was bound to come from you, François," said Tom. Torrente was naturally in favor, and Shaw had nothing against a drink, although it was only 11 o'clock.

"I think we should find out whether 'whatever that stuff is' from the Pink House is still drinkable," Cloutard said. He disappeared from the kitchen to fetch one of the bottles they had found in Christopher's basement.

Hellen could see that Leticia was in no mood to celebrate. Too much had happened, too much lay ahead, too much still had to be processed. She was reading through her mother's letter again. Hellen, from the corner of her eye, read a line or two, too. Suddenly, her sidelong gaze stumbled on a word.

"Now we will find out if Anne Bonny's whisky is as good as the rum the pirates loved so much," Cloutard said, about to go to work on the ancient bottle.

"Oh my God!" Hellen cried so suddenly that everyone jumped.

Cloutard was holding the bottle in his hand and was frozen in mid-movement, concerned he had done something wrong. Everyone turned and stared at Hellen, who was pointing nervously at the letter.

"Lisa," Hellen stammered. "Your mother writes that Lisa is the answer."

"Yes, and I never understood that. My mother had a good friend named Lisa, but I never found out what she had to do with it."

"What 'it'?" Tom asked.

"My mother was searching for the treasure," Leticia said, looking sadly at her father. "She was dead set on finding it. Obsessed, even. She sent this letter when she was following a lead in Charleston. But I never worked out why her friend was the answer. Lisa and I talked about it later, but she didn't know what my mother meant, either."

"But after the word is a little asterisk," said Hellen, pointing to a faded spot after "Lisa."

Everybody's eyes were now squinting at the word in question.

"And?" Cloutard asked. He still had the sealed bottle in his hand and was getting impatient.

Hellen had taken the letter from Leticia. She held it up to the light, turning it around, examining it closely. Tom smiled. He knew his wife's instincts.

"In one corner of the letter is a tiny M, in another an A, in the third a W, and in the fourth a little U."

"Mawu-Lisa," Torrente stammered. Leticia was also surprised.

"And who is Mawu-Lisa, if I may ask?" said Cloutard. He had resigned himself to leaving the bottle sealed for now and had put it aside. Shaw and Tom grinned—the Frenchman's patience was being put to the test.

"Mawu-Lisa is the male-and-female god from African Vodun. Vodun is the origin of the voodoo practiced in the New World."

"And here I was, thinking we were done with all that hocus-pocus after yesterday's fireworks," Tom said.

Torrente had turned pale. He shook his head and looked at his daughter in dismay. "Did your mother find Mawu-Lisa?" he asked, so softly it was barely audible.

"Found?" said Hellen.

"How can you find a god?" Tom asked.

"There's a legend on the island that's been told for hundreds of years. People say there's an old voodoo priestess in Haiti who is believed to be Mawu-Lisa."

"*Un moment*," said Cloutard, his interest in the whisky giving way to his interest in the treasure. "How can Leticia's mother say that an old voodoo priestess knows the secret if people have been telling that same voodoo priestess's legend for centuries? She would have to be centuries old."

Torrente gulped. "Because Mawu-Lisa *is* supposed to be still alive. They say that she still lives in a village in Haiti."

"Spell it out for me. I'm completely lost," said Tom. "They've been telling stories about this old woman for hundreds of years, but she's still alive in Haiti?"

Torrente nodded. "Mawu-Lisa is supposed to be more than four hundred years old. In Haiti, she's known as '*la vieille sage*.'"

"The old wise woman," Cloutard murmured, translating.

"So you're telling me there's a four-hundred-year-old woman in Haiti who might know where Anne Bonny's treasure really is?" said Tom.

Torrente nodded cautiously.

"Of course there is. Totally obvious," Tom said, turning in baffled amusement to Hellen. "I don't know how we could have missed that ourselves."

69

CAP-HAÏTIEN, HAITI

"Your mom's better than a taxi," said Tom, swinging his old duffel bag over his shoulder as he climbed down the Gulfstream's steps.

"Do not let La Mamma hear that. She will never help us again," said Cloutard, looking serious. The Frenchman was a bon vivant—he did not take much in life very seriously, and to him there were few problems that could not be solved easily. But when it came to "La Mamma," all joking ceased.

Leticia and Shaw exited the plane next, with Hellen behind them.

"My assistant has organized a rental car for us. But first, a little bureaucracy," said Leticia, leading the way.

"Ah, the energy of youth," said Cloutard. Recent weeks had clearly taken their toll on him.

"You know, François, maybe you shouldn't do any more jobs alone. You're not as young as you used to be," Hellen said with a smile.

Tom sighed and raised his eyebrows. He was also feeling weary, and for the first time, he found himself hoping that their assignment would soon come to an end. He was resolved never again to let himself go like this. His whole body ached. He shook his head in irritation. A year earlier, everything they'd been through would have cost him no more than a tired smile.

Hellen, reading his mind, kissed him on the cheek. "You'll be back in fighting shape soon," she said. "I'm pretty wiped out myself, but look what we've achieved. Not only did we find François, we're helping to bring justice back to a whole country."

Tom nodded. She was right. So far, their jobs had been exciting and spectacular, but that was all. Now, for the first time, they had a chance to make a real difference—to change the future of an entire country for the better.

Tom, Hellen and Cloutard followed Leticia and Shaw, who held hands as they approached a man. Leticia's assistant had clearly smoothed the way for them to enter Haiti, too. Leticia exchanged a few words with the man and turned and pointed at the others. The man nodded studiously and entered something on a list. Their passports were stamped, and the formalities taken care of.

"We should travel with politicians from now on," said Tom. "Everything is so much more straightforward." He patted his duffel bag, which contained his pistol. Entering the country like this meant not having to justify why he even had it.

Another man handed over the keys to an aging Mercedes G 460, and Tom swung in behind the wheel. Cloutard looked around the car's interior unhappily.

"Don't look so miserable, François. This thing's a classic. Listen..."

Tom started the old five-liter V8 engine, and the purr brought a smile even to Shaw's face.

The two women rolled their eyes. "Boys and their toys," they sighed together.

"It isn't far," said Leticia. "Sans-Souci is only forty minutes from here."

Torrente hadn't known exactly where the old woman lived, so Shaw had gotten in touch with some contacts he'd made during his "collaboration" with Graves, people he knew had been present at the mayor's rituals.

After a few calls, they had a little more information. "*La vieille sage*" was said to live close to the ruins of Sans-Souci Palace. They hadn't been able to discover anything more precise than that, but one of Shaw's sources had also suggested contacting Father Sherwin Eubanks, the priest at the Royal Chapel of Milot, which adjoined the ruins. He was rumored to be in touch with the old woman, so they agreed to make the chapel their first destination.

"Let's hope we get there without running into any problems," said Leticia.

"It's only forty minutes away. Or are we talking about something besides the time?" Tom asked, as they left the airport behind and turned onto Route Nationale #3, which led straight through the city of Cap-Haïtien and out to the chapel and the ruins of Sans-Souci.

"The island is not a safe place," Leticia replied, nodding. "Haiti is one of the most politically unstable countries in the world. Poverty levels are high, crime even higher. Governments don't last long."

"And if they do, then there's a guy like Graves on top," Tom added.

"Correct. Which means we may have to deal with roadblocks and armed separatists, even on a short journey like this."

The drive through the city passed without incident. The visible poverty all around weighed heavily on them. For tourists, the Caribbean seemed like heaven on Earth, but for the local population it was hell. Here, perhaps more than anywhere else on the planet, wealth and luxury existed side by side with bitter poverty and hopelessness.

Leticia interpreted their silence correctly. "Now, perhaps, you understand why I want to change things. Jamaica is not as badly off as Haiti, but under Graves it was heading in that direction. In fact, the entire Caribbean is in a terrible state. The treasure would give a valuable boost to the whole region."

Everyone nodded, but they said nothing. They felt a little relieved to see that they were gradually leaving the city behind. Farther out, the hardship of the locals was not so oppressively visible, though it was still there.

"So in the middle of the Caribbean, someone decided to build a palace modeled on Frederick the Great's summer palace, Sanssouci? How does something like that even happen?" Tom asked.

"Very good, *mon ami*. You found some time to read a little history. I would not have thought the name 'Frederick' meant anything to you . . . except *maybe* Frederick Forsyth," said Cloutard. He had removed his Panama hat and was wiping the sweat from his brow. He wasn't looking good at all. His face was still marked by the beatings he'd taken, he had lost several pounds, and, despite the Caribbean sunshine, he looked pale. Also, since they had landed, he hadn't drunk from his hip flask even once. Not a good sign.

"Absolutely untrue," Tom said. "It was a Frederick who started that Habsburg motto, AEIOU, the one that helped us when we were searching for the Chronicle of the Round Table."

Cloutard and Hellen nodded appreciatively.

"Chronicle of the Round Table? King Arthur's round table?" Leticia asked, and Hellen briefly recapped their adventures so far. "Wow. You really are the right people to find a pirate treasure," Leticia finally said.

"I'm impressed, old friend," said Shaw, and he boxed Cloutard playfully in the side. Cloutard let out a groan. "Oh, sorry. I forgot how hard Cabrera worked you over."

"Not only Cabrera. You did some damage as well."

"Sorry. It had to look real," Shaw said.

"Come on, Hellen," Tom said, steering them back to the question. "Tell us about this Sans-Souci palace here in the middle of Haiti."

70

HAITI, FARTHER INLAND

"Henri Christophe, a former slave, was king of North Haiti from 1811 to 1820, and took the title Henry I. He was one of the leaders of the revolution against the French and—"

Hellen was rudely interrupted by the sound of an explosion, and the car shook violently. Chunks of rubber flew through the air—the right front tire had disintegrated. Just a few minutes before, entering a more sparsely populated region, Tom had begun to push the vintage four-wheel-drive vehicle a little harder. Now he had his hands full just trying to keep it on the road. The car swerved hard to the right, leaving the asphalt and scraping past a patch of bushes before bumping to a stop in a ditch, jolting the occupants against their seatbelts. Tom had barely managed to stop them from rolling over, but they got away with no more than a scare. No one was hurt. Cloutard, who had been trying to take a nap in the back seat, was shaken awake. He looked around in confusion. "*Merde*, what happened?" he asked Shaw.

Tom and Hellen had already climbed out to inspect the damage.

"That's about as flat as a tire gets," said Tom. He went around to the back to get the spare, which was attached to the back door. "Let's hope there's a jack and a lug wrench."

"But how are we supposed to get the car out of the ditch?" said Hellen, pointing at the front of the car, which was stuck at an angle in the mud.

"Getting it back on the road won't be hard. There are five of us."

Tom began searching through the trunk for tools.

"There are more than five of us. Many more," said Cloutard, and he tapped Tom on the shoulder. Tom turned around slowly.

"I think we're about to get to know the locals much better than we were hoping to," Shaw added drily. "I guess these are the separatists Leticia mentioned."

Moments later, they were surrounded by a horde of men, all armed to the teeth and not looking at them in a particularly friendly way.

"This calls for a strategist," said Cloutard. He put on his hat and approached a man he believed must be the leader. He was the only one who did not look completely down and out. His trousers were as muddy as the others', but they weren't worn to rags. He was also the only one wearing a button-up shirt, though it had certainly seen better days. And the automatic rifle hanging from his shoulder and resting in the crook of his arm looked fairly modern: an AK-107, a successor to the classic Kalashnikov AK-47. The other men were also armed, although Tom couldn't see what they were packing from where he stood.

Cloutard raised his hat and unleashed a cascade of French at the separatist leader, whose expression did not change.

Tom and Hellen were leaning against the Mercedes, watching Cloutard's show. Tom sensed that Hellen had changed considerably in the last few days. She had always been courageous—if she hadn't been brave, she would never have made it through their past exploits. But now she had begun to show a kind of guts that impressed him greatly. Normally, in sticky situations like this, he had always had to play things cool, to stop her from worrying. But this time that wasn't necessary. Her eyes were on Cloutard and the men around them, and she wore a faint smile.

"I'm curious to see how Cloutard will get us out of this," she said softly enough for only Tom, Leticia, and Shaw to hear.

"In a fix like this, Cloutard is a maestro. No one can talk their way out of a difficult situation like he can," Shaw said. "There was this one time, I think it was in Casablanca. A game of poker." He paused when he saw the looks on the others' faces. He raised his hands apologetically. "Okay, perhaps not the right moment for anecdotes."

The others nodded in agreement.

Something had shifted in the negotiations. Cloutard waved in Leticia's direction. "*Madame, vite, vite.* The ivory rod and the medallions, *s'il vous plait.*"

Leticia frowned uncertainly first at Shaw, then Tom, and finally at Hellen. Shaw laid his arm around her shoulders. "You can trust François. He's got this," he soothed. "He knows what he's doing."

Shaw urged Leticia toward the group. She stepped hesitantly toward Cloutard, removed the rod from her bag, and held it up for the leader to see. All the blood seemed to drain from the man's face. The others around them began to mutter and look around nervously. Cloutard, meanwhile, had taken the medallions from Hellen's bag and now showed them to the leader as well.

When Tom picked out the words "*la vieille sage*" amidst all the others he didn't understand, everything changed. The men suddenly laid down their guns. Even the leader's unflappable expression was gone. He looked around.

Cloutard knew that he was in control. He put the artifacts away in his satchel, pointed at the spare wheel that Tom had already removed and leaned against the car. At first, the men hesitated, but with a nod from their leader they set about hauling the car out of the ditch and changing the tire.

"Like a NASCAR pit stop," said Tom, standing to one side and watching, glad he didn't have to get his own hands dirty for a change.

"This is Renaud," said Cloutard, who had exchanged a few more words with the leader while his men dealt with the flat. "He has promised to take us to the priestess."

They were mobile again minutes later. Ahead of them drove an old flatbed truck with Renaud's men sitting on the back. After a ten-minute drive, the Royal Chapel of Milot appeared out of the haze in front of them. Or rather, what was left of it. A stone's throw beyond it, high on a rise, they saw the ruins of the palace of Sans-Souci.

71

ROYAL CHAPEL OF MILOT, HAITI

THE SMALL CONVOY PULLED UP IN FRONT OF THE CHAPEL, AND the team stared in amazement. The structure was completely burnt out, and the once-magnificent dome was gone. Only the circular walls and the classical, columned entrance—not unlike the entrance to the Acropolis—still called to mind its former magnificence. There were definite similarities to the Pantheon in Rome.

"What use is a burnt-out chapel?" Cloutard asked.

Leticia and Shaw also looked as if they had a thousand questions. Renaud had climbed from the cab of the flatbed truck and was waving Cloutard over. The two men talked, gesticulating excitedly. Tom pointed to the ruins they could see beyond the remains of the chapel.

"Is that Sans-Souci?" he asked.

Hellen nodded. "The name actually has two sources. It was named after Frederick the Great's Sanssouci palace, of course, but also in memory of Jean-Baptiste Sans-Souci, a rebel leader—who, absurdly enough, was executed by Henry I, who built the palace."

"You mean he named his own palace after someone he'd killed?" Tom asked, shaking his head.

"Yes, but that's not the only interesting thing. It was incredibly luxurious; Henri Christophe even had a pipe system installed under the floor to provide in-floor heating."

"I haven't been around as much as you, of course," said Leticia, "but I've also heard that the palace did a lot more with water. Henri is supposed to have installed fountains, artificial cataracts, even an underground swimming pool, and was said to have received guests from all over the world there."

"So, basically, it was the world's first wellness hotel," said Tom.

"History lesson is over," Cloutard interrupted them, returning from his talks with Renaud. "I have to go to confession."

"Uh . . ." Tom looked uncertainly at Cloutard. "François, in case you hadn't noticed, the church is a charred ruin. Are you sure you understood the man correctly?"

"*Mon ami*, please, a little more faith in your old friend is warranted. Renaud says we should meet the old chapel priest, and he will lead us to *la vieille sage*."

Cloutard gave no more details but turned and went with Renaud into the circular remains of the chapel. Tom, Hellen, Leticia and Shaw followed him, all a little lost for words. Renaud's men waited at the vehicles. *This is a perfect trap*, Tom thought, but he did not share the thought with the others.

Not much was left of the once-magnificent building. "No one knows what caused the fire," said Renaud, now standing in the middle of the blackened ruin and looking sad.

Around them lay charred pews and the rubble of the old dome. Tom decided that a trap was unlikely. Renaud's men could have finished them off easily enough earlier, when they broke down.

"Well?" Cloutard looked encouragingly at Renaud. "*Que faire maintenant?*"

"There is a secret underground crypt beneath the chapel," Renaud explained. "The confessionals used to be down there. There was no room for them in the hall."

Tom looked at Hellen. "A crypt. I hope it's less spectacular down there than in the Sagrada Familia."

Renaud pushed aside pieces of a church pew and lifted the scorched remnants of a carpet, revealing a trapdoor underneath, then lifted the trapdoor and climbed down the stairs without another word. The others followed. Torches hung in brackets on the walls. Renaud took a lighter from his jacket pocket and lit the first torch. Then he took it out of its holder and led the way, lighting the rest of the torches that lined the passageway as he went.

"I thought we were meeting the priest down here," Tom said.

"After the fire, Père Badessy decided to use the vaults that connect the chapel to the palace of Sans-Souci for our purposes."

Hellen started at the mention of the priest's name. "Badessy is the name of a voodoo spirit," she whispered to Tom.

"And I'm not sure I like the sound of 'use the vaults for our purposes,'" Tom whispered back.

Leticia pressed close to Shaw, who was trying hard to act cool, but in reality was anything but. He was clearly out of his depth.

After about a hundred yards, the passage broadened into a large hall. Small pools had been built into the floor, and there were gargoyles around the sides. It looked like an ancient bathhouse.

Hellen frowned, her forehead creasing. Cloutard guessed what she was thinking.

"Someone has tried to combine every possible Greek and Roman architectural style. Unfortunately, it was someone who had no clue at all," he said, pointing to the columns, the gargoyles, and the remains of the mosaics on the walls.

Hellen shook her head and smiled. "Yes. It's a real jumble. Henry Christophe revered Roman culture, but his architects seem to have gone a little crazy down here."

"You go that way," said Renaud, and he pointed toward a colonnade visible at the far end of the room. "This is as far as I can go."

"I've got a very bad feeling about this. But then, that's why we're here, right?" said Tom. He lifted a torch from the wall and strode off toward the colonnade. Hellen and Cloutard followed, with Shaw and Leticia hesitantly bringing up the rear, all of them looking around nervously as they went.

The colonnade disappeared into the darkness somewhere ahead. To their left and right, about fifteen feet apart, stood beautifully preserved Doric-style columns. Tom kept moving, turning in circles as he went, taking in every detail.

Hellen studied the columns and the mosaics covering the walls between them. She recognized scenes from Roman history and Greek mythology, Christian imagery, and portrayals of fabulous creatures she could not immediately place. As so often before, she regretted not having time to examine all of it more closely.

The column-lined passage led them deeper and deeper into the hillside—Tom guessed they must be deep below the palace by now.

Cloutard dropped back. The anxious faces of Leticia and Shaw had stirred his sympathy, and he decided to join them at the rear.

Tom raised a closed fist, signaling them to stop. They saw a glow at the end of the colonnade and heard the low murmur of voices.

"We're here," said Tom.

"Wherever 'here' might be," Cloutard said from the back.

They moved on cautiously, and the light grew brighter. After another hundred feet, they found themselves in an impressive, vaulted hall, about the size of a football field. They saw men and women sitting on benches, apparently waiting for something. The room was lit by candles and torches. In the center was a circular fireplace thirty feet across, in which strange blue and green flames blazed.

In the front section of the immense vault sat a figure on a plain wooden throne. A skull topped the back of the throne, and the figure itself was shrouded in a plain robe and cowl.

"Père Badessy," Leticia whispered, pointing at the figure, as it rose to its feet and stretched an arm in their direction.

72

BENEATH SANS-SOUCI PALACE, HAITI

The figure moved slowly toward Tom and his companions, but its movements were strange. It did not look as if it were placing one foot in front of the other, but rather as if it were drifting toward them just above the ground.

Tom narrowed his eyes, but there was not enough light to see clearly.

"Is he floating?" Cloutard whispered, drawing a sharp breath.

"It certainly looks like it," said Hellen, also watching the figure intently.

"Remind me not to make any more deals with you," said Shaw. "This is all too weird for me." He and Leticia held on to one another—it was hard to say which of them was gripping the other more tightly.

The men and women on the benches had fallen silent. They sat wide-eyed and watched the cowled figure move. Their faces were filled with a mixture of horror and astonishment, as if they hadn't known the figure could move at all.

A few yards in front of the group, it slowed and took up a position in front of them. These movements, too, were odd; they didn't look like a normal process of slowing down and stopping.

"How is he doing that?" asked Tom, fascinated. "It's like Michael Jackson's moonwalk, but in the right direction."

"No kidding," Shaw said. "I feel like I'm in the 'Thriller' video."

"By the way," Hellen said, "It's not 'how is *he* doing that?'" The figure had pushed back its cowl with bony fingers. "You should be asking 'how is *she* doing that?'"

The flames in the room illuminated the face of a woman. At first glance, she did not look old at all. But when one looked closer, her face changed to the face of an ancient woman, only to shift a moment later and become as young and fresh as a teenager. Seconds later, it became old again.

All five stared at the woman, none of them able to properly process what they were seeing.

"We have found '*la vieille sage*,'" Leticia whispered.

"No," came the surprising answer. The voice was as strange as the figure's appearance. Old and venerable, and at the same time young and almost exuberant. She sounded hoarse and crystal clear, both at once. "You did not find me. I found you. The prophecy is true. The savior of the islands has come," she said, looking directly at Leticia. Then she raised her bony hand and pointed at Cloutard's satchel.

"You want to show me something." It did not sound like a question but was more like a statement, perhaps even an order.

Without hesitation, Cloutard took out the ivory rod and the medallions. A smile spread across the face of the ageless woman. She reached out her hands, suddenly no longer old, but young and vital. She touched the ivory rod. Cloutard watched creases, liver spots, and knotted joints form on her hands in a fraction of a second, only to vanish again a heartbeat later.

"I haven't seen you for a very long time," said the woman, gazing at the ivory rod. "The last time was when I said goodbye to Anne."

At the word "Anne," everyone instinctively gasped.

The women noticed their reaction. "Oh, yes. I knew her," she said, as if it were obvious. "She was a wonderful woman, a strong woman."

Hellen was the first to find her voice. She screwed up her courage and said, "You knew Anne Bonny personally?" knowing how crazy the question sounded.

The woman nodded. "She had a radiance about her. She was very special. She had no interest in wealth, fame, power, or gold. Inside her burned the flame of goodness. She wanted only to help people. The slaves, especially. They were brought here by the hundreds of thousands."

Tom tilted his head. "You KNEW Anne Bonny?"

A cheerful smile appeared on the woman's face. "I know everybody," she said, and this statement, too, sounded unquestionably true. "You seek her treasure," she went on, and her smile and radiance faded instantly.

"Yes. But only to help the islanders," Leticia said quickly. She had stayed in the background, stepping forward only now.

The eyes of the two women met.

"I know. You can use it for good. The time is certainly ripe. Anne wanted to take the treasure away from here. Back then, it was better to take it far away. All anybody wanted was gold. They were only interested in enriching themselves and living the high life. So Anne decided to take the treasure somewhere safe."

Tom, Hellen and Cloutard raised their eyebrows as one. But before any of them could say a word, the woman continued. "No, not to Charleston. Of course not."

Can she read minds? all three immediately wondered.

"Anne took the treasure back home. She wanted to give it to Mawu-Lisa."

Cogs were turning in Hellen's mind. "But what did Anne Bonny have to do with Mawu-Lisa?"

"Mawu is the chief goddess of voodoo, the creator, in case you forgot," Cloutard explained, baiting Tom. "Lisa was her husband."

"I'm not stupid. I remember these things," Tom hissed back.

"Anne was a believer," said the woman. "She came to know our faith through the many slaves she helped gain their freedom."

Hellen nodded.

"Yes. The Republic of Pirates also freed slaves," Cloutard whispered.

"For Anne, freedom was the greatest good. No one should have to live in captivity. She found her fulfillment in our faith, and here,"—the woman swept her arms wide—"right here, she celebrated many rituals. It was also here that she made up her mind to take the treasure to Ile-Ife."

Cloutard leaned over to say something to Tom.

"I know, the holy city of the Yoruba in Nigeria," Tom headed him off. "You think I'm some kind of chowderhead, don't you?"

"No, *mon ami*. I just like winding you up."

The woman smiled when she overheard the exchange between the two men. Then she looked at Hellen. "You three are doing the right thing," she said.

"So . . . you're saying that the treasure of Anne Bonny is in West Africa?" Leticia said, her spirits falling.

The old woman nodded. "Anne had to deal with many who envied her. There were traitors among those closest to her, as there are everywhere." She sighed. "But with a small deception, she managed to get the treasure into the holy city."

Silence. The treasure was now farther away than ever.

"The prophecy says that the time will come to return the treasure and use it to do good." Almost imperceptibly, *la vieille sage* had begun to move again. "You are the prophecy. Do what you must."

With that, she lifted her cowl back over her head, then turned away and floated back to her throne.

"That's becoming our motto," said Tom. "Off to . . . uh . . ."

". . . Ile-Ife," grinned Cloutard.

73

AIRBUS ACJ320NEO, VAN RENSBURG'S
PRIVATE JET, SOMEWHERE OVER THE
ATLANTIC OCEAN

"No disrespect to La Mamma, François, but van Rensburg's plane is in a completely different league," Tom said, leaning back comfortably and stroking the pure white leather of the velvet-soft armrests.

Cloutard was standing behind the well-stocked cocktail bar, busily checking the stock of wines.

"*Je suis impressionné!*" he said. He picked up one of the bottles. "Château Lafite Rothschild from 1951."

Without a second thought, Cloutard removed the cork, took a red wine glass and poured the dark red liquid into it. He sniffed it, sipped, held the wine in his mouth for a few seconds, and finally allowed it to flow slowly down his throat.

"*Magnifique*. Born in 1951 and better than ever. That is what I like about wine. Women from the same year cannot compete," he said, with a wink at Hellen.

Hellen rolled her eyes but could not resist a smile.

"Before you start guzzling thousands of dollars' worth of wine," Tom said, "did anyone else think van Rensburg sounded a bit strange on the phone?"

Meanwhile, Cloutard had taken out more glasses, filled them, and arranged them on a silver tray. He expertly picked up the tray and distributed the glasses, starting with Leticia and Hellen, then handing one to Shaw and finally to Tom. Cloutard raised his glass and looked around at the others. "Life is too short to drink bad wine," he said.

"Hear, hear," said Shaw, and everyone raised their glasses. And though no one else was the sommelier Cloutard was, they all enjoyed the moment and the expensive wine. They had been through a lot in their short time together, a lot of highs and lows, and West Africa was still waiting for them.

Hellen set down her glass. "You're right, Tom. Van Rensburg definitely seemed reserved, abrupt even."

"Well, perhaps we have been stretching his patience a little thin," said Cloutard. "To start with, I spend months researching while you two put your feet up. Then we create a scandal by exposing the respected mayor of Kingston and future prime minister of Jamaica as a gangster and con man, and now we need van Rensburg's brand-new private jet. He has not even flown in it himself yet. Maybe he is simply getting annoyed with the whole affair?"

Tom looked around at the mahogany-paneled interior and snorted. "His stress level can't be too high if he can afford something like this and hasn't taken it for a ride since he bought it."

Cloutard savored another mouthful of the wine. "Actually, he does not need this thing at all. It is his second plane. He just wanted to snap it up before a sheik got it. Apparently, the sheik had ordered this exact configuration from Airbus. Some old feud."

"If you're racing people to buy private jets, then you really don't have much to worry about in life," said Leticia, and she laid her head contentedly on Shaw's shoulder. She seemed to have moved on, at least a little. She had the election sewn up and a man at her side that she loved. Finding the treasure would be the icing on the cake. With that, she could really change her homeland for the better and fulfill her mother's life dream.

"So what do we do when we reach Nigeria?" Shaw asked. "From what I hear from François, you've got a pretty good record for finding ancient artifacts and treasures."

Hellen sighed loudly. "The trail is very, very thin. I think we need to start directly in Ile-Ife, the holy city of the Yoruba. They're a West African ethnic group, and their mythology runs very deep. Their religion is so widespread that many people call it a world religion in its own right. Many other belief systems stem from it, including modern voodoo."

The group nodded with interest. Hellen was on her feet, walking through the cabin with her wine glass in her hand. She was the scientist again, fully in her element. "Ile-Ife, for the Yoruba, is the origin of the world," she went on. "There are deep-rooted myths and legends, but most of them aren't especially relevant right now. My gut, however, is telling me we should start with the king."

"The king?" said Tom.

"The Oòni, as he is known. He is the spiritual leader of all the kings in Yoruba territory," Hellen explained.

"President and pope, rolled into one," said Tom.

Hellen nodded. "Not undisputed, however—there's the eternal question of bloodline. European nobles have the same problems. He's said to be a fanatical collector of artifacts and cult objects that support his claim to the throne."

"So we simply walk up to this king's front door and knock?" Leticia asked, looking around doubtfully.

With a quick glance at each other, Tom, Hellen and Cloutard smiled. "Yes," said Cloutard. "That is our usual procedure."

"When Tom starts knocking, the strangest things happen," said Hellen, touch Tom's shoulder lightly. He was still sitting comfortably in his armchair.

"If this Oòni has something to hide, we will find out," said Cloutard, emptying his glass.

"So, back to the guy that you're working for . . . how are you planning to tell him that he's not getting the treasure?" Shaw asked, looking uncertainly at Tom, Hellen and Cloutard. "Your word still stands, doesn't it? That Leticia can use the treasure to improve conditions in Jamaica?"

Hellen nodded immediately. Tom and Cloutard also nodded, but with some hesitation.

The captain's stern voice came over the intercom "Would all passengers please take their seats and fasten their seatbelts. We are beginning our descent into Lagos," he said.

"We don't know van Rensburg well enough to guess how he'll react, you know," Tom whispered in Hellen's ear. "The man sure as hell didn't become a billionaire by being Mr. Humanitarian. We may have some persuading to do."

"One thing at a time," said Hellen, pressing a kiss to his cheek. "Let's find Anne's treasure first before we start fighting over who gets it."

Tom nodded and leaned back. Somehow, they had switched roles a little. In the past, it had always been Hellen voicing misgivings. Tom shook his head a little grumpily. He didn't like being the "sensible" one in the team at all.

74

VAN RENSBURG'S VILLA, GRAND CAYMAN

The sun had just risen and Eon van Rensburg was already sitting on the terrace at his villa. Whenever something was troubling him, he rose early and enjoyed the sunrise. It was one of his better habits, and in those quiet moments, he never failed to find the solution to his problem. He always made his best business decisions at sunrise. Van Rensburg smiled as he thought back on how it had all begun—wealth hadn't just fallen into his lap. He had had to get his hands dirty often enough and there had even been moments of ruthlessness, although too often for his taste. Not until Kiara entered his life had he found peace. She grounded him and helped him focus on what truly mattered in life. It was she who had awakened in him the spirit of patronage for which they were now famous around the globe.

But this morning the solution would not come. He simply did not know how he was supposed to respond to Baron von Hohenfeldt's demand.

A sound behind him made him turn around. "Awake already? I can't remember the last time you were up so early, darling," Eon said.

His wife stood before him, as naked as God made her—and he had really tried his best the night before. And although he had seen his wife naked countless times, it was a magic moment. One of the many he had already experienced with Kiara. His eyes roamed her body. Not even Michelangelo could have crafted her more perfectly. The orange glow of the early sun falling on her skin from the horizon almost drove Eon out of his mind. In other circumstances, they would already be all over one another, would be making uninhibited love and giving free rein to all their fetishes, the private inclinations that could never be made public. Not that there weren't plenty of ultra-rich and powerful people who dabbled in far worse, truly abhorrent practices. But some things simply had to be kept private. No money in the world could repair the damage their image would suffer.

But they both knew this was not the right moment to indulge their sensual proclivities.

"You're thinking about what Baron von Hohenfeldt told us."

Eon nodded. "We have to tell the team the truth."

Kiara said nothing. She was thinking.

"Or do you disagree?" Eon asked, looking at her in surprise.

"No, we must, of course. We have to be fair to them. But we could not really blame them if they then decided to break off the mission."

Eon sighed. He had stood up and had his arms around his wife. She snuggled against him. Despite their erotic attraction, despite all the sexual escapades and the deeply intimate moments they had shared in their life together, they had seldom been as close as they were just then.

This is what love feels like, Eon thought, and even as the thought occurred to him, he felt his wife nod her head slightly, as if she could read his thoughts.

They stood like that for several minutes. Neither moved, and neither would have minded if the moment were to last forever. But they knew it was not to be. They broke their close embrace, kissed fervently, and smiled at one another.

"We have to take the risk. If they cut the assignment short, so be it. They would never forgive us if we weren't open with them. And at the end of the day, that kind of dishonesty is simply not us," Kiara said.

"We have so many plans," said Eon. "There is still so much for the team to do. We spent so long searching for people who support our vision and who can help us uncover the greatest secrets of humankind. It would hurt me greatly to lose Tom, Hellen and Cloutard now."

"You know, since we left behind all the questionable business practices, you and I have slept much better. And it hasn't made us any less successful," Kiara added.

Eon nodded. "Maybe I should send Tom a message and tell him what the search is really all about." He looked around for his phone.

"Of course. But I'm sure it can wait a few more minutes," said Kiara, deciding the right moment had come after all. Her hand parted the silk dressing gown Eon was wearing. His body reacted instantly. He closed his eyes and luxuriated in his wife's skillful touch—her hands could make him forget the world around him in a split second.

He sighed and agreed. "Yes, a few more minutes," he answered, but at the same time he decided to put off messaging Tom for now. He would try to call him in a few days and explain things. But that was as far as he got. Kiara quickly turned his mind to other matters, and they gave themselves over to their lust.

Meanwhile, on another cellphone, the "record" button was pressed. Wikus de Waal, van Rensburg's right-hand man, had been starting to worry that they wouldn't get down to business again at all.

75

ROYAL PALACE, ILE-IFE, NIGERIA

"Frankly, I'm a little disappointed," said Cloutard, looking up at the building.

"François, we're in Nigeria. What did you expect? Versailles? Schönbrunn Palace? Neuschwanstein?" said Hellen, climbing out of the car herself to take a look at the palace.

After landing in Lagos, Nigeria's biggest city, they had rented yet another a car. This time, they chose a Ford E350 wagon. They were five people traveling together and needed something with a little more legroom. Besides, the choices were limited. They turned down the offer of a driver, which was included in the price—but the price remained the same. It meant a little more strain on van Rensburg's credit card, but they did not want anyone they didn't know behind the wheel. Too many unforeseen things had happened so far, and the last thing they needed was another element of uncertainty.

"Check the air conditioning first," Cloutard said. He had spent the short walk to the E350 dabbing the sweat from his forehead with a cloth handkerchief. "I know every car rental office from Cairo to Cape Town. It is all but impossible in these countries to find a car with a working air conditioner." Ninety-five degrees Fahrenheit and ninety-two percent humidity were taking their toll.

To everyone's surprise and great relief, the air conditioning worked perfectly. The vehicle was otherwise in very good shape, too—certainly compared to the other cars roving the streets in this city of fourteen million inhabitants.

The drive from Lagos to Ile-Ife had taken around four hours and had passed without incident, which surprised Tom in particular. After the clash on the island, he felt he was slowly but surely getting back to his old form. He was feeling fit again, at least mentally. His instincts were back, his reaction time was back to a functional level, and his sense of danger and awareness of potential surprises had been sharpened. Now he only had to work on his body. He had to regain his earlier strength and stamina as quickly as he could. He was certain that, once they had recovered the treasure, their adventures would continue. He had to be ready.

"I knew we were not expecting Buckingham Palace, but this really is a bit of a letdown," Cloutard went on.

All five were now outside the car, standing on the sandy street and looking up at a white-painted building that looked more like a central European town hall than a royal palace.

"François is right," said Tom with a little disdain. "Vienna's City Hall is at least twice as big."

"True," said Shaw. "But as you know, it's not surrounded by a high cast-iron fence. And there's no army guarding it." He nodded toward the heavily armed soldiers on duty at the gated entrance and patrolling the palace grounds.

"Sure," Tom agreed. "But the statues up there do remind me a little of the good old *Rathausmann*." He pointed to the golden statues standing on the square columns to the left and right of the iron gate. He was right. They really did look similar to the statue standing atop the highest of the five towers crowning Vienna's City Hall.

"When you two are done playing tourist, can we move on to the treasure?" Hellen groused, growing impatient.

"*Mon dieu*," said Cloutard, and he patted Tom sympathetically on the shoulder. "She really does wear the pants, doesn't she?"

"*Ferme la bouche*," said Tom, grinning.

"Ah, I see you have learned at least the most important words. It took you long enough," Cloutard countered.

Hellen looked at Leticia and shook her head. "Yes, it's like this all the time. I'm used to it now. Come on. Let's get started while the Lords of Creation here are busy one-upping each other."

The two women approached one of the sentries. Hellen took out her old UNESCO ID and held it up while she spoke to the man, who listened to Hellen's request expressionlessly. Finally, though, he shook his head and went back to staring into space. It seemed to be too much effort to reply verbally. Leticia and Hellen tried to persuade the man, but his reaction did not change.

Meanwhile, Cloutard, Tom and Shaw had approached the second soldier, posted on the other side of the gate. His reaction was similar: a small shake of his head, no more.

"Admittedly, the guards at Buckingham Palace are generally not allowed to speak, either," said Cloutard.

They worked on the guards for a quarter of an hour but got nowhere. The sentries said nothing, and the gates stayed closed.

Then Tom noticed a radio message coming through on the headset of one of the guardsmen. There was movement, and through the fence, Tom saw servants taking positions near the palace entrance. More security appeared. The number of soldiers suddenly doubled. A small group of sentries marched toward the gates, which slowly swung open.

"The king's coming," said Tom. "The line-up's a bit like in Downton Abbey, when the lord and lady show up."

Cloutard looked at him in astonishment. "*You* have seen Downton Abbey? But there are no explosions. No body parts or car chases. The characters just talk to each other."

Tom glanced toward Hellen. Cloutard understood right away and let out a laugh. "Ha! She not only wears the trousers, but you are wearing slippers and have lost the remote control."

They were interrupted by the soldiers at the gate bundling them aside. At the end of the street, a large, black Mercedes appeared. The soldiers saluted. The Mercedes drove in through the gate and they watched as the king got out, nodded to his staff, and disappeared into the palace.

What no one noticed, however, was the soldier staring in dismay at Leticia.

76

IN FRONT OF THE ROYAL PALACE, ILE-IFE, NIGERIA

AFTER GETTING NOWHERE WITH THE SENTRIES, THEY CALLED A meeting. The sun was already low in the sky. "We're not going to get any further here, not now," said Tom. "We should find a hotel and sleep on things for a night."

There were nods of agreement all around. "Looking at this area and the houses, I do not want to take any risks with a hotel," Cloutard said.

"There's a Hilton here," said Hellen. She had taken out her phone and was checking Google Maps for nearby hotels. "We won't have any unpleasant surprises there. And it's not far at all."

"The Hilton it is," said Cloutard.

They returned to the car and set off. The mood was subdued. Getting into the palace and gaining an audience with the king seemed hopeless, and they had no other real leads. Where things were supposed to go from here was anybody's guess. Hellen tried to lighten the mood a little and cheer the others up.

"Once we've got our rooms, let's all meet in the hotel bar. I've was thinking about where we can continue our search on the drive here, if the palace really turns out to be a dead end," she said, trying to radiate optimism. The result was not overwhelming, however, not least because she wasn't really convinced of it herself. Cloutard brightened a little at the sound of "hotel bar," but Leticia just gazed absently out the window, while Shaw held her hand, not really knowing what to say.

"François, I don't want to bring you down, but this Hilton isn't going to win Hotel of the Year," said Tom. They had just turned a corner and the hotel came into view. "It looks like a pile of shoe boxes. If this is the best hotel in the city, I don't want to see the others." He stopped the car in front of the entrance.

"Maybe it's not such a great choice. I've just read a few horror stories about kidnappings that are supposed to have happened here," Hellen said. She had been checking reviews of the hotel on the short drive. Cloutard made a face, but said nothing.

The formalities were quickly dealt with. They took three rooms: one for Tom and Hellen, one for Leticia and Shaw, and a single room for Cloutard. Tom made sure they got adjoining rooms with connecting doors.

"You do not think you are being a touch *too* careful, *mon ami*?" Cloutard asked. "No one would have followed us all the way here because of the treasure, *n'est-ce pas*?"

"Better safe than sorry," Tom replied. Then, to them all, he said, "Hotel bar in an hour? Long enough to freshen up?"

Everyone nodded and went into their rooms.

"So do you really have a plan for where to go from here?" Tom asked as soon as they were alone.

"Not really, but I wanted to give Leticia a little hope. We can't leave here empty-handed."

Tom nodded.

"I'm going to take a shower," said Hellen, and she went into the bathroom. A moment later, Tom followed.

"This will save time," he said with a grin, joining her in the shower.

"I'm not so sure about that. It might take quite a lot longer," Hellen whispered, and she kissed him.

Cloutard, Leticia and Shaw were already in the bar when Tom and Hellen appeared on the stairs.

"Sorry we're late," Hellen said, joining them at their table.

Tom smiled at her and took the seat beside her. He looked around. Apart from them, there were only four men sitting at a table in the corner.

"We'd like to go through our options. We need to figure out where we go from here," Hellen said, when they each had a drink in front of them—in Cloutard's case, his third.

"Our first priority is still the palace," Tom began. "Just walking in obviously didn't work, and an official request, even if it were approved, would take too long." He turned to Cloutard. "What are our chances of finding another way in? Without getting shot, of course."

The Frenchman frowned and tilted his head thoughtfully. "I would need to make some preparations. I will have to get the floor plans and contact a few people. It would be good to know the security arrangements."

"So it's possible?"

"I think so, yes. Everything is possible. It is not Fort Knox or the Louvre. We can get in, but I will need a few days to come up with a workable plan. Whether we get out again without causing an international incident is another story," he said, and he sipped his drink.

"All right. Get started with that and see how realistic it is," Tom said.

Cloutard nodded. "Bradley can help me." He grinned mischievously. "Two crooks are always better than one."

"Works for me," said Shaw, rubbing his hands in anticipation.

"Garçon!" Cloutard raised his hand to order another drink. He looked around for the bartender. His gaze fell on the men in the corner, who were glancing covertly in their direction. He drummed his fingers impatiently on the table.

"You going to have to dry out for a few minutes," said Tom. "The bartender just went out the back with the receptionist."

"While François and Brad are working on a break-in, we can look at something else," Hellen said. "I did some research on the flight about what the old woman told us. Like I mentioned earlier, voodoo has its roots in the Yoruba religion. Besides the palace, that gives us two more leads."

Leticia looked hopefully at Hellen, her face showing her relief. "Tell me," she said curiously.

"One possibility is the Sacred Grove of the goddess Osun," said Hellen. "It's actually a group of smaller groves, each dedicated to a different Yoruba god. It may be where Anne Bonny took the treasure."

"Another magic forest?" said Cloutard, with an exaggerated shudder. "I am glad I get to break into the palace. You could not pay me enough to go into an enchanted forest after that business with the Fountain of Youth," he added, and he looked around again for the bartender. The four men in the corner had gotten up and left, and his optimism was dwindling. "*Foutu*. The fewer the guests, the longer it takes," he murmured. He had lived long enough in Africa to know the work ethic here. He knew it was a stupid prejudice, but too often it proved true, as he'd discovered while renovating his estate in Tabarka.

"No magic forests, François," Hellen reassured him. "It's a sacred area that is now a UNESCO World Heritage Site—largely, in fact, because of the efforts of an Austrian artist, Susanne Wenger, who lived among the Yoruba for many years. I believe that's our best chance of finding the treasure. Another possibility might be the Ifa oracle, but that's for later. You, Tom, and I will head to Osogbo tomorrow," she said to Leticia. "The Osun Sacred Grove is on the edge of the city, about an hour from here."

"We should see if we can dig up another car," said Tom. "François and Brad will need one, too. I'll find the receptionist. Their little backroom date has gone on long enough."

"While you are at it, send the bartender over," said Cloutard.

Tom stood up, went to the reception desk, and rang the bell several times. "Hello?" he called, ringing again.

He looked around. There was no one in sight, which struck him as very strange. After the four men had left, they had been the only ones left in the hotel bar. The barman and receptionist had disappeared several minutes earlier, leaving the reception area unattended. And they had seen no other hotel staff or any other guests. Suddenly, the hotel felt eerily deserted. From the reception area, Tom looked back into the bar. His eyes met Hellen's, and his eyes told her instantly that something wasn't right.

"I've got a very bad feeling about this," he murmured.

77

HILTON HOTEL BAR, ILE-IFE, NIGERIA

Tom turned around, went to the hotel entrance, and looked out at the parking lot. A rickety old truck with a canvas cover over the back was standing in front of the hotel.

That wasn't there before, Tom thought. It was too late for the hotel to be taking deliveries. He returned to the reception area, jumped the counter, and opened the door to the back office. Empty.

"Now where have our two sweethearts gone?"

Without warning, the lobby went dark. The power seemed to have gone out for the entire hotel. That might have been an everyday occurrence in this part of the world, but to Tom it seemed too big a coincidence that it would happen just then. He looked out the window. Lights were on in the buildings all around. *So it's just the hotel*, he thought. Quickly searching the small office, he found a flashlight in the first-aid cabinet.

"Tom, where are you?" Hellen called, coming into the lobby, using her phone to light her way.

"Over here," Tom said, emerging from the office. "We have a problem." He hopped back over the counter.

"Yes, the power's out—I figured that much out already. Even worse, François still doesn't have a drink."

"No, I think we're about to—"

A sharp cry from the bar made Tom and Hellen freeze. Tom's hand automatically reached for his pistol, as it had so often recently, but found nothing. The gun was lying up in his room. In the wake of their shower rendezvous and their delay in getting to the meeting, he had left it upstairs.

He snapped off the flashlight, moved in front of Hellen, and raised his finger to his lips. Hellen turned off the flashlight on her phone. Cautiously, they crept through the lobby to the archway leading to the bar. Tom spotted two chrome stanchions beside the entrance, with a braided cord connecting them. During the day, they were used to close the bar. He grabbed one of the hip-high stands, removed the red cord, and carefully unscrewed the metal post from its base. As he swung his improvised weapon up, he heard the unmistakable sound of a pistol being cocked behind him. He and Hellen froze.

The post clanged loudly through the lobby when he dropped it. He kept his hands raised. Hellen followed his example.

"Go. In there," ordered one of the two men who appeared from the darkness behind them. They were African, tall and slender, and well-dressed in normal street clothes: good trousers, short-sleeved shirts, and sandals, but with gold Rolex watches on their wrists. One had a pistol, the other a machete, and the looks on their faces were not friendly.

Tom and Hellen did as the man ordered and went back into the bar. In the light cast by two flashlights, they saw Cloutard and Shaw kneeling in the middle of the floor, their hands cable-tied behind their backs. Black fabric sacks had been pulled over their heads.

"Where's Leticia?" Hellen cried, when she realized she wasn't with Cloutard and Shaw.

"They took her away," said Shaw, struggling uselessly to free his hands.

"Kidnapping seems to be a complimentary service here," Cloutard murmured through the stinking material covering his head. Compared to Shaw, he was completely relaxed.

"What do you want from us? Where's the other woman?" Tom growled, as the men forced him and Hellen to their knees. Their hands were fastened behind them with heavy-duty cable ties, and sacks were pulled over their heads, too.

His question went unanswered. A moment later, he felt something prick his neck, and he lost consciousness.

78

SOMEWHERE IN NIGERIA, SEVERAL HOURS LATER

The rattling and bumping woke Tom from his invroluntary nap. His head was pounding: the headache that comes from being put under with a tranquilizer has a character all its own. Where was he? What had happened? He tried to turn, but he could hardly move. He was lying on his side, the plastic cable ties cutting painfully into his wrists. With an effort, he managed to sit upright and lean against a wooden wall. A tarpaulin flapped beside his head. Through the coarse fabric of the sack over his head, he could only vaguely make out his surroundings. It was daytime, the air suffocatingly hot and dusty. Gradually, his memory of the previous night returned. As far as he could tell, he was in the back of a truck, most likely the same one he'd noticed at the hotel just before the power had gone out.

He tried unsuccessfully to shake the cloth sack from his head. Breathing was difficult, and he realized that he was panting. He heard a groan and looked around, as much as he could with the heavy cloth half an inch in front of his eyes. Three bodies were lying in front of him. Reaching out with his feet, he prodded gently at one of them.

"Hellen? Cloutard? Shaw?" Tom said, loud enough to make himself heard over the rumbling, rattling truck. The way they were being shaken around, they had to be driving on an unsealed road, somewhere far from civilization.

"*Oh ma tête. Que s'est-il passé?*" he heard Cloutard grumble painfully. The Frenchman also sat up.

"Hellen!" Tom repeated, louder still. Another groan. Something moved to his right.

"What happened?" Hellen croaked.

"Are you okay?"

"Yes. But dear Lord, my head." She twisted around and also managed to sit up. "What's going on? Where are—" Hellen suddenly remembered everything. "Oh, God. Leticia."

"I don't know where she is or what's going on with her. But I promise we'll find her," said Tom.

"Hey, Shaw, *se réveiller*," Cloutard called, kicking at the last unmoving body.

Shaw woke with a start. "What the fuck? Where . . . ooohhh fuck, my head," he spluttered.

"Welcome to this year's S&M safari," Tom said. "We hope you're as uncomfortable as possible, the cable ties are not too loose, and the sack over your head is making it hard to breathe. We wish you a really shitty time."

Hellen and Cloutard had to laugh.

"Wow, I'm impressed. How can you crack jokes at a time like this?" said Shaw.

"You get used to it. It's how he deals with these things," said Hellen. "Sometimes they're pretty funny, and for a moment you forget the horror you're stuck in." She paused, then added, "And sometimes they're not. Then you get angry at him and his stupid joke, and then *you also* forget the horror you're stuck in."

"I'm not in a laughing mood. Leticia has disappeared, these sons of bitches are doing God knows what with her, and you're sitting here making stupid jokes." Shaw twisted furiously and tugged at his bonds, but they only dug more painfully into his skin.

"Calm down," Tom snapped at him. "I'm sorry about what's happened to Leticia, but your temper isn't going to get us anywhere. Get a grip," said Tom.

"He is right, *mon ami*," said Cloutard.

Shaw tugged aggressively one last time but then settled down and leaned in resignation against the side wall. "So what do you suggest?"

"First of all, I want this thing off my head. Hellen, I'm going to lie on my side, and I want you to pull the hood off."

"Okay," she said, and she soon had the sack off Tom's head. Then they repeated the procedure, with Tom freeing Hellen from her hood. Cloutard and Shaw did the same. Very soon, all of them could breathe easily again.

"What now?" said Shaw, already much calmer.

Tom struggled to his knees, wobbled across to the side wall, and was able to look out through the flapping tarpaulin. "Oh, boy," he sighed.

"What do you see?"

"Where are we?"

"Talk already!"

"We're in the middle of nowhere," said Tom, sitting down again. "There's nothing outside but savannah. Where we are is anybody's guess."

Shaw lost his cool again and writhed furiously. "Aaarrgh, can someone get these damned cable ties off me!?" His rage transformed into pitiful sobbing. "I don't want to die here."

"Brad, that's not going to help," said Hellen soothingly.

"How can you all be so damned calm?"

"Oh, *mon ami*. Because this is not the first time we have been in a hopeless situation," said Cloutard, looking at his old friend. "Tom will think of something. He always does," he went on, looking now at Tom. "Correct?"

Hellen and Shaw now turned to Tom, too. He grinned, a little abashed, and stared back into three expectant faces. Suddenly, his expression changed, and he became serious. He looked around, taking in every inch of the truck. A plan was forming in his mind.

"I've got it!" he exclaimed, looking at the others. Hellen smiled.

"Well? What's the plan?" Shaw said, suddenly hopeful.

"Okay, listen up," said Tom. He leaned toward Shaw, and Shaw wriggled a little closer. Tom looked secretively left and right.

"Your part is the most important," Tom whispered. Shaw looked at him with huge eyes. "You're going to shut up, lie back, and relax. And we're going to wait until this damned truck gets to wherever it's going."

Shaw's face turned ruby red. Cloutard and Hellen smirked and shook their heads. "Asshole," Shaw growled, and he leaned back against the side wall again.

"What did you think? That we could undo cable ties by sheer willpower? That I'd jump onto the cab roof while we're driving, throw the driver out, and grab the wheel?"

"I thought that was the kind of thing you did."

"Sure, but this situation is different. We have no clue where we are. We have no phones and no GPS. We don't even know if we're still in Nigeria. Even if I managed to overpower the guy or guys up front, who's to say that the truck has enough gas or which direction we're supposed to go? We're on the largest and by far the most dangerous continent in the world. Sometimes there's nothing but savannah and wild animals for hundreds of miles, and that's leaving all the Kalashnikov-toting warlords out of the equation completely."

Cloutard smiled. "All right, I think he gets it," he said.

"We'll get through this. Our best chance is to wait until we've reached our destination. Then we can work out a plan," Tom said, calming down. Shaw nodded.

Hellen edged closer to Tom and snuggled against his shoulder.

"And don't worry," Tom continued. "There are hardly any cannibals left. We're not going to end up in a cooking pot."

Before Shaw could reply, everyone tumbled sideways as the truck came to an abrupt stop. They sat up again. Doors flew open, they heard footsteps, voices mumbled incoherent words, and the tarpaulin covering the cargo bay was thrown back.

They were staring down the barrels of three rifles. Two men jumped onto the cargo area, pulled the sacks back over their heads, and dragged them out.

79

SOMEWHERE IN NIGERIA

The temperature suddenly dropped by at least twenty degrees. A soft, blossomy scent filled the air-conditioned air—Tom could smell it even through the sweat-drenched sack over his head. They had been led across a dusty square before passing through a gateway and into a building. Through a gap at the bottom of the sack, Tom could make out a decorative mosaic floor underfoot.

Where the hell are we? he wondered. "Hellen? Are you there?"

"Yes. Where are they taking us?" Hellen replied, a note of fear in her voice.

"What do they want from us?" asked Shaw.

"*Cést la fin*," Cloutard murmured.

"Come on, François. Don't be so negative," said Tom. Then, turning to the men who were pushing them through the building, he said, "Where is our friend, Leticia? Where are you taking us?" As before, he got no answer.

A few minutes later, they seemed to have reached their destination. They were ordered to stop. A strong hand pushed Tom onto a bench, and Hellen, Cloutard and Shaw were also forced to sit. Tom's adrenalin level jumped a little as he felt a cold blade slide down his forearm. He held his breath. Then there was a jerk and the cable ties binding his wrists fell away. Another hand pulled the sack off over his head.

Without hesitation, Tom jumped to his feet, turned, and threw himself onto the man behind him. His military instincts had taken over. Surprised, the man crashed onto the hard floor. Tom pulled his fist back, ready to smash it into the man's face.

"Tom, don't!" a female voice cried, ringing loudly in the circular room. He spun around and froze. Double doors of heavy, dark wood had creaked open, and Leticia Ortiz had entered the room. With her was an elderly woman.

Tom was speechless. He rolled off the man, who was instantly back on his feet. He moved to attack Tom, but a raised hand from the old woman stopped him in his tracks. He nodded obediently, moved back, and left the room, along with the three other men. Tom stood up and looked across at Hellen, Cloutard and Shaw. They were also untied and on their feet, standing in front of the circular arrangement of benches and staring open-mouthed at Leticia. Their expressions shifted quickly from confusion to joy and relief.

The old woman and Leticia stepped closer. Leticia was not wearing the same clothes she had worn the previous night in the hotel. She was swathed in a colorful dress with a matching headscarf, knotted at the side. Around her neck hung a golden chain with a round pendant. Hellen recognized the symbol on the pendant immediately: two snakes coiled around a rainbow. It was the same symbol she had seen in the Pink House, on the seal of Anne Bonny's letter.

So far, none of them had managed to say a word. Then Shaw stepped forward. He threw his arms around Leticia and kissed her ardently.

"I thought I'd never see you again."

The old woman smiled. Tom, Hellen and Cloutard looked around inside the windowless room. The walls were painted white. On the ceiling, dark wooden beams radiated outwards from the center, like an enormous version of the wheels that steered old sailing ships. A huge chandelier hung from the hub at the center. Around them stood small columns on which ancient artifacts were displayed, museum-like, beneath glass domes: voodoo figurines, masks, small statues, and artfully designed bowls.

"Where are we?" Hellen finally managed to ask.

"If I had to guess, I'd say a museum in Zamunda. But I don't see Eddie Murphy anywhere," Tom quipped. He looked around at the artifacts and pointed at a kind of headdress topping one of the columns.

"Yes. That's the crown of Baron Samedi. That's what Graves was after," Hellen whispered.

"*Merveilleusement*," Cloutard breathed, moving toward a pedestal standing by itself in the center of the room. On top of the pedestal was an ancient ship's bell.

"Old instincts coming back, François?" said Tom.

Cloutard ignored him. "Is that really . . ." he said, his voice failing him as he stared in disbelief at the elaborate old bell. Hellen stepped up beside him.

"Yes," said the old woman who had entered with Leticia. "It is the bell from Anne's ship, the 'Liberté,' the ship on which she arrived in West Africa three hundred years ago." She smiled.

"This is Thabani," said Leticia. "She is the leader here."

"Leader of what?" asked Tom.

"I know you have many, many questions," the old woman said, and she gestured invitingly toward the double doors. "But first, come and have something to eat, then rest awhile. Tomorrow we will explain everything. And we will take you to Anne Bonny's treasure."

80

THE NEXT MORNING

"You're . . . what?" Hellen said. She almost choked on her coffee and now stared at Leticia in shock. The five were sitting together on a roofed veranda in an unpretentious but well-maintained complex. Several white two-story buildings were arranged in a circle around a small plaza. They were reminiscent of old thatched-roof wattle and daub huts, although these buildings were bigger, more modern, and with wooden roofs instead of straw. A few children were playing on the lush grass in front of the building. The morning sunshine shimmered golden over the surrounding forest.

"I'm a direct descendant of Anne Bonny and Calico Jack. A great-great-seven-or-eight-times-granddaughter," said Leticia. "My ancestors go back to Anne's first daughter, Ayida, who she gave birth to in Cuba and left behind with a foster family. Thabani tells me that Anne always regretted giving Ayida up, but her pirating life left her no choice."

"Ayida?" said Hellen. Leticia nodded. "Ayida-Weddo is a female spirit in African and Haitian voodoo. Her symbol is the rainbow." Hellen pointed to Leticia's pendant. She drank a mouthful of coffee, then said, "The snake represents her husband, Damballa. He is the spirit of fertility and keeper of the traditions and roots of all peoples."

Leticia held the pendant in her hand and studied it. "Thabani says it belonged to Anne. She is also a descendant of Anne's, by the way, and a distant cousin of mine. Anne settled here, in what we call Nigeria today, and started a new family."

"But how did these people even know about you?" said Hellen. Leticia lifted her finger to the twin birthmarks beneath her eye. "These birthmarks are typical of my family. My mother had them, too. They go all the way back to Anne Bonny herself."

"Like the Habsburg lip or the Medici nose?" Hellen asked.

"More or less," said Leticia. "A guard at the palace saw me and was able to contact Thabani. After they took me from the hotel, I was flown here in a small plane, and Thabani explained everything."

"Then why did they knock us out and stuff us into the back of a decrepit old truck and cart us hundreds of miles across Nigeria? Why not just take us along in the plane, too?" Cloutard asked in annoyance.

"I can answer that for you." Thabani had just stepped out onto the veranda and now sat beside Leticia at the table. She looked to be about sixty-five, and radiated pride and wisdom. She wore her white turban like a crown, and her long, cream-colored dress accentuated her ebony skin. Large gold earrings completed her outfit, and she wore the same pendant as Leticia. But she seemed more like a businesswoman than a tribal chieftain. "We did not know you, and we could not take any chances. I apologize for that. But Leticia assures me that we can trust you."

Tom looked closely and saw that she had the same birthmarks beneath her eye as Leticia did. "What is all this?" he asked.

"We are in the middle of Yankari National Park. In the 1950s, my father was a member of a regional commission that wanted to start a pilot project for setting up a game reserve. In the 1990s, through my foundation, I had it reclassified as a nature reserve. There is no better place to stay out of sight than in the middle of hundreds of miles of untouched nature." She spread her arms wide.

"Through your foundation?" said Hellen in surprise.

The old woman smiled at Hellen but did not answer the question. Instead, she said, "We should be getting on. No doubt you would like to see the reason you have come all this way."

All five nodded, drank the last of their coffee, and followed the old woman to the courtyard in front of the house. Two Mercedes G-Wagons were waiting, engines idling. Tom, Hellen and Cloutard climbed into one, and Leticia and Shaw got into the other, along with Thabani. Dust swirled as the two cars drove off.

"I wonder where they're taking us now?" said Tom.

"To Anne Bonny's treasure, *stupidité*. She told us that already," Cloutard replied.

"I'm not so sure," said Hellen. "When I look at all this, I can't believe there's much treasure left."

"She's right," said Tom. "Think about it. We're sitting in two Mercedes G-Wagons. These things cost well over a hundred grand. And the guys who kidnapped us were all wearing decent clothes and Rolex watches. And apparently, they work for a 'foundation.'" He made air quotes around the word.

Cloutard and Tom turned in alarm when Hellen shrieked. The moment the car left the trees and entered the open savannah, Hellen had screamed for joy. Now, she had her head out of the open window. A herd of elephants ambled serenely across the plain, and in the far distance they could see a few giraffes, too, plucking leaves from a solitary tree. On the other side of the dirt road, a pride of lions lay in the sunshine. For a while, they watched the animals and drank in the indescribable beauty of Africa. The sight made them completely forget all the hardships and dangers they had overcome to get there.

"I don't care what's ahead of us or what we'll find when we get where we're going. This view alone makes it all worthwhile," said Hellen, snuggling against Tom.

"*Oui*," Cloutard agreed. "But we could have booked a safari much more easily than this." He fanned a little air over his face with the straw hat they had given him at Thabani's complex.

A little farther on, the two all-terrain cars entered the forest again and stopped in front of a small wooden house on the banks of the Gaji River. They climbed out and followed Thabani and the two drivers to the shore of the river. Overgrown along both banks, the river flowed from one side of Yankari National Park to the other.

At the river's edge, they boarded a long, flat-bottomed canoe. One of the men with them started the small outboard motor, while the other helped Thabani into the boat and cast off. They puttered slowly upstream, and the old woman spoke as they went.

"When Anne Bonny arrived in West Africa on the "Liberté," they welcomed her with open arms. Her crew were all freed slaves, and she had promised them that she would take them back to their homeland. The only condition was that they had to take her to Mawu-Lisa's temple. In voodoo, Mawu is revered as the creator of heaven and earth. Anne had made up her mind to offer the treasure—or 'blood money,' as she called it—to the voodoo spirits as restitution. Through the treasure, she wanted to ask forgiveness for all the cruelties inflicted on the people of Africa."

"And you're taking us to the temple that holds the treasure?"

Thabani only smiled.

"My tribe, into which Anne finally married, has been watching over the treasure for centuries."

"And no one has ever come looking for it?" asked Cloutard.

"No. Anne made sure of that," Thabani said, but offered no further explanation.

The boat eased into a small branch of the Gaji. Treetops leaned out from both sides, forming a rooftop over the shimmering water. The boat glided calmly upstream, the purr of the small motor barely audible over the lively jungle sounds in the rainforest around them. When they reached the end of the overgrown river, they saw the sun burning brightly on a rock wall.

"We are almost there," said Thabani, and she pointed ahead to a small waterfall that tumbled over the rocks and into the river.

81

A CAVE IN YANKARI NATIONAL PARK, NIGERIA

The man at the back had cut the motor and switched to a paddle. The shower they took when Thabani's assistant steered the long vessel straight through the waterfall and into a narrow cave entrance behind it was soon forgotten. The man lit torches and handed them to Tom and Shaw. Wide-eyed, they stared up into the gap in the rock overhead, now lit by the flickering flames. The steady sound of dripping resonated through the silence.

"Where are we?" Hellen said breathlessly, almost inaudibly, afraid to destroy the moment.

"When Anne passed away after a long, wonderful life, the tribe—in particular the children of the men and women she'd rescued—came up with something very special for her final resting place," Thabani replied.

"Do you mean—" Cloutard began.

"Yes. We are on our way to visit Anne Bonny's grave," Thabani said softly.

No one spoke. Only the distant, steady dripping, the crackle of the torches, and the gentle ripple of the water could be heard as the canoe slid deeper and deeper into the cave.

A sigh escaped all five when the narrow waterway abruptly ended, and they entered an enormous cave. Through a gap overhead, hung with branches and vegetation, rays of sunlight found their way down into the natural hall, similar to a Mexican *cenote*.

"*Sainte mère de dieu*," said Cloutard.

Hellen and Leticia were utterly speechless, while Shaw managed only, "Wow."

"Holy shit," Tom whispered.

Like spotlights illuminating a stage, countless rays of sunlight illuminated the "Liberté," the ship of Anne Bonny, almost perfectly intact. Thabani had to smile when she saw the amazed, excited faces of the five newcomers. A thin smile even appeared on the face of her otherwise stoic assistant.

"We're hundreds of miles from the coast. How is this possible?" Hellen breathed, still in disbelief.

"More than a hundred men and women worked for more than two years to dismantle the ship, transport it here, and reassemble it," Thabani explained proudly. "All to honor the woman who rescued them. My grandmother told me the story when I was a child, just as she had heard it from her grandmother."

Tom and Shaw looked at each other. They were both about the same age, and both were remembering a blast from the past. They nodded knowingly to each other, and for a moment both of them were seven years old again, recalling one of the greatest film experiences a seven-year-old boy could have.

"Goonies forever," they said as one.

Hellen, the only other person with any idea what they meant, just smiled and shook her head. "Men," she murmured.

Cloutard had heard none of it. He could not take his eyes off the ship. Thabani's escort guided the canoe to the shore and pulled it firmly onto the sand, and one after another they disembarked. The majestic galleon stood before them on the sandy bank, braced by enormous supports fashioned from tree trunks. Dust and pollen danced in the golden rays of sunlight.

"This is insane," said Shaw, still overcome with astonishment at the sight of the pirate ship. "How could they do something like that three hundred years ago?"

"Human beings have always outdone themselves, haven't they?" said Hellen. "Look at the pyramids. They're almost five thousand years old. Each stone weighs tons, and it's been proven that they were transported from quarries hundreds of miles away. Compared to that, a ship like this is a snap."

They gazed up at the richly decorated stern of the galleon, on which they could see "Liberté" spelled out in large letters.

A stairway constructed against the side of the ship led up to the deck. The timbers creaked as Tom, torch in hand, stepped aboard. He looked up. The creaking had startled a few birds that now flew up through the gaping hole overhead. The mainmast with its crow's nest rose almost to the roof of the cave.

"Somehow, I always imagined that a ship like this would be bigger. Weren't the crews normally between a hundred and two hundred and fifty men? This deck isn't much bigger than my grandfather's apartment," said Tom, after he'd walked around the upper deck.

"People back then were smaller than they are today," Hellen explained. "Remember the treasury at the Hofburg in Vienna, where the uniforms of the Imperial Army are on display? They look almost like children's costumes. Back then, on average, people were only about five-foot-two or three. That makes a huge difference in the amount of room you would need for them."

Leticia and Shaw were the last to step aboard, and they looked around in amazement. The ship looked as if it were ready to sail away at any moment. Everything was almost perfectly preserved.

"Come," said Thabani. She lit three waiting kerosene lamps, handed two of them to the others, and led them along the main deck toward the stern. Tom and Shaw tossed their torches overboard, into the sand. Thabani opened the door to the stern quarters, with its inlaid windows of leaded glass and went through. Tom and Cloutard had to duck to avoid banging their heads on the low frame.

"This is a ship for hobbits. I'm already feeling claustrophobic. Imagine being stuck for months on the high seas with hundreds of guys on a tub like this," said Tom.

Hellen punched him in the ribs. "Shhh," she hissed. "This is a tomb. Show a little respect."

When they reached the captain's cabin, they paused for a moment. Thabani murmured a few words in her own language before opening the door.

No one moved. Leticia stared uncertainly into the cabin. Hellen touched her shoulder gently, and the two women looked at one another for a moment. Hellen nodded almost imperceptibly. Leticia raised the lamp she was carrying and slowly entered the room. The timbers under her feet creaked lightly. A fresh, flowery perfume filled the room. Tom was about to follow her when Hellen stopped him.

"Give her a moment," she whispered.

In front of the leaded glass windows across the stern stood a large table. Numerous charts, a sextant, wooden rulers, a compass, and an old book were scattered across it.

Leticia drew a sharp breath when the light from her lamp fell onto the bed on the opposite wall. Heavy, red fabric draped from the frame of a four-poster bed. Leticia stepped back in shock and crossed herself, and for a while simply stood and stared at the bed. Her fingers rose to the pendant around her neck. An eternity seemed to pass before she finally stepped closer to where the mortal remains of Anne Bonny lay as if sleeping, surrounded by flowers atop the large bed.

82

A CAVE IN YANKARI NATIONAL PARK, NIGERIA

"Come in, what are you waiting for?" Leticia said minutes later, her voice tearful. She wiped away a teardrop and motioned to the others to come inside. Hellen knew what Leticia was going through. She put her arm around her and handed her a tissue. Discovering where you came from, solving the riddle of your own family, and confronting the knowledge that her dear mother had come so close to discovering the truth . . . it was too much to deal with all at once. Leticia was clearly struggling. But at least she had reconnected with her father, and in Shaw she had found someone with whom she could share her passion and her future, Hellen thought. She waved Shaw over, then released Leticia and moved aside. Shaw nodded and took Leticia in his arms. Even Tom looked a little moved. Hellen took his hand—she knew there were still a lot of open questions about his own family's history.

"It's the most beautiful grave I have ever seen, by far," Hellen whispered, looking at the skeleton, partially visible beneath the blanket. Cloutard, so rarely at a loss for words, was still speechless. He took out his little flask, raised it toward the bed in salute, and drank a long draft.

"Your ancestors did amazing work," said Tom. He went over to the table to look at the objects on it more closely, although he dared not touch anything.

"Yes. Every generation has watched over this shrine and looked after it. We bring fresh flowers in regularly, in gratitude for bringing back our people."

The book caught Tom's eye, and he turned to Thabani and pointed inquiringly at it. Thabani nodded and Tom picked it up. He turned a few pages.

"Hellen, look at this," he said, handing it to her. She scanned page after page excitedly.

"It's Anne's diary," she said. "Listen to this." Leticia, Shaw, and Cloutard moved closer to the table.

Cuba. 15 March, 1719

Five months have passed. I miss Jack less and less each day. I cannot say how it will be to see him again.

Boubacar has been a great help in these last few months. Despite the horrors inflicted on him and his kind, he is still an affectionate man.

Cuba. 14 July, 1719

Giving up Ayida was the most difficult thing I have ever had to do. But here in Cuba, she is safe. The people are decent, and they will take good care of her.

. . .

Leticia sighed and leaned against Shaw, who put his arm around her comfortingly. Hellen read on.

23 July, 1719

Today, Boubacar told me about his homeland. A land of such beauty sounds like a heaven on earth. I am not at all certain that Jack would appreciate that. His hatred of the Crown runs deep. Gold is all that interests him.

"Who was Boubacar?" Tom asked.

"He was Anne's bodyguard during her time in Cuba. He was a slave that Anne and Jack freed on one of their raids, and he was also the man who introduced Anne to my people's beliefs. He is also my ancestor," said Thabani, with a wink at Tom.

Hellen flipped forward a few pages.

17 September, 1719

Everything is prepared. The rod is hidden, the medallions distributed, and the treasure is safe. The trap is set. They are celebrating on deck, unaware that today is the end. If the Crown's lackeys follow my trail, they are in for a rude surprise.

"So we found exactly what Anne wanted us to find?" said Cloutard. "The treasure is no more than a few bottles of whisky?"

"Wait. There's more here," Hellen said.

Thabani was still standing in the entrance to the captain's cabin, observing her guests.

12 May, 1720

Day 25 of our crossing. The winds are favorable. I wish I could have saved more men and women. Boubacar was a great help. He assembled an excellent crew. With the gold we have down below, we can live for many generations. It does little to lessen the atrocities already inflicted, but in this way, at least, I can help the others. "Sacrifice means changing for the better the lives of those around you and those who come after you." I hope the priestess in Haiti was right about that.

"So the treasure's really here?" said Tom.

"Where?" said Shaw, a little too eagerly.

"Is it here on the ship?" Hellen asked, recognizing as she asked how absurd the question was.

Thabani laughed.

"Oh, yes, the treasure really existed," she began, looking around at the others' crestfallen faces. "And no, it is not aboard this ship. There are no barrels filled with gold coins, if that's what you mean." More disappointed looks. "On her deathbed, Anne voiced one wish. Her whole life, she had regretted having to leave Ayida behind in Cuba. And when she died, she asked that, if a descendant of Ayida's ever came to light, a portion of the treasure would be hers."

Leticia's eyes widened. Tom, Hellen, and Cloutard looked at each other in surprise.

"But if there's no treasure anymore...?" said Shaw.

"It is true that the original treasure no longer exists. That was three hundred years ago, after all. The gold is gone. But what that gold has yielded is still here. This morning, I mentioned my foundation, which I named after this ship. The Liberté Foundation is financed by the returns on investments made by the descendants of Anne Bonny, and today helps people all over the world. With Anne's help, my people quickly learned to use modern finance to their own advantage, and to profit from it. We do not appear in Forbes Magazine because we do not want people to know about us, but my family is among the richest in the world. And now you, Leticia, are part of that family."

Thabani removed a small USB stick from her turban and held it out to Leticia.

"Now you also have the opportunity to make a difference in your country. This contains the code to your wallet," she said with a smile. "I hope bitcoin is okay?"

83

AIRBUS ACJ320NEO, VAN RENSBURG'S PRIVATE JET, SOMEWHERE OVER THE ATLANTIC OCEAN

Tom watched Leticia. She was sitting by herself in one of the comfortable armchairs at a small table, fingering the USB stick in her hand. Through the small window, she gazed out at the expanse of passing clouds.

"How much do you think is on there?" asked Shaw, who was sitting with the others a short distance away. Leticia had wanted a little time alone.

"No idea," said Tom. "I only know that van Rensburg won't be overjoyed when we tell him we've donated the treasure to the people of Jamaica, especially without telling him about it first."

"Oh, come on. From what Cloutard says, the guy's made of money," Shaw said, looking again at Leticia, his eyes fixed on the USB stick.

"At least he'll get a chest of old whisky," said Hellen, and laughed.

"What? No! *Pour l'amour de dieu*, that chest belongs to me," said Cloutard. Hellen just looked at him and shook her head. "One bottle at least?" Cloutard asked with a sigh.

"You'll have to work that out with the boss," said Tom. He stretched in his seat and stroked his full belly. "That dinner last night was fantastic. I still can't move properly."

"*Oui, magnifique.*" Cloutard kissed his fingertips deliciously. "I spoke to the chef immediately afterward and he generously gifted me a few recipes. West African cuisine has been far too little on my radar. It is definitely something to explore more deeply."

"Thabani is an impressive woman, isn't she?" said Hellen.

"She sure is. And she knows how to party. My head is still pounding. What was that stuff they were pouring yesterday?" Tom groaned.

"Okay, well, apart from that," Hellen said, smiling. "What fascinated me most about her was that she took Leticia into her family so willingly. She welcomed her with open arms, on top of which she's given her God knows how much money. She hadn't even known her twenty-four hours."

"All I know is that Leticia will do the right thing to help the people in her country. Her family obviously shares that trait," said Cloutard. "And you, my friend, will give her all the support she needs." Cloutard clapped Shaw on the shoulder, and Shaw jumped. His eyes had not left Leticia.

"Yeah, sure, of course," said Shaw, taken by surprise. Tom looked at Shaw, then at Cloutard. He picked up his phone and leaned back in his armchair.

"I'm going to send van Rensburg a quick update, just so he's not completely in the dark." He tapped out a quick message and hit the "send" button.

A high-pitched squeal from Leticia had them all on their feet in an instant.

"What is it?" asked Hellen.

Leticia turned her laptop to face the others. The stick was protruding from a USB port.

"I just wanted to check my email. But then I thought I'd take a look at what's on the stick," she said, her voice trembling. Four incredulous faces, mouths agape, stared at the display. No one spoke. Seconds passed.

On the display, it showed 2,700 bitcoins. Beneath that was a conversion to dollars.

Shaw raised his hand and counted with a quivering finger. "Is that really nine digits?" he stammered.

"Looks like it," said Tom.

"A hundred million dollars?" Hellen said in amazement.

Cloutard, once again struck dumb, took out his hip flask with a shaky hand. When he finally managed to open it, he took a big swig and offered it to the others. Leticia, still in shock, took the flask and emptied it in a single draft. She coughed and handed it back to Cloutard.

"You can do so much good with that," said Hellen. "I'm so happy for you."

"We've done it, Brad," Leticia said to Shaw, who had dropped into the seat beside her. "Now we can do everything we've been planning."

Shaw put his arms around Leticia and kissed her.

"We should look after that stick," said Tom. "I'll put it in the safe until we land. If the key to the chain got lost, well . . . it wouldn't be the first time in bitcoin history."

Leticia nodded. She removed the stick and handed it to him. He went to the safe, put the USB stick inside, and locked it.

"Now we can sleep in peace," Tom yawned.

"Sleep? *En aucun cas*, this is something to celebrate," said Cloutard. He stood and hurried to the bar, returning a minute later with five glasses of champagne. Glasses clinked. An hour later, still worn out from the previous evening and the opulent farewell dinner Thabani had arranged for her new family member, all five made themselves comfortable and slept for the rest of the flight.

———

"This is your captain speaking. We will be landing in Kingston, Jamaica, in about thirty minutes."

The captain's announcement roused the team from their well-earned sleep. A brief "good morning," a quick coffee, and they packed their things. When the plane finally rolled to a stop, Tom went to the safe, opened it, and removed the USB stick.

The click of a pistol being cocked made him freeze.

"Shaw, what the devil are you doing?" cried Cloutard.

"Come on, hand over the stick," Shaw ordered, holding out his hand to Tom. He was waving Tom's pistol around wildly, keeping everyone at bay.

"You won't get away with this," said Tom.

"Hand it over!" he ordered again.

"Brad, what are you doing?" said Leticia, close to tears. "We had so many plans."

Shaw laughed. "Your plans. Did you really believe I'd stand around and watch you burn through a hundred million on total strangers?" He turned back to Tom. "Now give me the stick."

Tom handed over the stick and stepped back, hands raised. Shaw moved backward toward the airplane door and opened it.

"It's been a pleasure working with you. Cloutard, old friend, no offense, but a hundred million . . . I'm sure you understand. In my position, you'd do the same."

"A long time ago, maybe. Not today," said Cloutard in disappointment.

"Buh-bye," said Shaw, exiting through the airplane door.

Seconds later, he reappeared, walking backward. He had his hands in the air. At first, the team could see only a hand pointing an ancient revolver at Shaw's face. Two seconds later, Ignacio Torrente appeared. Unflinching, he drove Shaw back inside the plane.

"Perfect timing. I see you got my message," said Tom.

"Yes. And I called the cavalry, too. The police are already waiting outside."

Tom went to Shaw and disarmed him. He rummaged inside Shaw's jacket for the USB stick, which he handed to Leticia.

"Sorry, but I had a feeling."

Leticia nodded and accepted the stick back. Then she turned toward Shaw, took a step closer, and slapped him as hard as she could across the face.

"Get this son of a bitch out of my sight."

84

EMANCIPATION PARK, KINGSTON, JAMAICA, THREE DAYS LATER

LETICIA'S CHOICE OF VENUE WAS NO ACCIDENT. EMANCIPATION Park, known fondly to locals as EPark, carried considerable symbolic weight for the people of Kingston. It had opened in 2002 as a monument to the end of slavery, with two black bronze statues standing in a small, raised pool at the entrance to the triangular park. The figures—a man and a woman—gazed with hope toward the sky. Called "Redemption Song," the sculpture took its name from the Bob Marley song of the same name. In many places in the park, Adinkra symbols reinforced the relationship between Jamaica and the old homelands in Africa. Leticia could not have chosen a better place to celebrate her election victory, which also signified liberation from the corrupt rule of Grayson Graves.

"This looks more like a street party than the kind of celebration you'd expect after a landslide election win," said Tom, as he, Hellen and Cloutard climbed out of the taxi.

Bright lights lit the park, music filled the air, and people milled all around. The entire island seemed to be celebrating that night.

"I don't think Jamaica could have made a better choice than Leticia. She is far from a typical politician. And with the money Anne Bonny left her, she will be able to set a lot of good things in motion," said Hellen.

"It is not only a victory for her, but a victory for all the people of Jamaica," Cloutard agreed.

As they strolled through the park, the trio stopped again and again, not only to admire the countless stands and attractions, but in particular because of the park's fascinating flora.

"It is impressive, is it not?" Cloutard gushed. "How the designers brought together the flora of the entire Caribbean in this park. The majestic Cuban royal palm, the bull thatch palm, lignum vitae—Jamaica's national flower—and the blue mahoe, its national tree. And there is bougainvillea, poor man's orchid, poinciana, and the poui tree."

Tom looked at him in surprise. "Are you a master botanist now too, François?"

"*Non*. It is simply part of the general knowledge of a civilized person," Cloutard said indignantly.

"Those are roses," said Tom, pointing to a large rose bed they were passing just then on their way to Leticia's victory stage.

"Well done, Tom. Good eye," Hellen said, smiling. "Eight different varieties, to be exact."

"I would like to raise a rather delicate topic," said Cloutard, fanning himself with his hat. Although it was evening, the temperature reminded them that they were in the tropics. But that was not the only thing making the Frenchman sweat. "We have not yet discussed this directly, but where do we go from here?"

He looked expectantly at Tom and Hellen.

"What are you trying to say?" Hellen asked, trying to nudge the Frenchman a little out of his natural reserve. Tom saw it, and he could not suppress his customary grin. They both looked at Cloutard as if they had no clue what he was talking about.

"I don't know what you're getting at either, François," Tom said, pushing a little harder.

"*Mon dieu*, do not act so dense." Cloutard rolled his eyes. "If I did not know I would regret it, I would slap your face." Cloutard managed to look both annoyed and amused at once. He shook his head again. "All right, fine, you are forcing me to make the sentimental speech." He took a deep breath. "I enjoy working with you. I was not having nearly as much fun when I went off treasure hunting by myself. Oh, it was nice enough, traveling the world and tracking down clues, but it was not the same as . . ." He paused for a moment, as if to gather himself. "*Merde* . . . it was not the same as going treasure hunting with you."

Tom and Hellen looked at each other in amusement.

"If you're working up to propose, François, then I've got bad news," said Tom. "In case you hadn't noticed, we're already married. You're too late."

Cloutard sniffed. "*Tu es un cretin*," he murmured, trying to stifle a grin.

Hellen was more sympathetic. "If you're trying to ask if we want to stick together, searching for artifacts and tracking down the greatest myths of the human race, then all we can say is..."

She paused and looked at Tom. As one, they finished the sentence with a definite, "Yes!"

"But you have to promise that you'll choose your accomplices more carefully in the future," Hellen added.

Cloutard nodded, chastised, but then broke into a grin. He embraced first Hellen, then Tom, who grimaced a little when Cloutard hugged him tightly.

From the center of the park, they heard loud cheering and applause. Tom inhaled loudly when Cloutard released him. Someone sent a skyrocket soaring into the night, which was followed by the usual "oohs" and "aahs."

"Let's see if we can still get through to our victor," said Tom, and they began battling through the throng of people.

Cloutard's white Panama hat stood out like a beacon in the crowd, and Leticia spotted the trio as soon as they neared the stage.

"I'm so happy you came," she said joyfully, hugging all three. She had climbed down from the stage and led Tom, Hellen and Cloutard to the backstage area. Hellen could see that she was still suffering from Shaw's betrayal.

"I'm married to Jamaica now," Leticia whispered to Hellen, as if she could read her mind. "That's going to keep me busy enough."

Ignacio approached the group, carrying champagne goblets on a tray. "To a happy future for Jamaica," said Tom, and they all clinked their glasses together.

The band began to play Bob Marley's "Redemption Song." Cloutard took Leticia by the hand and pulled her up onto the stage. The improvised dance floor quickly filled with couples.

"Now all we have to do," said Tom, helping Hellen onto the stage as well, "is work out how to explain to the van Rensburgs that they're going to end up with nothing because we gave the treasure to its rightful owner."

Hellen frowned. "Let's think about it tomorrow," she said. She leaned against Tom's chest and closed her eyes. Holding each other tightly, they swayed in time with the music.

85

VAN RENSBURG'S VILLA, GRAND CAYMAN

"It's funny, isn't it?" Hellen said as they looked at the opulent villa in front of them. "We felt very comfortable here, almost at home," she said. "But something is different now." Tom put his arm around his wife but said nothing. "This phase was important. I needed to get some distance to see what I really wanted." She looked first at Tom, and then Cloutard. "Or to see what *we* wanted."

"Except that it's not entirely up to us," said Tom, with a nod toward the van Rensburg's multi-million-dollar house. "The two people in there have to play ball, too."

A few days had passed, and although they had talked a lot about how to explain the outcome of the mission to the van Rensburgs, they had not had any brilliant ideas. Eon van Rensburg had commissioned Cloutard to find the treasure of Anne Bonny. He had put in a lot of effort, invested a lot of money, and now his three treasure hunters were coming home empty-handed. It was not exactly the best basis for discussing future commissions.

They stood outside the house and leaned on their rental car. None of them wanted to take the first step. It could mean an end to the team on the spot, an eventuality for which they were not prepared at all.

"If van Rensburg doesn't like our decision, I don't know what we're supposed to do," said Hellen. "I'm not going back to some dusty office in a museum basement," she said bitterly.

"Wild horses couldn't drag me back to Cobra," said Tom.

Cloutard tilted his head. "I doubt very much, *mon ami*, that Captain Maierhofer would want you back."

Tom nodded in agreement.

"And I have little interest in spending my time among smugglers and grave robbers again," said Cloutard.

"You would be better off than us, though," said Hellen. "Fabio and Adalgisa would certainly be able to find some odd jobs for you."

"*Bien sur*. The difference is that, if something goes wrong with one of their 'odd jobs,' I'll spend the rest of my life in prison."

They continued to stand and stare at the house, still undecided.

"What are you lugging around there, François?" Tom asked, indicating Cloutard's satchel.

"It is something that might ease van Rensburg's wrath a little," he said, although he did not look particularly convinced.

They stood in silence for a few minutes before Tom summoned up his courage. "It's no good. Whatever happens, we have to go and make our report. But to be honest, I don't care that much what van Rensburg thinks. We did the right thing," he said, and he walked to the front door and pressed the bell.

Moments later, de Waal opened the door for them and led them silently out to the terrace.

Although Tom and Hellen had lived there for months, entering the house again made them both feel strange. They knew their life of luxury was over, whichever way things went with van Rensburg.

"I'm happy to see the team finally back together again," the billionaire said, greeting them effusively. Kiara, wearing her best camera-ready smile, also shook their hands. The couple looked a little ridiculous, as if they had just stepped off one of the Caymans' many golf courses. They wore identical, clichéd golf outfits: grass-green plus fours, socks, sweater-vests checked in yellow, brown, and green, and violently clashing golf caps, in a garish plaid. On Kiara, the outfit was strangely attractive, but on Eon it looked absurd.

Hellen knew that Tom would come out any second with one of his wisecracks, so she headed him off with a jab to the ribs. He got the message and bit his tongue, though the temptation, given Eon's and Kiara's preposterous outfits, remained great. Instead, he decided to just to throw everything on the table.

"We've got good news and bad news," he said, when they were all sitting down. De Waal had brought coffee for all of them and had set out a carafe of water and several tumblers on the table.

Van Rensburg looked up with interest. "And I have some news for you, too." He paused and glanced guiltily at his wife.

"Maybe we should go first," said Hellen. "What we have to say might make your news unnecessary."

"Now, now, Hellen. Don't be so negative," Eon said.

"The good news," said Cloutard, "is that we found the treasure."

The van Rensburgs' faces brightened.

"But the bad news is that we decided to hand the treasure over to Leticia Ortiz," Tom added.

The van Rensburgs' faces sagged again.

The team briefly related the story of the treasure and Leticia's connection to Anne Bonny. Van Rensburg listened to everything, with a grave look on his face.

"That is very disappointing," he said, when Tom, Hellen and Cloutard finished their story. "That was absolutely not what I hired you . . ." he looked at Cloutard, ". . . and later you . . ." he looked at Tom and Hellen, ". . . to do at all."

An awkward silence followed. The only sound was de Waal clearing things away in the kitchen. Tom, Hellen and Cloutard all had their eyes on the floor. No one knew what to say.

After a while, van Rensburg spoke again. "I also have a confession to make, though it hardly matters now."

Grateful that the conversation was moving in a new direction, Tom, Hellen and Cloutard looked up again.

"I did not want Anne Bonny's treasure for myself, but for one of my business partners. We had agreed on an exchange."

"An exchange?" said Cloutard, suddenly a little suspicious.

"Baron von Hohenfeldt, my business partner, has something in his possession that we want more than anything. Unfortunately, the man is impossibly rich, and money doesn't interest him in the slightest. I have tried to buy the object from him for years, but without success."

Tom was sitting up straight now. Hope was returning. Van Rensburg had not been completely honest with them, so they might yet be able to pull their heads out of the noose. "If the man is so rich, why does he even want the treasure?" he asked.

"The man is interested only in one part of the treasure," said Kiara.

Cloutard's expression changed. Graves had told him the same thing. "Is this about Baron Samedi's crown?" Cloutard asked. "The recently deceased Grayson Graves was also after the crown."

Van Rensburg's expression was inscrutable. He looked at Cloutard but did not respond directly to his question. He said, "That doesn't matter much anymore, not now that the treasure has been handed over to Leticia Ortiz."

"Baron Samedi's crown is safe where it is in Nigeria, where it belongs, and where it can't do any damage," Hellen said, perhaps a little too assertively.

Van Rensburg did not react to that directly, either. "What matters is that the exchange we had planned won't be able to take place."

The awkward silence settled again, but this time it was Cloutard who broke it.

"Perhaps we should simply put the matter behind us," he said. "We did not complete our assignment, and you left us a little in the dark as regards what our assignment actually was." He reached down for his satchel. "Now is maybe the time to look ahead. There are enough treasures in the world, and I am certain we will find something somewhere that you can use for the exchange, something that would be of interest to your business partner."

He removed one of the old whisky bottles they had found in the Pink House from his satchel and prepared to remove the cork.

Van Rensburg's face turned a strange color. He let out a horrified scream and literally jumped over the table to snatch the bottle from Cloutard's hands. Glasses crashed and coffee cups fell to the floor.

Tom leaned close to Hellen's ear: "I thought Cloutard had a drinking problem. But even when his flask was empty, I never saw François get that physical," he whispered, making Hellen giggle.

Cloutard looked at van Rensburg in shock. Eon was cradling the whisky bottle in his arms like a young girl holding her favorite doll. Slowly but surely, the team realized what had happened.

"It wasn't about the gold at all," Hellen said. "It was about the chest of old whisky all along."

Van Rensburg, who had calmed down again after his leap over the table, looked at Hellen in amazement. "Chest? There is more of this?"

"Sure. Out in the car," said Tom. Cloutard elbowed him in the side and glared at him.

Van Rensburg looked at the bottle. "This is an exceptionally rare whisky that one of the British governors of Port Royal had shipped especially from Scotland to the Caribbean. He couldn't stand rum and the local whisky was undrinkable."

"So you're saying we went through this whole circus so a rich guy could get hammered on ancient whisky?" Tom asked.

Cloutard looked indignantly at Tom. "Presumably, the baron is a collector of old whiskies. That is about pleasure, not getting drunk," he said grimly.

"Of course, François," said Tom with a laugh. "I knew you'd understand that."

Van Rensburg had waved de Waal over and now handed him the bottle carefully. "Put this straight in the safe," he said.

"May I keep at least one of the bottles?" Cloutard said with a grin, knowing that his request would fall on deaf ears.

Van Rensburg shook his head. "I owe you all an apology," he said, when they were all seated again. "We should have told you as soon as we found out about it ourselves. Baron von Hohenfeldt only revealed what he was really after just recently."

"Fuhgeddaboudit," said Tom. "You didn't brief us exactly, and we didn't exactly stick to your inexact particulars, and yet everyone's happy with the outcome. Win-win all round."

"I don't think there's anything to add to that weird logic," said van Rensburg.

"What exactly is this thing that you want so badly from the baron?" Hellen asked. "What are you going to get for the whisky bottles?"

Van Rensburg beamed at her. "One of the lost Fabergé eggs."

Cloutard raised his eyebrows. "Which one? There are six lost Fabergé eggs in total. I know who is in possession of three of them, but which one does Baron von Hohenfeldt have?"

Van Rensburg grew thoughtful, apparently weighing up exactly up how much he could reveal. "I think you will find out soon enough. Because you're going to make the exchange."

"Are we a messenger service now?" Tom asked drily. "Can't you just send the thing with DHL?"

"It's not that simple. But we'll get to the details later. Before that, I've got another job for you. Unless you have other plans?"

Tom, Hellen and Cloutard looked at each other and nodded.

"We're ready," said Tom. "What have you got?"

The end of
THE PIRATE QUEEN'S TREASURE
Tom, Hellen and Cloutard will return in
"THE MEDUSA'S SECRET"

GET THE PREQUEL TO

THE **TOM WAGNER** SERIES

FREE E-BOOK

robertsmaclay.com/start-free

THRILLED READER REVIEWS

"Suspense and entertainment! I've read a lot of books like this one; some better, some worse. This is one of the best books in this genre I've ever read. I'm really looking forward to a good sequel. "

———

"I just couldn't put this book down. Full of surprising plot twists, humor, and action! "

———

"An explosive combination of Robert Langdon, James Bond & Indiana Jones"

———

"Good build-up of tension; I was always wondering what happens next. Toward the end, where the story gets more and more complex and constantly changes scenes, I was on the edge of my seat"

———

"Great! I read all three books in one sitting. Dan Brown better watch his back."

———

"The best thing about it is the basic premise, a story with historical background knowledge scattered throughout the book–never too much at one time and always supporting the plot"

———

"Entertaining and action-packed! The carefully thought-out story has a clear plotline, but there are a couple of unexpected twists as well. I really enjoyed it. The sections of the book are tailored to maximize the suspense, they don't waste any time with unimportant details. The chapters are short and compact–perfect for a half-hour commute or at night before turning out the lights. Recommended to all lovers of the genre and anyone interested in getting to know it better. I'll definitely read the sequel."

———

"Anyone who likes reading Dan Brown, James Rollins and Preston & Child needs to get this book."

———

"An exciting build-up, interesting and historically significant settings, surprising plot twists in the right places."

THE TOM WAGNER SERIES

THE STONE OF DESTINY

(Tom Wagner Prequel)

A dark secret of the Habsburg Empire. A treasure believed to be lost long time ago. A breathless hunt into the past.

The thriller "The Stone of Destiny" leads Tom Wagner and Hellen de Mey into the dark past of the Habsburgs and to a treasure that seems to have been lost for a long time.

The breathless hunt goes through half of Europe and the surprise at the end is not missing: A conspiracy that began in the last days of the First World War reaches up to the present day!

Free Download!
Click here or open link:
https://robertsmaclay.com/start-free

———

THE SACRED WEAPON

(A Tom Wagner Adventure 1)

A demonic plan. A mysterious power. An extraordinary team.

The Notre Dame fire, the theft of the Shroud of Turin and a terrorist attack on the legendary Meteora monasteries are just the beginning. Fear has gripped Europe.

Stolen relics, a mysterious power with a demonic plan and allies with questionable allegiances: Tom Wagner is in a race against time, trying to prevent a disaster that could tear Europe down to its foundations. And there's no one he can trust...

Click here or open link:
https://robertsmaclay.com/1-tw

———

THE LIBRARY OF THE KINGS

(A Tom Wagner Adventure 2)

Hidden wisdom. A relic of unbelievable power. A race against time.

Ancient legends, devilish plans, startling plot twists, breathtaking action and a dash of humor: *Library of the Kings* is gripping entertainment – a Hollywood blockbuster in book form.

When clues to the long-lost Library of Alexandria surface, ex-Cobra officer Tom Wagner and archaeologist Hellen de Mey aren't the only ones on the hunt for its vanished secrets. A sinister power is plotting in the background, and nothing is as it seems. And the dark secret hidden in the Library threatens all of humanity.

Click here or open link:
https://robertsmaclay.com/2-tw

———

THE INVISIBLE CITY

(A Tom Wagner Adventure 3)

A vanished civilization. A diabolical trap. A mystical treasure.

Tom Wagner, archaeologist Hellen de Mey and gentleman crook Francois Cloutard are about to embark on their first official assignment from Blue Shield – but when Tom receives an urgent call from the Vatican, things start to move quickly:

With the help of the Patriarch of the Russian Orthodox Church, they discover clues to an age-old myth: the Russian Atlantis. And a murderous race to find an ancient, long-lost relic leads them from Cuba to the Russian hinterlands.

What mystical treasure lies buried beneath Nizhny Novgorod? Who laid the evil trap? And what does it all have to do with Tom's grandfather?

Click here or open link:
https://robertsmaclay.com/3-tw

———

THE GOLDEN PATH

(A Tom Wagner Adventure 4)

The greatest treasure of mankind. An international intrigue. A cruel revelation.

Now a special unit for Blue Shield, Tom and his team are on a search for the legendary El Dorado. But, as usual, things don't go as planned.

The team gets separated and is – literally – forced to fight a battle on multiple fronts: Hellen and Cloutard make discoveries that overturn the familiar story of El Dorado's gold.

Meanwhile, the President of the United States has tasked Tom with keeping a dangerous substance out of the hands of terrorists.

Click here or open link:
https://robertsmaclay.com/4-tw

———

THE CHRONICLE OF THE ROUND TABLE

(A Tom Wagner Adventure 5)

The first secret society of mankind. Artifacts of inestimable power. A race you cannot win.

The events turn upside down: Tom Wagner is missing. Hellen's father has turned up and a hot lead is waiting for the Blue Shield team: The legendary Chronicle of the Round Table.

What does the Chronicles of the Round Table of King Arthur say? Must the history around Avalon and Camelot be rewritten? Where is Tom and who is pulling the strings?

Click here or open link:
https://robertsmaclay.com/5-tw

———

THE CHALICE OF ETERNITY

(A Tom Wagner Adventure 6)

The greatest mystery in the world. False friends. All-powerful adversaries.

The Chronicle of the Round Table has been found and Tom Wagner, Hellen de Mey and François Cloutard face their greatest challenge yet: The search for the Holy Grail.

But their adventure does not lead them to the time of the Templars and the Crusades, but much further back into mankind's history. And the hunt into the past is a journey of no return. From Egypt to Vienna, from Abu Dhabi to Valencia, from Monaco to Macao, the hunt is on for the greatest myth of mankind. And in the end, there's a phenomenal surprise for everyone.

Click here or open link:
https://robertsmaclay.com/6-tw

———

THE SWORD OF REVELATION

(A Tom Wagner Adventure 7)

A false lead. A bitter truth. This time, it's all or nothing.

Hellen's mother is dying and only a miracle can save her... but for that, the team needs to locate mysterious and long-lost artifacts.

At the same time, their struggle with the terrorist organization Absolute Freedom reaches its climax: what is the group's true, diabolical plan? Who is pulling the strings behind this worldwide conspiracy?

The Sword of Revelation completes the circle: all questions are answered, all the loose ends woven into a revelation for our heroes — and for all the fans of the Tom Wagner adventures!

Click here or open link:
https://robertsmaclay.com/tw-7

ABOUT THE AUTHORS
ROBERTS & MACLAY

Roberts & Maclay have known each other for over 25 years, are good friends and have worked together on various projects.

The fact that they are now also writing thrillers together is less coincidence than fate. Talking shop about films, TV series and suspense novels has always been one of their favorite pastimes.

M.C. Roberts is the pen name of an successful entrepreneur and blogger. Adventure stories have always been his passion: after recording a number of superhero audiobooks on his father's old tape recorder as a six-year-old, he postponed his dream of writing novels for almost 40 years, and worked as a marketing director, editor-in-chief, DJ, opera critic, communication coach, blogger, online marketer and author of trade books...but in the end, the call of adventure was too strong to ignore.

———

R.F. Maclay is the pen name of an outstanding graphic designer and advertising filmmaker. His international career began as an electrician's apprentice, but he quickly realized that he was destined to work creatively. His family and friends were skeptical at first...but now, 20 years later, the passionate, self-taught graphic designer and filmmaker has delighted record labels, brand-name products and tech companies with his work, as well as making a name for himself as a commercial filmmaker and illustrator. He's also a walking encyclopedia of film and television series.

www.RobertsMaclay.com

Printed in Great Britain
by Amazon